COLD FRONT

CHRISTOPHER ANTHONY

❀ Created with Vellum

For Kyle and Ryan

COLD FRONT

"Life is not an easy matter...You cannot live through it without falling into frustration and cynicism unless you have before you a great idea which raises you above personal misery, above weakness, above all kinds of perfidy and baseness."

    -Leon Trotsky

PROLOGUE

Bucharest, Romania
December 26, 1989

A t 1:35 in the afternoon, the cab stopped on the corner of Calea Victoriei and Episcopiei Street. Richard Dunn opened the door and stepped out onto the curb. His breath escaped in a miniature cloud that vanished above his head. It had stopped raining, but a fine mist hung in the air. Water beaded on his navy-blue overcoat. Across the street, the black stain of a burned-out personnel carrier bled into a storm drain. He pulled one lapel over the other.

Leering down on him from the street corner was the Athénée Palace Hotel. An impressive concrete structure built in 1914, the hotel was a city landmark inspired by French architecture with a reputation for conspiring against its guests. Now, fresh pockmarks dotted the hotel's southeast façade and shards of glass littered the sidewalk out front. Dunn took in a lungful of cool moist air. It smelled of burnt rubber and oil. He exhaled deeply and then made his way through the lobby doors.

· · ·

Dunn was responding to a phone call he'd received the day before. Someone named Brewer from the American Embassy in Bucharest had called during breakfast. He was pushing cold eggs around his plate at the time and as always, he let the answering machine pick up the call.

His answering machine's female voice thanked the caller for their interest in Spa Group, apologized that no one was available to take their call, asked for a name and phone number and pledged to call the interested party back. The brief, ambiguous message was repeated in Flemish, French and German.

When the caller stated that he was not interested in any services provided by Spa Group, Dunn's attention was grabbed. This was the first time that someone outside of his organization had called this number on purpose. When the man who identified himself as Mr. James Brewer, rambled on about an associate of Spa Group that was "found" in the Palace Athénée Hotel in Bucharest, the color ran out of his face.

Dunn knew who the dead man was. A detailed map of the whereabouts of all his people was etched onto his brain. The hard copy he had hung on his office wall. He knew them all by their Christian names, real and otherwise, and could rattle off height, weight and birth date without pause. Interestingly, what he couldn't be sure of anymore, was what any of them currently looked like. Disguise being essential to their survival. For now, he identified them as different colored pins pushed into varying degrees of latitude and longitude on the map that hung on his office wall. Dunn returned Mr. Brewer's call and advised that he would meet him in the hotel lobby at 12:30 p.m. the following day and that he would be taking possession of the man's body.

Normally, this time of year, Dunn would have at least rudimentary decorations scattered about his simple home. But the circumstances of the last six months gave him reason to believe that his residency might not last the current holiday season. Therefore, it seemed a wise move to take a pass on the wreath and garland. The only evidence of the Christmas season being a pathetic little conifer leaning against the wall in the corner of the living room. After hanging up with the embassy man, he pushed himself away from the breakfast table. It was time to get moving and the eggs were no good anyway.

He walked heavily across the home's hardwood floors to the small second bedroom which served as his office. Facing the world map on the wall, he removed a blue pin from a city called Timisoara in western Romania. He dragged the pin eastward through the Transylvanian Alps, ripping a crude slit as he went. Upon turning south and reaching the capital city of Bucharest, he jammed the pin through the paper and into the plaster wall behind, bending it in half.

The room was barren save for a desk with a singular lamp and chair pushed against a wall nearest the door. On the desk sat a soft, black attaché. Dunn unzipped a side compartment and pulled out a flimsy, dog-eared folder. He spread its contents over the desk.

Two thirds of the way through the assortment of documents, letters and other filings, he found what he was looking for. A 5x7 picture of a fit, good-looking man in his late twenties, taken only a few years before. In the photo, the man wore a white buttoned-down dress shirt rolled up at the sleeves. He held a cigarette in one hand and a bottle of beer in the other. His forehead was damp with sweat and his lips curled into a mischievous, cheshire cat-like smile. A woman tugging at the man's bicep in the picture had been cropped off by the editor and was seen only as a pair of sinuous arms. In the background, a young groom danced with his bride.

He stared at the picture. A single moment frozen in time. A smile briefly crossed his lips before his face turned hard. The man mugging for the camera at the center of the photograph was more than a blue pin pushed into a one-dimensional paper map. He was a husband and father.

Dunn went back to the map. His eyes jumped from country to country. Beattie, represented by a green pin was stuck into Prague. He pulled it out. Williams, a red pin, jammed into Budapest. Dunn released him. Hall, a yellow pin, survived Warsaw. He freed her. He tore the map from the wall and the remaining pins popped out onto the floor, liberated. They would all be coming home now. All but one.

After he'd arranged for transportation and body retrieval, he called the dead man's wife. The first chore was simple enough. The latter was the single hardest thing he ever had to do. When he was finished, he packed up his meager belongings and prepared to walk out the front door of his Belgian home for the last time.

Inside the Athénée Palace Hotel's lobby people talked feverishly, stopping only briefly to stare when Dunn walked in. There was electricity in their conversations and a seriousness of demeanor. That there was a dead man in one of the hotel rooms hardly seemed scandalous.

It was impossible to tell if the lobby was populated with guests of the hotel or merely pedestrians who had come in off the street to join the conversation. In any case, everyone was propped up by either a drink or a smoke.

One of the smokers stubbed out his cigarette and approached Dunn. He walked with the assistance of a cane and stuck out a hand.

"Are you the gentleman from Spa Group?" The man asked.

"I am."

"James Brewer from the Ambassador's office. I spoke to you on the phone yesterday." He checked his watch.

"Circumstances beyond my control," Dunn replied.

James Brewer was thin and frail looking. He had more black hair than he knew what to do with, small teeth and girlish hands. Mouse like. He wore a wrinkled, dark blue pinned striped suit and looked much older than his age. "I'm sorry sir, what did you say your name was again?"

"I didn't."

"Right. Well, I hope you had a nice flight or ride in, whichever way you got here."

"Where is he?" Dunn cut him off.

"Third floor." Brewer spun petulantly on a heel. "I'll show you."

Dunn let the little rat lead. He followed the embassy worker through an orgy of marble pillars anchored by travertine tiles. Sparkling chandeliers trimmed in gold lit their way. Expensive furniture set in deep alcoves listened in on hushed conversation. The hotel lobby was cold, hard and wastefully extravagant.

The staff was neatly dressed and obvious. A couple of disinterested women sat in the lounge, chatted up by a heavy bartender. Three pairs of eyes followed Dunn and Brewer as they walked by. Dunn stared back until they lost the desire to compete.

When they reached the elevators, Dunn stepped inside first and took up a position in the back, Brewer near the control panel.

Once the door had completely closed, Brewer remarked, "These are quite remarkable times."

Dunn nodded.

"Did you see the footage last night?"

"I heard about it," Dunn replied.

"They executed Ceausecu *and* his wife."

Dunn said nothing. Of course, he'd seen it. For nine years he and his colleagues worked around the clock supporting an effort to overturn the communist regimes of the Eastern Bloc nations. The United States provided funding and organizational support for the dissenters while Radio Free Europe advanced the virtues and sensibilities of democracy.

By the summer of '89 their efforts had paid off. Poland and Hungary had peacefully ousted their communist regimes, Poland boasting the first non-communist government in Eastern Europe. In November, East Berliners had crossed over the notorious wall into Czechoslovakia without incident. A day later, Bulgarian dictator Zhivkov stepped down. A week after that, demonstrators in Prague forced the communists from power in Czechoslovakia. Romania was the sixth and the last of the Eastern Bloc.

"The whole thing was televised." Brewer's voice rose. "They were tried and executed all in one day. Unbelievable. Not a very merry Christmas."

"Depends on who you ask."

The events of the previous ten days started in western Romania in a town called Timisoara and had ended in the capital, Bucharest. On December 16, a protest broke out over the government's attempt to deport a popular Hungarian pastor, but before long, the pastor's cause had been abandoned and motivation then turned to the removal of the communist regime. The military intervened and battled the citizens of Timisoara for four days resulting in hundreds of casualties.

On December 21, Nicolae Ceausecu, the Romanian Dictator for the last 25 years, summoned the people of Bucharest to the plaza that adjoined the Central Committee Building. 100,000 people gathered in the capital to hear the Eastern Bloc's last dictator condemn the people's protests in Timisoara.

To Dunn and his colleagues, the fall of communism in Romania was nothing more than a formality, the last domino in the Eastern Bloc that was going to fall whether Nicolae Ceausecu cooperated or not. The events in Timisoara had already been bloodier than the whole of Eastern Europe and the situation was about to get worse.

The second story balcony of The Central Committee building in Bucharest faces west out onto a public square. It was from this vantage point, that Ceausecu would stand, undeterred by the reality that surrounded him in eastern Europe, and begin once more to laud the accomplishments and advantages of the communist state to the citizens of Romania, clearly misreading the writing on the wall.

As the Romanian dictator continued to read from the communist script, the people began to rebuke him. Tentatively at first, a few shouted from the back of the crowd: *We are the people, down with the dictator!* As their confidence grew, so did their voice.

An anxious Ceausecu attempted to chide the rising sea of dissenters *Sit quiet in your places.* He scolded them.

They would not, could not.

Having heard of the incredible steps their neighbors had taken, Romanians were eager to light the flame of freedom. They castigated Ceausecu and his party, ridiculed his pathetic attempts to appease the working class and mocked his collectivist plans for the future. They had given their blood for a chance in Timisoara and would give it again in Bucharest.

As the Romanian people continued their rebuke and Ceausecu retreated into the Central Committee Building, shots were fired into the crowd igniting chaos and sparking a standoff between Ceausecu's security forces and the Romanian Army.

The Revolution that started in Timisoara would end in Bucharest. In four days' time, Eastern Europe's last Communist dictator would become a fugitive, be captured, be tried and executed.

"He should have just stepped down like the others," Brewer said. "He shouldn't have run."

"He shouldn't have killed people."

When the elevator doors opened on the third floor, Dunn stepped in front of Brewer and headed down the hallway to the hotel room where inside, his friend lay dead. There was no need to ask which room it was. Bright yellow tape crisscrossing the door at the end of the hall gave that mystery away.

"The chief of the politzia said the body was discovered two days ago." Brewer picked up the pace, trying to keep up.

Dunn spoke over his shoulder. "And it took you until yesterday to call me?"

"It was quite chaotic around here as you might imagine. Nobody knew who to answer to, not even the military. The man being a foreigner, an American, the politzia did not want to get involved. They called the American Embassy. I did a little investigating on my own, but wasn't able to find or get a hold of any of the man's family," Brewer lamented.

"How did you get my number?"

"The chief of politzia gave me a bag of your colleague's personal effects. I found a card in there. I didn't want to waste any more time trying to find his family." Brewer scrunched his nose. "I couldn't imagine the man was getting any...fresher, the longer we waited."

"I wouldn't think so." Dunn stopped in the hallway in front of the taped off door. "You made the right decision." He held out his hand and Brewer gave him the room key. A little hand gesture and Brewer took the bag holding the dead man's personal effects from his coat pocket and handed them to Dunn as well.

Dunn put the key in hotel room number 316 and opened the door.

Brewer gagged.

Dunn breathed through his mouth.

They pushed through the yellow tape and into the room.

"Good god." Brewer gasped.

A man wearing clean blue jeans and a white button-down dress shirt lay stretched out on the queen-sized bed. His skin appeared gray-green in the hotel light. His mouth was slightly ajar and his eyes closed. His right arm lay across his stomach, his left arm by his side. A pair of shoes was set at the foot of the bed.

Dunn cleared his throat.

It would seem as though the hotel occupant kicked off his shoes and laid down for an afternoon nap in a nicely appointed suite and died a peaceful death while the world fell apart outside his window.

Dunn lifted the man's right shoe, inspected it.

"How do you think he died?" Brewer asked through a handkerchief that covered all but his eyes.

Brown leather dress shoes, size eleven, inexpensive. Dunn put the right shoe down and picked up the left, made eye contact with Brewer. "I'm not the coroner." He turned back around and scanned the light fixture overhead for any obvious signs of a listening device.

"It doesn't look like foul play," Brewer said. "He probably just had a heart attack."

"Yeah." Dunn answered with a hint of sarcasm. "That's probably all it was."

"I must admit, if you're going to die in a hotel room, there are worse ones to go in." Brewer noted through his handkerchief.

Dunn continued to inspect the left shoe. Its heel was loose, as though it had been removed. He picked up the right shoe again and checked its heel. It wriggled a little and started to come loose. The shoes weren't that cheap. He put them both back down.

"Is there something wrong with his shoes?" Brewer asked. His voice distorted as he pinched his nose.

Dunn ignored him.

He knew that in the last three days any number of people had already been in and out of this hotel room. Communist agents scurrying around the hotel room like rats desperate for scraps of intelligence to take back to the nest to feed whatever vermin remained, trying to keep their species from becoming extinct. They were meticulous, even searching the dead man's shoes.

Dunn walked up beside his friend and fought back the urge to vomit. Blocking Brewer's view of the body, he pinched a bit of Murdoch's shirt sleeve between his thumb and forefinger and gave it a tug, exposing the watch on his left wrist. The agent had pulled out the stem on his wrist watch the moment he felt threatened. Whoever entered room 316 had done so on December 21 at exactly 11:07 a.m. and 23 seconds. Not on the 23rd as the chief of politzia had told Brewer. Whoever it was had been unexpected. And they were responsible for Thomas Murdoch's death.

Dunn glanced back at Brewer. The embassy man was busy picking lint off of his suit jacket, his cane resting against his leg. He looked back over his friend's body. There were no obvious signs of foul play as Brewer had so accurately pointed out. Whoever killed him would have had to have been clever and quick.

To Dunn, *why* his friend had been killed was no mystery.

Once he was back in the States, the agency would figure out *how*. *Who* killed him didn't matter.

Not yet.

Dunn said, "I have people coming to claim my colleague's body."

Brewer stood holding the kerchief to his nose, his other hand propped up his elbow. He didn't get the hint quickly enough.

"Someone must be downstairs to meet them," Dunn added forcefully.

Brewer said nothing, but made a point of rolling his eyes before grabbing his cane and turning on the ball of his foot before heading out the door.

Dunn waited a moment after Brewer was gone and then once more looked up at the light fixture. This time, he spoke to it.

"I know you are listening." He stepped back and checked the hotel room door, made sure it was closed all the way. "I know you bastards killed him, but the game is over. You've lost." Dunn glared defiantly around the room as he spoke. A listening device could be anywhere. "This man believed in something bigger than himself. He wasn't afraid to die." He couldn't contain the scowl that was forming on his face. "He was a good man, a kind man. He believed in the decency of the human spirit and the redemptive power of forgiveness." Dunn rubbed his chin, maintained his composure. "I don't." He took a step closer to the bed so that he was positioned in the middle of the small hotel room. "So, when I find the son-of-a-bitch that killed my friend, I swear to God, I am going to kill him too."

1

One of the men grabbed his partner by the shoulder, stopping him before he stepped in it. *It,* was an expanding puddle of blood pooling on the apartment's white, tiled floor. And until a moment ago, it was contained inside the body of 64-year old Hinata Sakai. Now, too much of *it* was spilling on the floor.

Mr. Sakai couldn't move. The loss of blood made his limbs heavy and his head light. His glasses had fallen off when he hit the floor, leaving him unable to see with any degree of clarity. Conversely, he could hear just fine and from what he could tell, multiple assailants had broken into his apartment. He guessed three. They spoke to each other in a foreign tongue and rummaged through his belongings. He knew why they were here.

While working towards his retirement as an employee of the Waste and Environmental Safety department, a lower level subdivision of the International Atomic Energy Agency, Mr. Sakai was alarmed by a recent discovery. He noticed the discrepancy while auditing the shipping manifests of various supply chain entities associated with a Tokyo based logistics company. The company had contracted with a Japanese nuclear energy supplier to move 150,000 pounds of spent nuclear fuel waste distributed in ten casks, from their continuously growing stockpile, for reprocessing at the PA Mayak facility in Ozyorsk, Russia. Sakai discovered that only eight of the casks were scheduled to be shipped back.

This was not an accounting error. Somebody didn't accidentally transpose numbers. There were no missing digits or decimals. There was only missing cargo. 30,000 pounds worth of dangerous nuclear cargo.

Despite this fact, he was greeted with total apathy when he escalated his findings up the chain of command to the Division of Radiation, Transport and Waste Safety. Unsatisfied with their nonresponse, he decided go above their authority and raised the issue with The Office of Nuclear Security.

Before he even had the chance to formulate an email highlighting his concerns, he received a call from the Director of The Office of Nuclear Security. He found it odd given the sub-department's earlier disinterest.

The Director was an irritable man named Steiner. An Austrian-born Swede who enjoyed displaying his command of the English language through the use of condescension and sarcasm. Within minutes, it was obvious to Mr. Sakai that the Director cared less about the perilous nature of his discovery and was more interested in the storage of and potential dissemination or leaking of the disparate information.

Steiner demanded to know everyone he'd spoken to about his findings with regard to the logistics company. Sakai told him that he had not spoken to anyone except the Managing Director of the Division of Radiation, Transport and Waste Safety. He kept the fact that he had indeed questioned the Chairman of the shipping company to himself. Steiner appeared to accept his answer. Then, in what seemed to be an attempt at a threat, he asked Mr. Sakai if he were married or had any children. The question had made him uneasy, but it was one that he answered in the negative.

Finally, Sakai was reminded by the Director of his past failures as the top official in charge of the Nuclear and Industrial Safety Agency in Japan during the Fukushima nuclear disaster. An incident that marked only the second time, after the Chernobyl accident in 1986, that a disaster reached a Level 7 classification on the Nuclear Event Scale. The agency was abolished shortly after and Mr. Sakai left the country in shame, eventually finding new employment with the IAEA in its New York City offices.

The conversation with the Director was enlightening. Mr. Sakai suspected that senior officials of the IAEA were aware of the situation and may even be active participants in the plan to cover it up. His belief was reinforced when the Director strongly advised against investigating any further.

The men continued to move with purpose around the small apartment. They opened drawers and combed through cabinets, snatching folders and papers of any perceived relevance. They hunted through the books on his bookshelf and took his laptop and cell phone. It was all an exercise in futility. Fearing such a scenario, he had committed all damning information to memory.

Sakai was desperate to alert the international community, particularly those in Japan, before it was too late. However, having been shunned by his country of birth due to his past failure, he was certain that none of his old colleagues would have listened to him or taken his call.

He knew that even a small amount of unaccounted for fissile

material floating around freely posed an enormous security risk. One that could change the balance of power in the Middle East, threaten Europe and destabilize continents across the globe.

He knew that what he'd found wasn't an innocent typo. Destruction was coming. For him personally, the consequences of his discovery had already proved to be deadly.

Frantic, he determined that his childhood friend was the only one who was loyalty enough to listen to him and had the conviction to take the necessary action without any bureaucratic questioning. But, his friend too was ostracized and currently in hiding and therefore, was unable to be contacted directly. So, Sakai had reached out to his friend's only available next of kin and transferred what he knew verbally and in person in an urgent attempt to prevent a nightmare scenario. She left his apartment fifteen minutes ago.

His assailant's voices trailed off and he knew that he was slipping into the quiet abyss of death. He was correct to have suspected that someone would come for him. Still, he was surprised at the finality with which they'd chosen to operate.

Slitting his throat. He must have really pissed someone off.

The men left his apartment as abruptly as they had come in. Their departure caused a vacuum and lack of noise that was filled by the discomforting sound of his heart beating inside his head.

As he listened to the slow, deafening drumbeat of his heart pumping the final liters of blood from his body, he wondered if it was fair to have burdened his friend's daughter with information of such fatal importance. He replayed the conversation with her over and over in his head. He was confident that he'd made the right decision.

Then he realized.

He'd forgotten to tell her one other thing.

2

Ayumi stood with her hands over her head, leaning against the smooth tile. Warm water cascaded over her shoulders and down her back. After the 13-hour flight from Tokyo to New York, she arrived at JFK International Airport and took a cab straight to Mr. Sakai's apartment on 49th street, per his urgent instructions. As she watched the water trickle down the drain at her feet, she wondered if that had been a good idea.

Mr. Sakai is a dear and trusted friend of her family's, but considered persona non grata back in their home country. As the top official of the scrapped Nuclear and Industrial Safety Agency, he was the scapegoat for the Fukushima nuclear disaster after the tsunami of 2011. His relationship with Ayumi's father complicated matters and dictated that any contact between them be discreet. So it was that today, Ayumi met with her father's longtime friend in his absence and received alarming information that she was asked to pass along to him.

After leaving Mr. Sakai's apartment, she checked into her room on the 35th floor of the Millennium Hilton at One UN Plaza, procured for her by her father's friend. A return flight to

Tokyo departed early tomorrow morning. She was anxious to get home and untether herself from the information deposited on her by Mr. Sakai. In the meantime, she'd reserved a table for one at the Ambassador Grill with the intention of eating a good meal. She planned to skip breakfast tomorrow morning and not eat again until the following day.

The hot shower felt good and she was beginning to relax. She'd set her phone on the bathroom counter and tapped into a playlist for a little background noise. Her hips moved subtly as The Rolling Stones asked for sympathy for the Devil. A thin river of water flowed down the front of her neck and spilled out over colorful, tattooed breasts.

The Irezumi tattoo that covered her upper body was applied using the traditional Tebori process. A method that utilizes a needle attached to the end of a bamboo rod and that is tapped into the skin. The colorful artwork covered both of her arms and breasts as well as the entirety of her back. The ink stopped short of her hands at the wrists and below her neck at the top of her shoulders. Lengthwise, color flowed downward over her ribs to the middle of her waist. The tattoo was worn like a jacket. A two-inch gap of skin was left untouched down the middle of her chest and stomach, leaving her bellybutton unstained.

A red koi, a black serpent and a green dragon intermingled with pink cherry blossoms and rolling blue waves born out of bold, curling lines. A grisly blue Oni mask with fangs and bulging eyes was etched on her left shoulder. The dragon clawed up her right side from her waist to her underarm and reached out for the curve of her breast. On her back, a gruesome depiction of the severed head of a Samurai warrior or Namakubi. A warning to all those who understood its significance.

Water splashed off of the tiled stall and echoed in the small bathroom while the hissing of the shower competed with the

'Stones. She ran her fingers through her hair one last time to make sure she'd rinsed out all of the shampoo before turning the water off. It took both hands to wring out her hair, twisting it in multiple, foot-long sections before grabbing a towel and stepping out of the shower.

She'd decided on an all-black outfit for dinner, and after having dried herself off, slipped into a pair of panties and matching bra. She pulled on a long sleeved, button down shirt, but hadn't yet decided if she were going to wear a skirt or pants. She resolved to figure that out as she dried her hair.

Bent over at the waist with her hair nearly touching the ground, the hairdryer whined loudly as she waved it back and forth across a fluttering curtain of black silk. She noticed that her toenails weren't painted and upon realizing this, made the decision to wear pants to dinner. She had a pair of black Jimmy Choo's in her suitcase that were perfect for her outfit and would hide her naked toes.

As she continued to wave the hair dryer back and forth, she noticed a sudden, perceptible change in the temperature of the room. Cool air nipped at her ankles, having arrived along with the pungent smell of a recently exhausted cigarette. The bathroom door was open and a pair of ugly boots stepped into her field of view.

The boots were brown and worn. A speck of what looked like dried paint stained the tip of one of the shoes. She hadn't invited anyone to come into her hotel room. Certainly not into the bathroom. Anyone who knew anything about her wouldn't have made such a mistake.

Somebody was about to get hurt.

Ayumi stood up straight and fast. Her long hair whipped the face of the hotel room intruder, buying her a second which she used to level a solid kick to the groin. But her target was unfazed and responded with a quick, open-handed slap to her face that knocked her off balance and backward up against the toilet.

Ayumi shook off the blow and then launched forward striking her assailant in the side of the head with the hairdryer that stuttered for a moment, but was still plugged in and continued to whine loudly.

The stunned intruder fell sideways onto the vanity counter top. He was wiry and unattractive with a shaved head and narrow eyes. She wasn't fooled by the bogus maintenance attire and was sure that she hadn't seen him before.

She jumped on his back and wrapped the cord from the still whining hairdryer around his neck. Beneath the cord, a tattoo of a snake wrapped itself around his neck as well. A little lower down his neck, a dagger tattoo that appeared to pierce one side and exit the other.

Ayumi was all too aware that in certain societies tattoos were more than just ink stains on flesh. Sometimes, they were labels, wanted or not, that identified who a particular person was or what a person did or was willing to do. She recognized this man as a killer whose services were for hire.

She jammed the hot end of the hairdryer against his cheek under his eye and pressed down hard, branding his face and producing an audible response. The intruder cried out in pain and struggled to get free. Unable to get loose, he pulled the cord from the electrical outlet.

Ayumi was on his back and held the cord tight as the man thrashed around the confines of the small bathroom. He grasped at the hairdryer cord with one hand, while the other clawed at her. He was running out of fight and fell to his knees in front of the toilet. He focused both hands on the cord tightening around his neck. She could feel him starting to fade. His energy was almost exhausted.

She clenched her teeth and squeezed tighter. The Rolling

Stones continued to haunt the bathroom as "Gimme Shelter" rang out from her cell phone. The man's head was bright red. She stood over him like the owner of a disobedient canine, holding the cord like a leash as he knelt on the bathroom floor.

She was going to teach this dog a lesson.

She reached for her hairbrush on the counter. She planned to wrap the dryer cord around it to use as a garrote and finish him off, but it was just out of reach. She let go with one hand and took a half step sideways toward the counter, keeping an eye on the intruder on the floor in front of her.

Just as her fingers made contact with the hairbrush, she was stopped in her tracks. It was as if her hair had got caught on something. Then she felt the thick edges of a pair of heavy hands up against the back of her head. Before she could turn around and see who it was, she was ripped from the bathroom by her hair. Her hand slipped off the hairdryer cord and for a moment, she lost all conscious thought.

3

K yle slid the squeegee into his tool belt and arched his back. Sitting on a boson's chair four hundred feet off the ground doesn't offer too many agreeable positions, but it was the isolation that attracted him to the job. Where else could you work in a city of approximately 8 million people and never have to interact with any of them.

Except for Carl.

"Are you ready yet?" Kyle asked.

"Just a second," Carl answered.

The young man was meticulous. So, it had gone since the two men began working together four days ago.

Retired from his first career, Kyle had moved into the city to get lost amongst the millions of residents. He had long appreciated New Yorker's steely resolve to ignore each other even while forced to cohabitate in such cramped and close quarters. He enjoyed anonymity and the personality of the city suited him. And in a city this large, no one would miss you when you were gone.

When he accepted the job, he was advised that his position was a solitary one, but for the occasional need to complete a job quickly and thus incorporating another employee. The current job met the criteria and so Carl and Kyle were assigned to clean the windows of the Millennium Hilton New York. They were now a team, even if they never said so.

To Kyle, the team was everything. He had lived his entire adult life by the creed of leaving no man behind and this job would be no exception. Carl's attention to detail was countered by Kyle's efficiency and the two of them got along without having to think much about it.

"Dang birds." Carl pulled out his scraper. "What do they eat anyway?"

If the isolation is what drew Kyle to this line of work, then the view was a very good secondary benefit. He was surrounded by some of the most recognizable buildings in the world and at this vantage point he couldn't help but feel to be a part of a living work of art. And quite literally, closer to heaven.

He lifted his head and his eyes rolled passed tiles of green glass to the top of the high rise and into the heavens. Above, the tattered blue and white sky retreated giving way to solid gray clouds that drew a low, horizontal line. He wasn't sure anymore if Heaven existed, but if it did, then God was angry and it was not a good day to be an angel. Winter was getting anxious and it pushed at their chairs with a cold stiff hand.

"You ready now?" Kyle asked again.

"Almost." Carl scraped at the bird shit. "Stuff's like paint." He smiled.

Carl always smiled.

While he waited for Carl to finish the window, Kyle considered his reflection in the tinted glass. Staring back at him were his mother's eyes. Only, his were cynical. Forged by a lifetime of loss and the knowledge that sometimes, no matter how much you cared, no matter how skilled a person was, there was nothing you could do to save the ones you loved.

A substantial head of hair passed down from her father barely moved when taunted by the stiffening breeze. Two of his mother's dimples were barely visible, hiding underneath a day's worth of stubble.

The more severe features he had received from his father. His slightly pointed nose drifted to the left side of his face and was anchored by a solid, angular jaw. A vertical crease between his brows served to keep strangers from getting too close. The straightest line of all was the one formed by his lips, like the seam of an unopened box.

Carl sidled his bosons chair up next to Kyle in front of the green glass building. With their reflections, the two men appeared as four marionettes.

"I'm ready," Carl said.

"You sure?" Kyle asked Carl's twin in the glass.

"I swear." Carl smiled wide and answered Kyle's reflection. "I'm good to go, now."

Kyle checked his watch. "Okay. Well, then what do you think?" He asked. "A couple of more windows?"

"What time is it?"

"Five twenty-three," Kyle answered.

"Whoa." Carl stopped smiling.

"Something wrong?"

"Yeah. A little bit," Carl said. His voice fell off.

"What is it?"

"It's our anniversary today. And I promised Kim that I'd take her out to dinner tonight," Carl said.

The two men were still communicating via their reflections and the expression on Kyle's face said he did not understand.

"I made reservations for seven o'clock." Carl's eyebrows jumped to the top of his forehead. "There's no way I could make it home in time to pick her up and get to Angelo's by seven."

"Angelo's?" Kyle whistled. "You had better not be getting paid more than me," he teased. "How long have you two been married?"

"We aren't married yet. We've just been dating for two years."

It didn't register as a big event for Kyle and he remained expressionless.

"That's why tonight is so important." Carl turned away from the glass to look at Kyle. "Tonight, I'm going to ask her to marry me."

Carl's smile had returned and it was the biggest that Kyle had seen yet.

"Well, congratulations to you both."

"Thanks. What about you?" Carl asked.

"What about me?"

"Do you have a wife or girlfriend?" Carl hesitated. "Kids?"

"No."

"No to which one?"

"No to all three."

"Really? A good-looking dude like yourself."

"Really." Kyle's answer was flat and unemotional.

"You're a lone wolf, huh?" Carl jabbed an elbow at Kyle. "Out on the prowl."

"I'm not much for prowling."

"Yeah, me neither," Carl confessed. "That's why I'm getting married." He thought for a half second and then quickly added, "That, and the fact that I love her."

"I'd call her if I were you," Kyle said. "Let her know that you'll be running a little late."

"I hear that, loud and clear," Carl replied.

The two sat staring at each other until Carl broke the silence. "I forgot my phone," he said. "I was so excited thinking about this evening that this morning I ran out of the house without it."

"Use mine." Kyle handed his partner his cell phone.

"Wow, this is nice." Carl whistled. "Is this the new one?"

"Something like that."

Carl rolled Kyle's phone over in his hands. "I only got a prepaid. Trying to save for the wedding and all."

"You're sure she's going to say yes?"

"Look at me." Carl held his hands out wide. "Who could resist this?" His smile turned into a mischievous grin.

"Well, partner." Kyle patted Carl on the shoulder. "A wise man once said that all you need in this life is ignorance and confidence and success is assured. So, I think you've got it covered."

"Oh, I see how you are," Carl said. "I'm gonna take that as a compliment."

"Feel free." Kyle smiled and snatched the tool bucket off of Carl's chair and attached it to his own. "I'll get our gear topside." He nodded skyward. "Mother Nature is looking kind of angry." He pushed the jumar that held his lines and began ascending the building. "I'd call Kim quickly if I were you."

"I will." A gust of wind pushed Carl's chair sideways, but he hardly noticed. He was preoccupied with Kyle's cell phone. He looked up in time to see that his partner was already two and a half floors clear. "Hey." Carl shouted halfheartedly. His voice was stolen away on the breeze. "You'd better not be getting paid more than me."

4

Ayumi crashed into the dresser. She was still being held by her hair. Before she was able to get to her feet, she was jerked off the floor and swung over the bed and into the headboard.

She rolled onto her hands and knees and onto her clothes that had been spilled all over the bed. Her laptop bag was emptied onto the chair. She touched her face and confirmed that her chin was cut. A warm trickle of blood ran from her nose onto her upper lip. She spat it onto the pillow.

Her attacker paused for damage assessment. He smirked when he noticed that she'd been bloodied. He held on tight to the end of her long hair.

Compared to the man she'd wrestled with in the bathroom, this man was much larger. His hair was grown out, but short in style. His face was full of stubble and he too wore a maintenance uniform that wouldn't fool anyone. She caught a glimpse of some blue-black ink on his hands.

The thin man staggered out of the bathroom. The color was returning to his face as he rubbed at his neck. The branded, red circle from the hairdryer was noticeable on his left cheek. "Suka!" *Bitch!* He swore at her.

The big man seemed to nod in appreciation after seeing what Ayumi had done to his partners face.

She flashed him a disingenuous smile in return. "You like that?"

His amusement faded however, and now knowing what she was capable of, he reached into the front of his work uniform and pulled a combat knife from a leather sheath that was strapped around his waist.

He lunged at her with the knife, but she was able to keep herself at her hair's length. She jumped off the bed and negotiated the furniture in the room like an acrobat. He lunged again, but Ayumi was too quick and again dodged out of the way.

Frustrated, he yanked her hair to bring her within striking distance. She coiled up on her back in a protective posture as she was dragged to within his reach. When he slashed at her, she spun and used her feet to deflect his arm and guide the knife away from her body. The knife grazed his hand and cut her hair off where he'd held it. Separated, Ayumi rolled backward away from him.

She sprung to her feet and ran for the door where the thin man was kneeling down next to an oversized, black canvas duffle bag. He had a cellphone in his hand and appeared to be texting. He stood up to stop her as she ran his way. She met him with a perfectly placed jump kick to the chest, knocking him backward and into the wall. She opened the hotel room door and was about to get away when the door suddenly slammed shut, catching her right hand in the process.

The big man leaned heavily on the door. The diamond on the ring on her middle finger cracked and broke on impact. The ring had saved her hand from being crushed, but now she was stuck and had no way to escape.

The large man twisted her left arm up and behind her back while snaking a muscular arm around her neck. She was immobilized and in a choke hold, unable to move or make a sound. "Playtime is over."

He dragged her backward toward the bathroom. She could see the knife in his hand out of the corner of her eye. She pulled at the arm around her neck and struggled to breath. She was starting to lose the strength to fight back.

The large man instructed his partner to follow him into the bathroom. When the thin man hesitated, he was scolded. "Nemedlenno!" *Right now!*

Mr. Sakai was afraid that someone would come for him. Ayumi was certain that they had. And now, they had come for her too. She feared what might be coming next.

In the bathroom, the big man gave the knife to his partner and grabbed her other arm, holding them both behind her back with one hand. He lifted the toilet seat and pushed her head down and over the bowl with his free hand. Her nose dripped blood into the water as she was choked by the toilet bowl rim.

"Sdelay eto," the large man ordered. *Do it.*

Ayumi couldn't move and felt frozen in time. Breathing was difficult and she could hear her heart pounding heavily inside her head. Scenes from her childhood flashed before her mind's eye on a screen of black. First, her brothers as little children. Then, her father. Finally, a koi pond and her mother kneeling down beside it, feeding the fish.

The cool toilet water numbed her mind as it washed up against her head. The men's voices echoing from inside the bowl were drifting farther and farther away. Her fingers brushed up against her attacker's uniform and the sensation brought Ayumi instantly back to the moment.

The big man was over top of her, bent at the knees, almost

sitting on her to hold her down. She could feel his leg moving against her hand as he shouted urgent commands at his partner.

She processed the mental image that her fingertips were sending back to her brain. She needed her assailant to move a little to his right. When he finally did, she grabbed and squeezed with all the strength she had left.

He stood up and tried to pry Ayumi's hand from his crotch. When she wouldn't let go, he responded by forcing her head down and into the toilet until she released him and lie nearly lifeless over the rim of the toilet.

"Give me the knife," the big man ordered. "I'll do it myself."

The thin man hesitated. He leaned forward to take a look out of the bathroom and into the hotel room as if he was waiting for or expecting someone. Finally, he handed over the blade.

The big man gathered Ayumi's hair in a ponytail so that her neck was exposed. He pulled her head up by her hair and spat in her face. He shoved her head back into the toilet and set the blade of the knife against the back of her neck.

Before he was able to go any further, the hotel door swung open and a third man stepped inside. He was dressed in black jeans and a leather jacket. A full beard covered his face.

"Niko, stop. Don't kill her." He spoke calmly. "There's been a change of plans."

5

Kyle stopped and locked his line, thirty-five stories above 44th Street and four floors above Carl. The wind had gotten stronger and now whipped noisily against the side of the building. He looked down, saw that his partner was preparing to ascend the skyscraper, and decided to wait for him.

He braced himself against the glass with his work boots and used a suction cup attached to his chair for further support. He took a second suction cup from Carl's work bucket, attached it to the glass and used it to pull himself close to the building.

He stared down the length of the hotel, his forehead resting against the window. From his vantage point, people really did look like ants, cars appeared as toys and for a second, he felt as though he might get vertigo.

He lifted his head to shake the sensation. With the sky darkening outside and from this close proximity, the glass of the skyscraper had lost its reflective property and allowed him to see into the hotel room in front of him. The curtains were opened wide and the whole of the room was in view. He couldn't believe what he saw.

Kyle peered in to see two men in maintenance attire dragging a partially clothed woman from the bathroom. One of the men held her upper body under her arms with a hand over her mouth. The other held her legs. Her eyes were wide and she struggled desperately, but she was overpowered by the two men and unable to get free.

A third man, was also in the room. He had in his hand an oversized sports equipment bag which he set the on the floor and opened wide. All three men acted calmly. The sound of the wind whistling against the glass outside juxtaposed against the scene unraveling inside made for an eery soundtrack.

Kyle maneuvered himself so that he was able to hide behind a length of curtain. He made a mental note of the floor that the hotel room was on. His heart pounded.

Carl had ascended the building and was now stopped next to his window washing partner. The wind was constant and Carl held onto Kyle's rope for support. "Thanks for waiting," he said. He was oblivious to what was taking place in the hotel room in front of him. "Check this out. I recorded a video of me proposing to Kim. I was thinking that maybe you could send it to her phone while we're at dinner."

Carl smiled. When Kyle didn't respond, he continued. "You know, me and her sitting there eating at Angelo's and then her phone rings. Of course, she'd have to answer it 'cause that's what she does, and then there'd be me on her phone asking her to marry me while I'm also sitting there in front of her. It'd be great," he said. "There's no way she could say no."

Kyle didn't hear him. His attention was focused on the hotel room. The two men had pinned the woman to the floor. One of the men produced a syringe from the duffle bag and had removed its cap. The woman saw this and became frantic.

"Here check it out." Carl held the phone out towards Kyle. "I got a great picture of those nasty storm clouds overhead, too."

32

The third man helped hold the woman still. They rolled her onto her side and pierced her left buttock with the needle. She tried to resist, but they held her tight.

"Hey. Spiderman." Carl tapped the phone on the glass to get Kyle's attention.

Kyle turned and grabbed Carl's arm. His tapping had got the attention of the men in the room as well. They turned toward the window. The woman locked eyes with Kyle and tried to scream.

Carl was still pointing to the video on the phone. The men in the hotel room saw him. Surely, they believed that Carl had just taken a picture of them.

Kyle grabbed Carl's ropes. The expression on his face and the intensity in his eyes caused Carl to lean back, perplexed, and concerned about his partners intentions. Kyle wanted to scold him for being so careless. He had brought them unwanted attention. Mostly, he wanted to tell Carl to get out of here. Get up to the rooftop and call for help. But it was too late. Out of the corner of his eye Kyle saw it coming, a large, dark blur rushing the window.

"Hold on!" Kyle kicked Carl's chair away as hard as he could. The suction cups holding his own chair popped and sent him sailing in the opposite direction. Between them, the window exploded. Shards of glass floated and then sank onto the street below.

Physics brought their chairs back together in front of the open window where the blur had materialized into a large man that reached out and took a firm grip of Carl's rope.

"Hey, what the-?," Carl yelled, trying to pull his rope free.

"The camera." The man held out his right hand.

He was a broad man with deep set eyes sheltered under an overstated brow. He had short dark hair and a pale complexion that was exaggerated by a navy-blue maintenance uniform. On the middle finger of his left hand, a solitary skull. It was obvious that English was not his first language.

"I don't have a camera." Carl tried to pull free. "Get your hands off my rope."

With her mouth uncovered for the moment, the woman in the room shouted, "Tora!"

The big man holding Carl's rope yelled over his shoulder for his partners to keep the woman quiet. "Shut her up."

She repeated the word Tora several times as if she desperately didn't want the two window washers to forget it. "Tora!"

Kyle assessed the situation. He kept one eye on the room. Inside, the woman was fading, her eyes were closing and her voice trailed off as she tried to speak. The other two men knelt on the floor beside and started fitting her inside the sports bag.

The large man instructed Carl once more. "Give me the camera."

Carl was indignant, "It's a phone. See." He held it in front of the man's face and took a picture. *Click.* "A *cell phone.* Do you know what that is?"

"Give it," the man insisted.

Carl craned his neck around the man and saw what they were doing with the woman. "Hey, screw you, man." He handed the phone to Kyle, who dropped it into his tool belt.

"Alex." The man holding Carl's chair called over his shoulder.

Alex was thin and lanky and had a protruding Adam's apple and a shaved head. He picked up a pair of bolt cutters from off the bed before making his way to the opened window. Shadowy blue-black tattoos crept up out of his collar and down from his shirt sleeves, indistinct symbols, words and pictures, few if any, professionally done. A raised, circular, red burn mark on his left cheek under his eye looked newly acquired. He pulled apart the long wooden handles, separating the cutter's short powerful blades.

The third man approached the window, having finally secured the woman in the duffle bag. He had dark hair and matching beard. His English was better and he spoke with confidence. Unlike the other two men, he was not wearing a maintenance uniform. He came to the window wearing a black leather jacket. "Vile words inspire neither man nor swine," he said. He gave Carl a penetrating stare. "Isn't that right, Niko?"

"Da," *Yes,* the large man replied.

"Svin'ya," *Swine.* Alex shouted. The bolt cutters opened wide.

Niko grabbed Carl's left hand and pried his fingers apart.

"It is the prod that motivates both," the third man continued. The accent was Eastern Europe. "Do you know what it is that separates men from beasts?" He asked.

Carl didn't answer.

"The thumb." The man continued, "Without it, we might as well have hooves."

"Svin'ya." Alex shouted again and put the blades to Carl's thumb.

"Wait, leave him alone," Kyle shouted.

Alex squeezed the handles of the bolt cutters and Carl's thumb clipped off with no resistance.

The screaming didn't seem human. Carl's eyes were clenched and he struggled to hang on to his rope with his right hand. Blood streamed down to his elbow and ran off one droplet after another in quick succession, carried by gusts of wind, speckling the side of the hotel.

Kyle felt in his tool belt for his razor knife.

The leader of the group turned his attention to Kyle. "Give Niko the phone."

Carl's breath came in short groaning bursts. "Don't give it to him." His eyes were pinched shut. He tucked his damaged hand under his right armpit to try and slow down the bleeding. The dark stain on his shirt grew larger by the second.

Kyle motioned to his co-worker. "Let him go. He needs medical attention."

The tall man nodded his head and Alex knew what to do. With one quick clip, he cut the rope holding Carl's bosons chair. Carl cried out in terror as his chair fell out from under him and left him dangling by his safety line.

"Alright, alright. Just stop," Kyle demanded. "I'll give you the phone."

Carl was going into shock.

"You need to let him go," Kyle pleaded once more.

"Let him go, Alex," the man ordered.

Alex spread the blades of the bolt cutter and reached out the window towards Carl's safety line.

"No!" Kyle yelled.

Carl yelled obscenities faster than they could be interpreted. Kyle pleaded for them to let him go. Their voices clashed in a maddening crescendo.

Alex cut the rope.

"Carl!" Kyle watched helplessly as Carl fell head over heels, his arms instinctively covering his head in a futile attempt to absorb the impact. Kyle turned away, sick to his stomach. He prayed that Carl died before he hit the ground.

The man in charge turned to Kyle, emotionless. He seemed to take no pleasure in what he had done to Carl, nor was he repulsed. He just stared with heartless intensity and again asked Kyle for the phone.

Other than a picture of one of the men's face, there was nothing on the phone of any value, a photo of the Chrysler building and a few empty phone numbers. He could give it to them and they might let him go. Or, he might still end up like Carl. He fished through his tool belt while assessing the three men. His fingers ran over the smooth contoured edges of his cell phone.

"Alright, alright," Kyle said.

Alex, who was nearer, reached his hand out for the cell phone. Kyle pulled his hand out of his tool belt and slashed with his razor knife, opening a white, gaping wound on the back of Alex's hand. The man dropped the bolt cutters on the floor and fell back from the window.

Niko charged forward. Kyle raised up on his boson's chair and met him in the face with the heel of his boot, stunning the man and giving himself a moment to think.

Kyle looked up. The rooftop of the hotel was still a lengthy four stories away. If these men had gotten the hotel's uniforms, they most certainly had access to the roof. There was no way he could outpace them to safety that way. He looked down.

451 feet.

A crowd circled below. Onlookers thrilled by the gruesome or respectful citizens concealing the carnage, Kyle couldn't tell which. He only knew that Carl was at the center, a dark stain on the sidewalk. The decision was made for him as Alex again came forward with the cutters.

Down it is.

Kyle unlatched the rope lock and the chair dropped instantly. Windows zipped by at a furious pace. He pinched the lock to slow the chair.

How much line did he have? 400 feet?

He couldn't remember.

The rope hissed as it passed through the lock. The bastard Alex was reaching out from the shattered window with the bolt cutters.

Halfway down.

Kyle could see that there were two bodies on the street. Carl's broken body on top of another.

He was descending too fast.

He squeezed the lock, and then let it go.

The crowd below was uneasy, pointing at him. The rope continued to hiss through the lock.

Almost there.

Alex refused to quit on the bolt cutters.

He was close now. Four stories to go.

He wasn't going to die. Couldn't die. Who would speak for Carl? The girl?

"Get out of the way!" He shouted, hoping that the people on the sidewalk could hear him.

They fled.

He squeezed the lock to slow his momentum one last time. The hissing of the rope passing through the lock stopped.

Kyle didn't.

Twenty-five feet from the pavement, he flailed his arms and tried not to land on Carl. The last thing that went through his mind were the words of the woman in the room.

Tora.

6

Frank Merylo hunched over his desk, reading glasses perched on the end of his nose. The downward turn of his mouth was natural. He opened a tan, dog-eared file folder and spread its contents in front of him. A paper clip held a series of photos together in the top right-hand corner. They were pictures of a blond-haired woman lying face down on the pavement. He pulled one from the stack and pushed it under his lamp.

"Excuse me," a voice said from the doorway.

Merylo didn't hear it. He was concentrating on the photos.

The woman was on her stomach, her head turned to the left. Her eyes were closed and her left hand lay flat on the pavement a few inches from her chin. Her left breast was partially exposed.

"Excuse me, detective?"

The woman looked as though she could be asleep, painfully at odds with her surroundings, lying in a damp, sunless alley, naked except for a pair of pink panties and matching socks. An overstuffed dumpster spilled its insides at her feet. This was no place for slumber.

There were close-ups of the woman's face. Her eyeliner had run down her cheek and there was a dirt smudge on her chin. Dried blood crusted around a nostril. Full body shots captured the scene from different angles. Pieces of debris on the pavement next to her were labeled with folded over index cards like some kind of a morbid science experiment. Each photo was worse than the one before.

Looking at the pictures, Merylo could feel his back tighten and his jaw clench. The brass thought it best that he transfer to a different department. Twenty years of dealing with organized criminals and his partner's recent murder had bought him some administrative leave and then a change of scenery. To Homicide.

Merylo didn't find that the scenery in Homicide was all that much different. He'd seen his share of dead guys over the years, organized criminals not being a very sensitive group. But at least one could make the argument that they knew what they were in for. Not so for the poor woman in the pictures in front of him.

He pushed the photos aside and was startled by a large man standing next to his desk.

"Detective Merylo?" The man asked.

"Jesus." Merylo barked. "How long have you been standing there?"

"Just a few minutes," the man chuckled. "I'm sorry. I didn't mean to scare you."

"Don't you know that there are rules about sneaking up on cops in the office?"

"No, sir."

"This ain't the healthiest of professions and some of us are prone to heart attacks."

"I'm sorry, sir."

Merylo stood up and was immediately conscious of the noticeable difference in height. "So what brings you to the seventeenth precinct Mr.-?"

"Joe Cavasano, sir. I'm your new partner." He held out a meaty hand.

"My new partner?" Merylo ignored the man's hand.

"Yes, sir."

Merylo sat down. "Already?"

"I'm sorry?"

"They don't fuck around do they, the brass?" Merylo said. "Benny's barely been gone a month."

Cavasano dropped his hand down to his side. "I'm sorry about detective McCarthy,"

"You keep saying you're sorry, but it don't look like you're old enough to be sorry about anything besides pissing the bed."

Cavasano didn't respond.

"I'm the one who's sorry. I should've been the one killed that night?" Merylo stood back up. "If it wouldn't have been for me, Benny would still be here." He ran a hand through his hair. "You have no idea how pathetic your little life is until somebody with everything to live for loses theirs because of you," he said. "Because Benny's gone, I get to wake up every morning and suck in a lungful of polluted air. Because Benny's gone, I get to fall asleep alone at night to the soothing rhythm of gunfire outside my window." Merylo looked down at the pictures on his desk. "Most of all, I have the privilege of seeing what happens when the scumbags of this city have too much free time on their hands." Merylo pushed the pictures off his desk.

Cavasano didn't flinch.

Merylo sat down and turned in his chair not wanting to expose himself emotionally. "Man, I hope you never have a friend like that."

Cavasano cleared his throat, "Actually, I had three friends like that. We all graduated from the academy in August 2001. A month later-"

The older detective swung his chair around, "Save your

breath, Cavasano. Every man, in every department in this city lost someone that day. Don't think for one second that you have a monopoly on that story."

"Please call me Joe," the younger detective said.

"I'll call you whatever I want." Merylo spat.

Just then a short, bald, bespectacled man in plainclothes poked his head into Merylo's office and rapped on the door molding. "Got a possible one eighty-seven on forty fourth and first."

Merylo got out of his chair, "How so?" He asked.

"Splat." The bald man clapped his hands together for effect.

"Pushed?"

"You're the fucking detective."

Merylo grabbed his jacket from the back of his chair and put it on. "How long ago?" He asked.

"It just got called in. I don't know, maybe ten minutes."

Cavasano had cleaned up the scattered pictures and was finishing putting them on Merylo's desk.

"Good. Perfect timing." Merylo adjusted his jacket. "It was getting stuffy in here."

"You want me to drive?" Cavasano asked.

Merylo laughed at the suggestion. "No way," he said. "I looked you up. Two speedings, a parking and a failure to yield all before you joined the force." Merylo hurried out of the office with Cavasano close behind. "The car may be a department issued piece of shit, but I've grown very fond of it."

7

U nder the shadow of a construction crane and the twenty-story apartment building she temporarily called home, Ingrid Garcia hustled northward up First Avenue. Litter tumbled by on the sidewalk and the rain had begun to fall in tiny drops to which the gusting wind had added a little sting. "Despacito" by Luis Fonsi rang out and she pulled her cell phone from her back pocket to check the caller id.

"Hi, Edward." She tried to conceal the displeasure in her voice.

"How's my Colombian beauty?" He always started the conversation with those words. Lately, she was beginning to be bothered by the constant reference to her country of origin. It came off as condescending.

"Yes. Eight o'clock is great," she lied. "I'll be on my way shortly. Thank you. I know, it's beautiful." She looked at her watch. "You really shouldn't have." There was more than a hint of honesty in her voice.

It was a gaudy thing, her watch. Encrusted in pink diamonds with a gold face, the watch kept great time, but was obnoxious and expensive, two characteristics that couldn't suit her less. The watch was one of a number of rings, earrings and bracelets that VanRoy had given her since they'd met four months ago. It was as if he saw her as a pitiful Christmas tree on which to hang his ornaments in order to disguise her modest South American upbringing.

She refused to refer to him as her boyfriend, even if that was what he'd liked to consider himself. Edward VanRoy was a well-educated, dark-haired, good looking, highly compensated executive. All of which, by its self, would not be enough to keep Ingrid interested after the third date. Add narcissism, a fifteen-year age differential and an ugly watch to the equation and their relationship was destined to go nowhere. But in spite of that and his refusal to accept that he and Ingrid were anything less than boyfriend and girlfriend as well as his near constant accentuation of her ethnicity, Ingrid had her reasons for maintaining the relationship, as long as it was at arm's length.

While Edward rambled in her ear, she and a half dozen New Yorkers were huddled at the corner of 23rd and First. Some of the pedestrians faced the rain head on, shielding themselves with umbrellas, briefcases and newspapers. Ingrid turned her back to it. When the light finally changed, she migrated with the herd, crossing over to the east side of First Avenue.

Ingrid had rebuffed Edward's earlier proposition to have a driver pick her up, opting to walk instead, but given the dramatic turnabout in the weather, she was beginning to regret her decision. The Yankees were playing in the World Series and VanRoy had reserved the best table at a new upscale sports bar in the Gramercy neighborhood from which to watch the game. She hadn't yet acquired an appetite for American bar food and so chose to grab a bite at a little Latin American eatery a couple blocks down. It too was new, if hardly upscale. But she liked the empanadas, even if they were made by Argentines.

Continuing north, the stiffening breeze cut through her thin layer of clothes and bit at her skin. She hugged herself with her free arm. What started out as a beautiful fall day had quickly degraded into what looked to become an ugly early winter storm. She had left her apartment wearing only a light jacket over the long-sleeved t-shirt, jeans and a pair of running shoes, a small purse slung over her shoulder. And as always, a small religious pendant on a thin chain around her neck. Her choice of footwear proved to be the smartest move she had made all day.

Suffering through the elements, Ingrid wished she were back home in Medellín. With an average daily temperature of 72 degrees, it was little wonder why her birthplace was referred to as the "City of Eternal Spring." As she hustled up First Avenue, she tried to tune out the worsening weather and focus on the reason she had come back to New York in the first place.

Her niece.

Four months ago, her sister's twelve-year-old daughter, Marlena, had gone missing from their home in Medellín. The family initially suspected the FARC, a left-wing rebel insurgent group that has operated inside Colombia for the last half century and is known to have used kidnapping and extortion to finance its cause. However, Marlena's family is considered middle class and they reside in a strata 4 neighborhood, and no ransom demand was ever made.

The fear then shifted to another, more sinister probability. Human trafficking. Hundreds of women and children are abducted and sold as sex slaves throughout South America every year. Young Peruvian, Ecuadorian and Colombian girls have been found thousands of miles away in Brazilian and Argentinian brothels, turning up on brochures for the underground sex tourism industry.

After weeks of searching without any leads, Ingrid's mother, who had lived in New York with her father until his death, decided to move back to Medellín to be with her youngest daughter in her time of grief. Ingrid was granted a leave of absence from her job with the Colombian National Army to assist with her mother's transition from the United States back to Colombia.

But a rumor circulating the streets of Medellín around this time involving a "gringo" who posed as a Chilean National caught her attention. The rumor stated that the man sold kidnapped Colombian girls for sex with American men. Undesirable girls were sold to Kings, Princes and Sultans in the Middle East for use as house servants. The stories varied wildly, but the description of the man was always the same. A tall, pale, American with reddish brown hair.

It was only moments after receiving a complimentary upgrade to first class on the New York bound Avianca flight from the Jose Maria Cordova International airport, en route to JFK that she met Edward VanRoy. Or more accurately, Edward VanRoy had met her. Seated across the aisle from her in the aircraft's front row of seats, he mentioned that he was on his way home from Colombiamoda, the Latin American equivalent of Fashion Week and an event held yearly in Medellín, the fashion center of South America. VanRoy claimed to have had attended on business. An added perk or necessary evil, he had boasted. Depending on how one looked at it.

Over the course of the five-and-a-half-hour flight from Medellín to New York, VanRoy turned on the charm, compliments and humor in an obvious attempt to win Ingrid's favor. She humored him, laughing graciously at his attempts to communicate in Spanish even after she assured him that having grown up with an English-speaking father, she was well versed in his native tongue.

VanRoy offered her a chance to be on the cover of one of the magazines his company owned on the spot. As well as being an heir to the VanRoy publishing empire, he was also the editor of one of the largest weekly woman's glossies in the country. It was a ridiculous offer as she'd never posed for anything more than a passport, driver's license or military ID in her life. She saw through the façade and politely rejected the offer.

They exchanged contacts and kept in touch and over the weeks that followed, VanRoy introduced her to a number of celebrities and New York royalty. Wealthy, good-looking people she had only heard about or seen through television shows and magazines. She'd been given the opportunity to sit front row at Madison Square Garden and in a luxury box at Yankee Stadium.

None of these things impressed or interested her much. They were only distractions in her search for the truth about her niece's disappearance. And VanRoy, she suspected, was not at all who he seemed. The more time she spent with him, the more he acted suspiciously like a friend who had planned a surprise for her, but was desperate for her to discover it on her own. And so, she played along at arm's length, waiting and watching for the big reveal.

"Alright, then. I'll see you later. Goodbye, Edward." Ingrid shoved her cell phone back into her pocket as she crossed 23rd Street and then started into a hasty jog.

The wind was more forceful, the rain heavier. Horizontal sheets of rain marched down First Avenue like curtains of water challenging all comers head on. Pedestrians scurried like rats, unable or unwilling to confront the ugly prelude to winter.

Ingrid leapt over a puddle in front of the Board of Education. She kept running and crossed 25th street. The sky was spitting on her now. The rain was heavy and hit everything with an audible smack. She crossed 26th Street without even looking, sped passed a fenced off green area and then darted for cover under an overhang at the entrance to Bellevue Hospital where she stopped to catch her breath.

The iconic hospital at 462 First Avenue attends to over

100,000 emergency room visits a year. On any given day, there could be over two hundred people rushed through its doors. Today, a conversation regarding one particular patient caught her attention.

As Ingrid stood under the overhang at the entrance to the hospital drawing shelter from the storm, she overheard a security guard as he spoke openly on his shoulder mic to a colleague stationed elsewhere on the hospital campus. She guessed him to be either Puerto Rican or Dominican. Either way, he spoke in Spanish and was within earshot.

"Who, the Chilean guy?" The guard was only half concerned with hospital security. He was excited and mostly interested in the information coming over via his earpiece. "Yeah, I heard a couple of guys fell off the side of the Millennium Hotel onto a guy on the sidewalk below," he exclaimed. "And one guy was a people trafficker. That's some crazy shit. Huh? My little cousin texted me. She works in fingerprinting." Suddenly aware of his surroundings, the guard gave Ingrid a quick look then turned his back to her and took a step away to create some distance.

The words "Chilean" and "people trafficker" sent a hot flash down Ingrid's spine. And even though she had only heard one side of the conversation, she knew it was worth looking into.

"And he's still alive?" The security guard continued his conversation. "You're still on the Head Trauma Ward? Right, fifth floor. Yeah, keep me posted. That's some crazy shit." Conversation over, the guard turned to give Ingrid another look, but she was already gone.

8

Prodded by a gentle rocking motion, Ayumi's head cleared and she rose out of the depths of unconsciousness. She opened her eyes and blinked several times, but darkness enveloped her and her eyes wouldn't adjust. She tried to stretch her limbs, but couldn't.

She was trapped.

Her thoughts raced back to the hotel room and the three men. She could still taste the dirty hand that had covered her mouth. With only the slightest range of motion, she moved her hands along the inside of the lightweight confinement until she felt the familiar tracks of a zipper and recalled being fitted inside a large bag.

She remembered the two window washers outside of her hotel room window and how she'd made eye contact with one of them. They saw what was happening and she hoped that they'd be able to help. Then her mind replayed the screaming. The horrific, hideous screaming. It was the last thing she remembered before she blacked out.

With her head now fully clear, she was able to discern that

she was being transported by automobile. With the exception of the constant whirring of tires through water, and the soft murmur of the radio, the space surrounding her was quiet. A bump in the road stung her buttocks and she was reminded of the needle.

At the hotel, her captors had spoken some English while confronting the window washers. Now, they began a conversation in Russian. She was fluent in five different languages herself and understood everything they said, each time they had spoken. The proximity of their voices assured her that she was not stuffed in the trunk and she listened closely, hoping to piece together information that would give her an indication of where they were or where they were going.

"Let's get rid of the woman now," Niko said.

Dmitri gave Niko a stern glance. "We can't."

"Of course, we can." Niko pulled a 9mm from the glove compartment.

"Someone else wants her alive." He eyed Alex who was slouching in the back seat.

"Who?" Niko checked the magazine. It was full.

"I'm not sure, yet," Dmitri admitted. "But it's none of your concern."

"It is my concern," Niko countered. "I was told that I would be paid to complete a job." He pulled back the slide to make sure there was a cartridge in the chamber. "I have to get paid."

Alex sat up straight in the back seat and squirmed uncomfortably.

Dmitri placed a hand on Niko's arm. "I'm going to make sure that you – we, get paid. Don't you worry about that."

"I am worried." Niko continued to express his concern over his payment and the new direction that their operation had taken.

A news story in the radio caught Dmitri's attention and he ordered Niko to shut up. "Zatknis." *Be quiet.* Dmitri said.

The radio was turned up as a newswoman recited the day's top story: "Two men are dead after an accident at an east side hotel. Paramedics responded to a call outside of the UN Millennium Hotel just after five o'clock this afternoon. A police spokesperson says that one window cleaner is dead after he and his co-worker fell from the side of the building on Forty Fourth Street. The second co-worker remains in serious condition at Bellevue Medical Center's Head Trauma Center. A pedestrian was also killed by the fall. Names are not being released until all the victims' family are notified. Police would not say at this time what caused the men to fall. In other news, an early season snowstorm is expected for much of the East Coast this evening..."

Dmitri turned the radio off and slowed the car quickly. He turned sharply to the left, changing directions.

"What are you doing?" Niko asked.

"We are going to Bellevue hospital," Dmitri answered.

Niko held onto the handle above the passenger side window. "What for?"

"The window cleaner is still alive."

"So, what?" Niko said. "Who cares about the window cleaner?"

"I do," Dmitri responded. He turned the vehicle again. "Somebody thinks they can fool us."

"What do you mean?"

"I don't think they were real window cleaners," Dmitri said. "I think they were imposters. I think that they were after me. After us," he said.

"What are we going to do if we find them?" Niko asked.

"We're going to go to the hospital and ask him some questions." He kept an eye on a suddenly disinterested Alex in the back seat. The thin man had stayed quiet the whole time and avoided eye contact as much as possible. "And then kill him."

Ayumi's head bumped against the wheel well as the vehicle made another sharp turn. The force of acceleration almost rolled her over.

They were on their way to Bellevue Hospital to kill the window washer who was still alive according to the report on the radio. This sudden detour could provide her with the opportunity she needed to try and escape. It might be her only chance to get away and find help.

She contorted herself to try and maneuver her right arm over her head, hoping to find where the zipper began. Her movements were slow and calculated. She was careful not to alert her captors to the fact that she had gained consciousness. She gave her arm a final push and was able to get it into position above her head.

Cramped by the tight space, she ran her fingers along the top of the bag until she located the seam. Finding it, she walked her fingers farther behind her head, following the tracks until she reached the smooth, flat underside of the zipper. Using her middle and index finger, she dug her nails behind the zipper and pulled. The zipper would not move. Her body was putting too much pressure on the overcrowded bag. She exhaled and drew her left arm in close to her body, trying to free up space and reduce the tension on the zipper. This time it moved.

She held her breath and pulled at the zipper some more, moving it one tooth at a time. When she had moved it far enough to stick her index finger through the opening, she stopped. When the opportunity arose, she would be ready.

While she waited, her thoughts turned to the window washer who had first seen her. The image of his face was burned on her brain. It was his eyes. They were penetrating. He had a steely resolve and she was sure that it was he who had survived the fall. She wondered how badly he was injured and if he was able to talk. Was he able to tell anyone what he had witnessed?

They were coming for him, just as they had come for her. She feared for him. Ayumi had devised a plan for herself. She hoped that the window washer had made one too.

9

Merylo ran a finger inside his collar. His tie was too tight. "I hate these places," he said. "They smell bad."

"That's the disinfectant."

"That's death." Merylo changed the topic. "What room did they say he was in again?"

"Right here," Cavasano answered. "Bed number two."

The double occupancy hospital room smelled of antiseptic and fresh plastic. Like a new shower curtain or cheap Halloween costume.

"How do you know which is bed two?" Merylo yanked back the privacy curtain. On the bed behind it was an elderly man with plastic tubing snaking out from his nose. A coffee mug full of flowers sat on an end table, a pair of slippers on the floor. A Styrofoam cup of soup sat on a plastic tray with a plate of limp vegetables.

"It says so on the footboard." Cavasano tapped the foot of the bed. "This is our guy, over here."

Merylo snapped the curtain back into place. "I thought so."

Bed number two's occupant was much younger. His head was completely bandaged in white gauze. Electrodes stuck to his chest monitored his heart rate. A pulse oximeter was clamped on the end of one finger.

Merylo walked over and waved a hand in front of the man's face. "How long's he been out?"

"It's been a couple of hours." Cavasano looked at his watch. "Since he hit the ground."

"Good-looking fella," Merylo said. "Lucky for him he didn't land on his face."

K yle was aware of his surroundings. He had been conscious for some time now, but had decided against opening his eyes. At the moment, he thought it better to play "dead" and gather as much information as possible before answering the barrage of questions that were sure to come his way. Once visiting hours were over and the ward settled down for the night, he'd figure out how he would make his escape.

He discovered from the doctor who had visited earlier that he was doing fine considering the fall. His scan was normal and there was no swelling of his brain. He had suffered only a slight skull fracture and a badly bruised elbow and tailbone. A minor inconvenience the doctor had termed it. Demerol had been used to block the pain. Along with the back of his head, his elbow had also been stitched up, although he would have to wait until he opened his eyes to confirm this.

Carl and another man were dead. That much he knew. Both men had broken his fall. He'd heard the gossip between the doctor and one of the nurses.

Now, two new men had entered the room and Kyle easily identified them as detectives. It was the way they spoke to one

---

another, the manner in which one of the men asked questions and the other one answered. New York's finest.

Kyle had been expecting them. They were the reason he had kept his eyes closed. When he was young, his father used to say that if you kept your mouth closed, you'd be the smartest person in the room. You'd know what you knew and you'd know what everyone else in the room knew. It was time to see if his father was right.

One of the detectives waved a hand in front of his face. Kyle felt the air move. The confident tone of voice and the fact that he was the one that asked all the questions suggested that this man, closest to him, was the one in charge. Kyle's mind's eye painted the two detectives as physical opposites and he was tempted to open his eyes just to see if he was right.

"If they wrapped this guy up any more he'd be a friggin' mummy," Merylo noted.

Cavasano chuckled. "A few more wraps and a pair of sunglasses and he'd look like Jack Griffin."

"Who?"

"Jack Griffin. You know, The Invisible Man."

"No one knows that." Merylo stared blankly at his new partner. "Why don't you just say, The Invisible Man. Jesus, Cavasano. Who was it that thought we'd be good partners?"

A nurse entered the room sparing the detective further indignity. "Good evening guys." Her voice was sweet. She had blonde hair pulled into a long ponytail and zero makeup. Her powder blue scrubs highlighted a fair complexion.

Merylo stuck his hand out. "Detective Frank Merylo." He hooked a thumb at his partner. "This here's Cavasano."

The junior detective held out his hand. "It's Joe."

She shook both of the men's hands. "Katie Davis, RN." She pointed to her badge and smiled.

"Ms. Davis," Merylo started.

"That's right." She smiled and made eye contact with Cavasano.

Joe Cavasano smiled back uncomfortably.

Merylo continued. "What's the prognosis for head wound Harry over here?" He watched over the nurse's shoulder as she unwrapped gauze from the patient's head, quickly at first, then slowly as she neared the wound.

"Short term or long term?" She answered.

The man still had hair on his head. The paramedics had shaved only where necessary to get at the wound. The result was a four-inch diameter bald patch that resembled a yarmulke. She made sure the wound was clean and redressed it.

Merylo was fascinated by the skill and speed at which the nurse worked. So much so that he did not hear her reply. He decided to rephrase his initial question. "When can we expect him to wake up?" He asked. "We'd like to ask him some questions."

Cavasano's cell phone chirped, but before the nurse could give him the lecture, he answered it and took it out into the hallway.

The nurse continued to float effortlessly about the hospital room, checking blood pressure, changing the saline drip, and entering data on the patient's electronic medical chart. "That's impossible to say." She stopped typing and looked up from the tablet. "Head injuries are tricky. It could be any time in the next five minutes or the next five years. You never know with these things."

"This guy is pretty banged up then?"

"I'd say Humpty Dumpty here had a great fall." She snatched the dinner tray from the old man in bed number one and squeezed passed Cavasano as he reentered the room. "Goodnight gentlemen." She winked at Cavasano and then disappeared out the door.

"Do you want me to call down to the station and have 'em send up a beat cop to stand watch?" Cavasano asked.

"Nah," Merylo responded. "This guy isn't going anywhere anytime soon." He smoothed out his mustache. "Maybe not for five years."

"What?"

"Nothing." He noticed Cavasano had out a note pad. "What have you got?"

"I've got some info on our DB's, Shirley called it over for me."

"Shirley, the one with the big-" Merylo held his hands out in front of his chest.

"Yeah, I think that's her."

"What'd she say?"

Cavasano referenced his note pad. "She said that our first dead body, the one with the clipped thumb, and also the one found directly under the invisible man here." He paused for effect. "Window cleaning company says his name is Carl McCree. Twenty-five years old, from Queens."

"And the other guy?"

Cavasano licked his thumb, flipped a page. "This guy's a bit more interesting. A passport found on his person says his name is Tobias Welke from Chile. A used boarding pass from Medellín, Colombia to New York was found in his coat pocket."

Merylo furrowed his brow. "A Chilean guy goes to Colombia and then comes to New York."

Cavasano shrugged. "Also, a key and keychain from the Armsport Apartments in Brooklyn was found in his pocket. Maybe he was some sort of traveling business man," Cavasano speculated.

"Right," Merylo said. "Have you ever seen the Armsport Apartments?"

The big detective hadn't.

"Alright, have they run the prints on these guys, yet?" Merylo asked.

"I haven't heard."

"Ok. Well, let's send someone over to McCree's house while we're waiting on the prints," Merylo said. He glanced at the patient in bed number two. "We'll check out the Armsport, see what we can find out about Mr. Chile. Look and see if there's any family members he might have been traveling with or any personal items that would be helpful, a phone number or something."

"We've got two guys continuing to interview staff and customers at the Millennium Hotel," Cavasano added.

"We'll circle back on that. Set up a sit down with whoever's the most interesting. Somebody must've saw something. Any word on the occupant of the room?" Merylo asked.

"Other than her name, no. Not yet."

"Jesus," Merylo sighed. "Get someone on the security footage."

Cavasano pushed his chin out. "What about him?"

"What about him?"

"He might have all the answers," Cavasano said.

"Well, when he wakes up from his nap, he'll tell us all about it." Merylo was confident. "He's got no reason not to."

K yle opened his eyes just enough to catch a glimpse of the back of the two detectives as they left the room. They were as he'd imagined. And his father was right. *If you keep your mouth shut, you will be the smartest man in the room. You'll know what you know. And you'll know what everybody else knows.*

One thing Kyle knew for certain was that he had to get out of this hospital soon. There wouldn't be much time before the charade would be impossible to keep going. And besides, the Demerol was beginning to wear off and the pain was making a huge comeback. Strangely, it had been a long time since he'd felt this alive.

10

The elevator came to a stop on the fifth floor. When it opened, two men in suits were standing against the opposite wall talking over a yellow legal pad. One of the men was tall with impossibly thick hair. He held a cell phone up to his ear. The other was older and shorter with wiry gray hair, spiked in a military kind of way. He had a mustache to match. Ingrid figured the two men for cops, detectives more precisely. She stepped out of the lift.

The older detective looked up from his legal pad and eyeballed her as she walked by. Ingrid flashed him a friendly smile. All he could manage to do in response was raise his eyebrows. The taller, younger detective was distracted with his cell phone and out of the loop, but he had enough sense to give her the compulsory once over that he probably gave to all women.

She paused a few steps after she'd passed the two men to unzip her wet jacket and smooth out her shirt. It was a good bet that the two detective types were here to see the same man she was, but probably for very different reasons. She pretended to rummage through her purse which was only home to a pack of tissues, a tube of lip balm and a small notepad and pen. She hung out nearby hoping to catch a bit of their conversation.

Cavasano was off his phone. "A little more on the guest from room thirty-five seventy-one. Her name is Ayumi Kagawa. The hotel says she had a reservation at their restaurant this evening, but she never showed up. No surprise there," he said. "Security is in the process of retrieving the surveillance video."

Merylo scribbled the information on his notepad. "Someone watching the room?"

"Officer Perkins," Cavasano said. His cell phone rang again. "Hold on."

The older detective grunted and nodded his head. He flipped a page of his notebook and then closed it.

Detective Cavasano paced in a tight circle. "Uh, huh. Really." He grabbed his partner's suit coat, mostly to keep from pacing, but partly to get his attention. "Okay, thanks." He ended the call. His eyebrows were raised so high they threatened to get tangled in his hair. "Our boy, Tobias Welke, is not from Chile after all."

Merylo subtly wrested his suit coat from his partners grip. "No kidding. What I could see of him, he looked Irish Catholic. Straight outta Boston."

"His prints came back."

"And?"

"And he's American. On the Fed's list." Cavasano was excited at the progress they were making. "He is accused of violating the involuntary servitude, forced labor and sex trafficking statutes."

"A real alter boy."

"I know, right. His real name is Richard Allen Sawyer. Last known residence was Colombia," Cavasano said.

A bell sounded and the elevator doors opened. The younger detective stepped in first and held the door for his partner. Merylo gravitated to the back of the carriage. He said, "The Bureau is going to come knocking. They're gonna ask for our report and everything we've got. Call the station and make sure someone's on their way to McCrees'. I'd like to head over to the Armsport Apartments and take a quick look around, see if we can't find anything interesting before the Feds get there." The elevator door started to close. "If we do, it'll look good on your resume."

Ingrid waited while the elevator door closed. As a Special Forces operator in the Colombian army, Ingrid's antennae had been raised. And although she wasn't able to discern from the conversation who, exactly, was in the hospital room on this floor, the fact that the detectives mentioned an American from Colombia who posed as a Chilean national excited her. Her gut was telling her that she was close to finding out what happened to Marlena. She had to keep going.

If Tobias Welke or Richard Allen Sawyer had anything to do with Marlena's disappearance, Ingrid wanted to be the first to know. She used her phone to send an email to her colleague, Carlos, back in Colombia. Carlos had been working leads back home and might find this new information useful. In the meantime, she decided to see for herself just who it was that had captured everyone's attention.

In front of her was a set of double doors and the entrance to the Head Trauma Center. Ingrid could see through the chicken wire enforced glass, a solitary nurse sitting at the nurse's station. She held up her visitor's pass.

An intercom near the door crackled. "Visiting hours are only 'till eight." The nurse announced.

Ingrid looked at her watch. It was five after. "I'm here to see my brother," she lied.

"I'm sorry dear, but you'll have to come back tomorrow," the nurse replied.

The nurse was a softie. Ingrid could tell from her tone of voice. It wouldn't be too much of a challenge to get her to forgo hospital policy. She'd probably done it a hundred times before. All she needed was a little persuading.

"Please, please, please," Ingrid pleaded. "My brother had a bad accident today and I need to see him." She let her head fall against the window for dramatic effect. She had always wanted to be an actress.

The nurse stared at Ingrid and then looked around the ward. It was a slow night with only four patients in the entire center. There were two nurses on duty with another two at home and on-call. The attending physician had already made his rounds and was retired to his office. What the hell. She pushed a button and a buzzer sounded. Ingrid opened the door and walked in.

Showtime.

Ingrid played up her act as she approached the nurse's station. She took a tissue from her purse and wiped an invisible tear from her eye.

"Thank you so much," Ingrid said as she approached the nurse's station.

"Who are you here to see, hun?"

"My brother. He had an accident this afternoon."

"At the hotel?" The nurse asked.

"Yes."

"Oh dear, yes. Poor fella. He's in room five eleven bed number two, down the hall on your left."

"Thank you," Ingrid said. Before she could turn away, the nurse stopped her.

"Don't forget to sign in." The nurse pushed a clipboard across the counter. "Name and address please. When you write in the time, be sure to put seven fifty-five. Just in case someone asks." The nurse winked.

Ingrid signed in using her mother's address. She flashed the nurse a fake smile. "Thank you. You are so kind." She sniffled.

"Oh, don't mention it." The nurse leaned across the counter and whispered, "I do it all the time."

Ingrid put the clipboard back on the counter, spun on her heel and headed toward room 511. A wicked smile crossed her lips and she whispered to herself, "So, do I lady. So, do I."

11

R oom 511 was a dimly lit double occupancy room with the two beds separated by a nylon curtain. In the first bed, closest to the door, an old man was lying with his head tilted in Ingrid's direction. One eye was open and his mouth was agape. Ingrid smiled and gave him a brief wave, but he did not respond. She hoped he was sleeping.

Bed number 2 was behind the curtain on the opposite side of the small hospital room. She kept an eye on the old man as she walked past his bed.

A chart hung from the foot of bed number two and as she passed by, Ingrid paused to get a look at the name. The name wasn't Welke or Sawyer as she had hoped. This man's name was Murdoch, Kyle. And although he wasn't the man she was looking for, she was desperate to know if he knew anything at all about Tobias Welke.

She took up a position towards the head of the bed to get a better look. A stand with a full saline drip stood next to her. Latex tubing snaked its way down his shoulder and past the bedrail where a spiny tip entered his hand under white surgical tape. The top of the man's head was completely wrapped in clean white gauze. The same for his left elbow. The monitor above the bed indicated that he was still alive.

Kyle Murdoch looked pained. Not physically or externally, as one would expect given the severity of his situation and the bandages that adorned his body, but internally. Emotionally. The expression on his face, even in an unconscious state, expressed a kind of warning to back off. Ingrid, never one to give care to such warnings, set her purse on a chair next to the bed and leaned in for a better look.

Her eyes traced the hard lines of his face. An angular jaw and square chin. He had the beginnings of crow's feet at the corners of his eyes that she guessed were more a result of squinting in the sun than from smiling and laughing. Ingrid noticed his eyes roll under his eyelids. Her hand slowly moved toward his face. A nurse in blue scrubs entered the room and she pulled her hand back.

"Hi," the nurse said.

Ingrid straightened up to greet her. "Hi," she replied back.

"My name is Katie. I've been taking care of Kyle since he was admitted this evening."

"Thank you. It's nice to meet you, Katie."

"The front desk nurse tells me that Kyle is your brother."

"Yes, that's right."

The nurse stole a quick glance at Kyle. The differences in appearance between Kyle and Ingrid were stark. Ingrid's dark hair and Mestizo features contrasted with Kyle's European accents. Katie Davis winced noticeably.

The expression did not escape Ingrid. "We were adopted."

The nurse breathed a sigh of relief. "Of course. I didn't want to say anything, but you two do look very different."

Ingrid put her best fake smile forward and then changed the subject. "Is he going to be okay?"

"That's hard to say," the nurse answered. "Doctor Lewis just left. Would you like me to call and see if he's still in the building?" She started to move toward the door. "He's very nice."

Ingrid motioned for the nurse to stay put. "No, that's not necessary. I can come back in the morning to speak with his doctor."

"Are you sure?"

"Absolutely." Ingrid hated to lie but, the fact that the patient was suffering a possible brain trauma gave her confidence that her deceit would survive for one more day. "Is there any swelling of the brain?" She asked.

"The MRI didn't show any. So far, as far as we can tell, Kyle has only suffered a slight concussion. He's breathing on his own and his vitals are good, but obviously the fact that he's still unconscious and unresponsive is a concern."

"Has anyone else been here to see him?" Ingrid asked.

"Only a couple of detectives," the nurse said. "They asked us to call them if and when he wakes up."

"Any particular reason why there were detectives here to see him?" Ingrid asked.

"I can't say for sure," Katie replied. "I don't want to give any false information. I hope you understand."

"Absolutely," Ingrid said.

Before she left the room, the nurse tapped an armoire on the wall across from the bed. "His belongings and the clothes that he was wearing are in a bag in here. He's going to need some new ones because these are badly soiled."

"Thank you so much, Katie," Ingrid said.

"You stay as long as you like and if you need anything, there is a nurse call button on the bed rail to his left. You just press that button and I'll come as quickly as I can."

Ingrid found the call button and gave the nurse a knowing smile, "Thanks, again."

"My pleasure."

Once the nurse had left the room, Ingrid rummaged through her purse and pulled out the little notebook. She bit the cap off of a pen and started writing down the information she had accumulated so far. She noted the conversation overheard between the two detectives and jotted down a few details regarding the patient in bed number two.

She tapped the pen against her lips trying to think of anything else. She checked her watch. Eight fifteen.

"Shoot!" Her scheduled dinner with VanRoy. Violating hospital policy, she grabbed her cell phone and called him. When Edward answered, Ingrid stood up and pulled the curtain aside and looked out the window. "Hi, Edward. I'm sorry," she said. "I'm going to have to ask to reschedule for tonight." Rain was coming down hard and streaked the glass.

She glanced over her shoulder at Kyle Murdoch. His eyes were still closed, but to Ingrid there was something about him that was off. He didn't look unconscious to her anymore. The old man in the bed next to him "looked" unconscious. She lowered her voice, "I'm at the hospital visiting an old friend."

Edward VanRoy was used to getting his way and wouldn't let something as trivial as a hospital visit stand in the way of a dinner date. The conversation continued with a lot of nodding, grunting, and pacing back and forth. Ingrid looked at her watch. "I'll try to be there by nine. I promise." She powered off her cell phone.

All of her pacing about the room had left her facing the old man in bed number one. The man's mouth was still agape and to her, he still looked unconscious. It was his mouth.

Unconscious people don't breathe with their mouths closed, do they?

That is what looked off about the man in bed number two. He was unconscious and breathing with his mouth closed.

As she spun around to take a look, she was startled to see

Kyle Murdoch out of his bed and standing in front of her in a hospital gown. She dropped her cell phone.

The expression on his face was distressed, but non-threatening. He propped himself up with one hand on the bed. He brought his other hand up to his mouth and touched his index finger to his lips, asking her to stay quiet. He said, "I think I'm going to need your help."

12

The SUV stopped. Ayumi wasn't claustrophobic, but the combination of darkness and immobility was making her very uncomfortable. If she didn't get some fresh air soon, she was afraid that she might pass out again. She continued to work the zipper one tooth at a time, until the opening was large enough to squeeze three fingers through and she could breathe more easily.

Parked in a dark corner of the hospital's parking lot, the three men in the vehicle sat in silence. Dmitri was behind the wheel, while Niko rode shotgun. Alex slouched alone behind them, one arm thrown over the back seat.

Niko reached into his coat pocket and pulled out a small packet. Inside were two sodium thiosulfate tablets. He handed one to Dmitri and put the other on the back of his tongue and swallowed. He gave a reassuring nod and waited for Dmitri to follow suit.

After Dmitri had swallowed the pill, Niko gave him an ampoule of amyl nitrate. "For afterward," he said.

Dmitri knew what the amyl nitrate was for. He was

impressed that Niko had been prepared in the event that the operation not go as planned, although he was not surprised. Niko was a professional all around. He was a master at extracting information or incapacitating those reluctant to agree. The big Russian began his apprenticeship as a journeyman in the RUOP, Russia's Regional Department for Combating Organized Crime. He perfected his trade during the Second Chechen War as an operative for the FSB, Russia's latest incarnation of the infamous KGB.

It was in this capacity that Dmitri and Niko first met. While Dmitri was building a reputation in the Rostov-on-Don crime scene, Niko had attempted to arrest him. Niko soon discovered that Dmitri wasn't the archetypical Russian mobster, a reckless and arrogant fool, eager to demonstrate how many bullets his gun would hold. Dmitri was composed, polite, charming and intelligent.

The problem with Russia, according to Dmitri, was that Russian mobsters knew little discretion. A problem Dmitri assured Niko he did not have. At least in Italy and the United States he argued, the mafia had tact and respect for the uninvolved. People could be "persuaded" or "convinced" in a civil society. In Russia, they were just shot.

Dmitri sold himself as akin to the mob bosses in the popular American gangster movies, when the truth was, he had yet to reach the big time, himself. Niko bought into the dream and instead of arresting Dmitri, found himself with a nice little "side job" that eventually evolved into a permanent full-time position.

Alex, in the back seat, came highly recommended. He was the least refined of the three and there was nothing that he wouldn't do for money. A convicted murderer, Alex spent eight years in a penal institution in Siberia for the slaying of a private oil company executive. He was eventually and controversially, pardoned by the office of the President of the Russian Federation.

Upon his release, he found that his services were in high demand. A committed alcoholic and drug addict, Alex often worked for under the going rate and held allegiance to no one group in particular. Whether it was prostituting himself at a sleazy Moscow disco, putting a knife in the ear of a wayward lover or decapitating the elderly resident of a sought after downtown flat, there was nothing that was beyond Alex's code of conduct as he simply just didn't have one. Couple his inability to say no with his discounted asking price and the wiry, tattooed man from Tver had no trouble finding work.

As unpredictable as they were individually, the combination of Niko and Alex gave Dmitri confidence that the operation would be a success. Each man was unique in his talent. And each was very much expendable.

Both Niko and Alex had obtained fraudulent passports from countries that were covered under the United States' visa waiver program. This allowed them to travel freely to and within the US. Niko's passport was from Latvia, while Alex's stated that he was a resident of Finland.

Dmitri had been living and operating in the United States after having gained admittance along with 2,500 other Ukrainian nationals two years earlier. He found moderate success working the streets of southern Brooklyn by following the usual tract of extorting recent emigres and insurance fraud while also dabbling in the heroin trade.

Dmitri had not personally met the man who ordered the current job, but was advised that the man wished to be called "Koba." The particulars were setup through an intermediary in the Brighton Beach neighborhood in Brooklyn and Dmitri was assured that successful completion would fetch him a quarter of a million US dollars. An amount that would enhance his reputation as well as his bank account. All he had to do was kill Mr. Hinata Sakai.

A ten percent down payment was left under the front seat of an unlocked Lincoln on Brighton Beach Avenue, just outside of the Georgian House restaurant. Dmitri imagined that he'd picked up the money under the watchful eye of a sniper's rifle. Having taken the money, he had agreed to the job and was now either fully committed or had signed his own death warrant. The balance would be paid upon the job's successful completion and would be divided three ways.

But the situation had now become complicated with the decision to seek out Mr. Sakai's associate, Ms. Kagawa, who had seemingly met with him mere moments before the trio had broken into his apartment and taken his life. They'd found her itinerary and hotel information on Mr. Sakai's desk. Today's date was circled on his day planner with a message to "*Discuss with Ayumi @ 17:00.*" Having discovered this useful information and after eliminating the target, per the contract, Dmitri informed Koba of his intention to demonstrate his ruthless proficiency by killing Mr. Sakai's confidant as well.

To his surprise, the woman, Ayumi, looked to be more valuable than her associate. If not monetarily, then personally. At least she was to the person who'd called him while they were at the Millennium Hotel.

Dmitri suspected that the caller was of Japanese origin, but the man had spoken Russian well enough to be understood clearly. The caller knew the details surrounding the job Dmitri had undertaken as well as the alias of the man who had hired him. The caller stated that "Koba" had no intention of paying the remainder of the contract and that by involving the woman, he had increased his troubles tenfold.

Dmitri wasn't sure how much to believe from the caller, but he was advised to be very careful with the woman and to let her go unharmed. So far, he hadn't been offered any money for her, but rather an ultimatum. If he did not let the woman go, Dmitri's daughter, Valentina, would suffer an unfortunate fate. A photo of the little girl and her mother was sent to him via text as proof of the caller's sincerity. Still, he believed there was an opportunity to monetize the woman's life if he could discover the identity of the caller himself.

With that in mind, he was convinced that the window washers they encountered earlier were not window washers at all, but rather agents for the caller engaged in a failed attempt to take his life. And according to the news reports, one of them was still alive and in the Head Trauma Ward of Bellevue Hospital.

Dmitri handed out simple orders to his two accomplices. Alex would mind the woman while he and Niko would enter the hospital and find the second window washer. When the driver's door opened and the dome light came on, Alex shielded his eyes with his bandaged right hand to protect his fully dilated pupils. Dmitri told him once more to make sure the woman did not escape all the while the interior light was threatening to blind him.

"Ya panimayu," I understand! Alex barked. He was keen for Dmitri to close the door and shut off the dome light. Alex held Dmitri's gaze through the rear-view mirror, rolled his shoulders and then spat out of the open back window.

Before stepping out of the vehicle, Dmitri gave one last order to Alex. "No smoking in the car. You make it smell like shit." He got out and slammed the door.

"Atebis," *Fuck off*, Alex muttered under his breath. He watched as Dmitri and Niko hustled into the darkness and toward the cover of the hospital. When the two were out of sight, he pulled out of his coat pocket a pack of cigarettes and a flask of alcohol.

His cellphone rang.

"Hello." Alex sat upright.

"Is the woman unharmed?" The caller asked.

"Yes," Alex barked. He threw his arm over the backseat and touched the duffle bag that held the woman captive. "I'm grabbing her little ass right now," he hissed.

The caller was not impressed and chose to remind Alex of the potential consequences. "If her ass has even a scratch on it, I will flay you open like a butterfly and serve your insides to the pigs."

Alex barked into the phone. "You just make sure to have my money."

"A word of caution, Mr. Alex," the caller said. "The woman can be uncontrollable. I'd be careful with her if I were you."

The caller started to laugh as Alex shouted into the phone, "Fuck you!" He tossed the phone on the seat next to him and touched his burned cheek.

From the back of the vehicle, Ayumi heard the scratchy flick of a lighter and seconds later, the potent scent of cigarette smoke stung her nose. The hand that had landed on her arm a few moments ago had lifted. She knew that two of the three men had left the vehicle and this would be her best chance to escape.

Alex slouched coolly in the back seat smoking his cigarette. Dmitri had gotten under his skin. Mind the woman. Twice Dmitri had told him, as if he were stupid. He took a drag on his cigarette. The woman was going nowhere. He turned, blew a plume of smoke out the window and shook his head. He took a sip from the flask.

Over the pinging of rain that battered the vehicle, Ayumi could hear the sloshing of liquid as he pulled the flask away from his lips and could picture the shape of his lips when he blew out the toxic smoke.

She continued to pull the zipper, one tooth at a time. Slowly, the bag began to open up. She knew that the lone man in the car was the one that had surprised her in the bathroom. She could smell him. The bag separated some more. In a few moments, she would be the one to surprise him.

13

"You need my help for what?"

Kyle was rummaging through the armoire. "I need you to watch the door," he said. He pulled his shirt and pants from the cabinet. Both were soaked with blood. His shirt had been cut up by the paramedics. He threw them both on the bed. Next, he retrieved his tool belt and found his cell phone. It still worked. He grabbed his boots.

"Excuse me," Ingrid said.

Kyle shimmied passed Ingrid and the foot of the bed, cell phone in mouth, boots in hand. He opened his roommate's armoire and took the phone out of his mouth. "Please watch the door." He put the cell phone back between his teeth. He sorted through the old man's items, finding a light blue zip up hoodie that that he felt like he might be able to squeeze into.

Ingrid kept a lookout at the door as he'd asked, although she didn't know why. Maybe because his request came across as polite. She peeked out into the hallway. Nurse Katie was nowhere to be found. Only the front desk nurse was visible.

"What-," Ingrid started to speak, but Kyle was pulling on his jeans and she caught a glimpse of him in his underwear from behind. Her face flushed red and she turned away.

"You're not watching the door," he said.

"What do you want me to watch for?"

"A doctor or a nurse. Police, maybe," he said. "If any one of those comes by, I need you to stall them."

"Stall them, how? And what makes so sure that I'm going to help you?" She asked.

"Because." He zipped up his pants and squeezed into the old man's hoodie.

"Because why?"

Kyle stepped into his boots. The old man's hoodie was tight and the seams threatened to split with every move that he made. He shoved his cell phone into his front pants pocket. "Because I've known you for a whole ten minutes now," he said. "And in that short amount of time you've claimed to be both my sister and my friend. Neither of whom actually exist."

"I was hoping you were someone else."

"Sorry to disappoint you."

"I can explain," Ingrid said.

"I'm sure you can." He knelt down to tie his boots. "And I'd love to hear your explanation, but that's going to have to wait until I-we, get out of here." Finished with his boots, Kyle stood up. Still woozy, he held onto the bed for support. "I see that you're pretty skilled at - *improvising*," he said. "We might need you to do some more of that."

N iko stepped into the elevator and took up a position in the back. Dmitri followed and positioned himself in front. As the elevator climbed upward the two men stood in silence, Dmitri's arms folded across his chest. Niko stood stoically behind him clutching a handful of flowers recently plucked from a planter on the first floor. Hidden among the stems and leaves was a plastic, tube shaped device no larger than a cigar.

The elevator opened on the fifth floor and the two men stepped out. Niko adjusted the cylinder to make sure it was hidden. Dmitri approached the double doors to the Head Trauma Ward. A single nurse sat behind a counter reading a magazine. A minor obstacle.

Dmitri rang the buzzer.

The nurse behind the desk abandoned her magazine with a frown and turned her attention to the door. She saw two men peering through the chicken wire enforced window.

"I'm sorry guys, visiting hours are over," the nurse squawked through the intercom.

Niko held up the flowers and smiled. Again the nurse's voice crackled over the intercom, "You'll have to come back tomorrow morning."

Dmitri gave Niko a nudge, "Apyat," *Again*, he ordered.

Niko pressed the call buzzer once more and waited for the nurse to look his way. This time, after he got her attention, he held up the flowers once more and moved his lips without uttering a sound.

Frustrated, the nurse hit the buzzer that would let the two men in. Reaching through the tangle of stems and roots, Niko pulled a rod out of the bottom of the plastic tube, cocking it.

The two men casually approached the nurse's station. This section of the hospital was particularly quiet and the blank expressions on the men's faces gave the desk nurse a sense of unease. She set her left hand for the security button, ready to push it.

Dmitri said, "We're looking for our friend. He is a window

washer who had a very bad accident today." His best English came out wanting.

The nurse's eyes darted back and forth between the two men. "You're going to have to sign in," she said motioning to a clipboard.

Niko pushed the flowers across the counter at her, his fingers resting gently on the trigger mechanism. "These are for you," he smiled. His eyes glued to hers.

Dmitri shielded his face with the clipboard.

The nurse didn't move. The flowers were inches from her face. The roots were visible and still had dirt on them, dangling out from the man's grip. A crumb of dirt fell onto her computer keyboard. Her eyebrows arched questioningly. Her left hand slid over to the security call button.

"Smell them," Niko said. He pushed the flowers closer.

The nurse glanced down for an instant. She inhaled the earthy, floral aroma. She recognized the flowers from the first-floor lobby. There was something tubular and black in the middle of them. The object had an opening on the end and it appeared to be made out of plastic. Something was terribly wrong and that realization was expressed on the nurse's face. Her jowls sagged. The bags under her eyes were darker and more pronounced. She'd aged in a second. As her eyes rose to meet the bulky Russian's, his friendly smile from a moment ago was gone.

Niko squeezed the trigger and the firing mechanism shattered a small glass vial of acid inside the plastic tube and pushed the vapor into the nurse's face. She lurched back in her chair, unable to stand up. Deadly droplets latched onto capillaries in her nose and quickly rode the sinuous highway to her brain. The poison snaked into her airway, infiltrating her lungs. Within seconds, the cyanide molecules were pumped into her heart where they grabbed hold and sent the nurse into cardiac arrest.

Niko nodded to Dmitri. The two men took the amyl nitrate ampoules out of their pockets, broke them, and inhaled the antidote as a precaution in case they accidentally breathed in any of the deadly gas themselves.

The nurse clutched at her chest trying to remove the invisible attacker within her. Her legs stiffened and she could gain no traction on the smooth tile floor. She lunged forward and only managed to ram herself into the desk, still a captive of her ergonomically designed chair. And then suddenly, before she could make another move, her body went limp. Her arms fell to her sides and her head landed on the computer's keyboard next to the handful of flowers.

A nurse in blue scrubs entered the area from a room down the hall. She was carrying a tablet and typed as she walked. Niko positioned himself to block any view she might have of the deceased desk nurse.

Dmitri pined for her attention. "Excuse me," he called to her.

The nurse looked up from her tablet and walked his way. As she neared him, she discreetly tried to look past Niko who stood in front of the station desk. "Can I help you?" She asked.

"I'm here to see my friend. He is a window washer. He had a very bad accident today. We've come to see if he is okay." Dmitri smiled.

"Visiting hours are over at the moment," the nurse said. She craned her neck trying to get a look at the desk nurse. "Maybe tomorrow would be a better day to see him."

"What room is he in? I only want to leave him a get-well card." His smile faded.

"He's in room five eleven." Her voice trailed off as she caught a glimpse of the slumped over nurse behind the desk.

Before she had the chance to make a sound, Niko grabbed her around the neck and pushed her hard against the wall.

Unable to scream, Katie Davis dropped the tablet and kicked as hard as she could.

The big man ended the struggle quickly. He drew the nurse toward him and then in one smooth motion, smashed her head against the wall. She fell in a heap, listing sideways. Her left cheek lying against the cold tile floor.

14

A dull thud rattled the wall.

"What was that?" Kyle asked.

"I don't know." Ingrid chanced a look out the door. Two men were now standing near the nurse's station. She saw nurse Katie lying slumped on the floor with her hair splayed across her face.

"That was your nurse's head," Ingrid said. "Is someone looking for you?" Her tone was urgent, but not panicked.

"Possibly."

"A couple of ugly guys?"

"Yeah, that sounds about right."

"I think they're here."

"Which way?"

Ingrid pointed down the hall in the direction of the nurse's station. "They're at the front desk."

"Then we have to go this way." Kyle tried to grab her hand and pull her out the door with him.

Ingrid held him up. "Un momento," she said. "You can barely walk, yet. You go and I'll catch up."

"What?"

"Don't worry, I'll improvise," she said.

"I don't think these guys will appreciate your improv the way I do."

"Vamos." Ingrid waved him off. "I'll be right behind you."

Kyle hesitated for a moment, pulled the hoodie up over his injured head and then started off down the corridor. Ingrid stepped out of the room into the hallway.

Both men turned away from the nurse's station when they saw movement down the hall. Ingrid stood in the middle hoping to shield Kyle from their view as much as she could.

"Perdón, tiene hora?" *Excuse me, do you have the time?* She tapped the gaudy watch on her left wrist as if it were broken.

The bigger of the two men turned and marched down the hall straight towards her.

"No? Ok, gracias."

"The window washer," the other man barked. "He's getting away."

Ingrid looked back and saw that Kyle had just rounded the corner.

The big man started running.

Ingrid felt that now would be a good time to run as well. "Hasta la vista," she said. She turned and took off down the hall ahead of him.

An abandoned housekeeping cart sat idle up against the wall at the end of the hall. As Ingrid ran by it, she snatched the first bottle of anything that she could get her hands on. In this case, toilet bowl cleaner.

She opened the bottle as she ran. Once she was around the corner, she sprayed its contents all over the floor creating a slippery green coating. Kyle was waiting for her. He propped open the door to a room at the end of the hall.

"C'mon," he called to her.

Ingrid ditched the bottle and ran toward him as fast as she

could. Her heart was thumping and the adrenaline was pumping. The big man chasing her was not far behind. He slipped on the cleaning agent as he rounded the corner and slammed into the wall.

"In here." Kyle kicked the doors open to a room that read LINENS above the frame.

Ingrid hurried inside and closed the door. "We can't stay here," she said. She was breathing excitedly.

Kyle pushed a housekeeping cart in front of the door. It wouldn't prevent anyone from entering, but it would slow them down for a second. "The stairs are too slow and the elevator is unreliable," he said.

"So, you chose here?"

"It seemed like a good idea, yes."

"We're trapped." Ingrid looked around the room hoping to find an alternative exit point.

On the far wall, a laundry chute advertised "Soiled Linens." Kyle grabbed a fistful of sheets out of the laundry cart. "There!"

Ingrid turned and read the signage. She saw the chute. "Oh, no. No way," she said. "I'm not going down that chute."

Before she could say more, Kyle had wrapped her in the sheets and carried her toward the open laundry chute. "Tuck your chin down," he said.

"Let me go." She tried to wriggle out of his arms. "No, no, no."

"Trust me," Kyle said. He stuck her feet through the opening. "It's our only chance." He let her go and could hear her protest in Spanish as her voice echoed back up through the sheet metal laundry chute.

He climbed into the opening himself just as the linen room door burst open. The laundry cart was pushed away and sent crashing into a set of shelves on the far wall. The familiar profile of large man from the hotel stood in the doorway.

Kyle waited as long as possible before letting himself drop. He had already fallen on top of one person today and was in no hurry to make it two. He had lowered himself into the chute as far as he could and held on to the opening by his fingertips. When the man who had chased them appeared at the opening, Kyle let go and slid into the darkness.

He spread his legs and arms as wide as he could, applying maximum pressure to try and slow his descent. His knees and elbows absorbed the shock of every joint in the sheet metal laundry shaft.

There was no light at the bottom as far as he could see and no way to tell how far he had slid or how far he had left to go. "Get out of the way!" He shouted. He was sliding fast and hoped that the woman below could hear him. He replayed the horrible image of Carl over in his head. How broken he was. And how he had tried but couldn't stop himself from falling on him. He yelled again down the chute. "Get out of the way!" He closed his eyes.

For the second time today, Kyle landed on something soft. This time, it was a mountain of unwashed hospital bedding. Sheets and blankets that reeked of antiseptic, body odor and urine. He lay there a moment in the stillness of the darkened room. His body was numb. Adrenaline was still the world's greatest drug.

"Are you alright?" A voice in the room asked.

"I am," Kyle responded. "Where are you?"

Before she answered him, Ingrid turned on her cell phone. The light on her home screen shone like a beacon. "I'm over here."

Kyle rolled off the laundry pile. The blood in his brain seemed to drain all at once leaving him faint and lightheaded. The after effects of a concussion. He reached out and steadied himself on a laundry cart. The light of Ingrid's cell phone floated toward him like a radioactive firefly.

"Are you okay?" She asked him, moving closer.

"Just a little dizzy that's all."

Kyle had intended to ask how she was, but before he could get the words out of his mouth, Ingrid had put her fist into his jaw, knocking him over and onto the pile of dirty laundry. The adrenaline had gotten to her as well.

"How dare you." She was still offended that he had picked her up against her will and dumped her down the laundry chute.

Kyle massaged his jaw. He could taste a little blood under his bottom lip. "I just saved your life."

Ingrid lunged at him, cursing in Spanish and determined to inflict pain. She knocked him backward and jumped on top of him, knees on his chest. He grabbed her arms before she could start swinging.

"Who are you?" She shouted.

"Who are you?" He said. "You're the one who showed up in my hospital room claiming to be my sister one moment and my friend the next."

"Let me go." Ingrid struggled to break free, but Kyle held on tight and was too strong for her.

"Those men would have killed you," he said. The adrenaline was beginning to subside and Ingrid stopped struggling. "You saw that poor nurse." Kyle loosened his grip, but kept his hands up in a defensive posture in case she decided to hit him again. "We didn't have a choice."

Ingrid rolled off of him and onto the pile of dirty laundry. She pushed a band of unruly hair from her face. "Since you have all the answers, what do you suggest we do now?"

"We have to get out of here," he said. "Beyond that, I'm not sure."

A red "EXIT" sign provided the way. Kyle put his phone in flashlight mode and followed the beam of light around metal shelving and past industrial sized washers and dryers until he found a solid metal exit door.

He kicked aside two five-gallon pails of laundry detergent so that Ingrid wouldn't trip. He leaned into the panic bar and the door spread open to a concrete landing adjacent to the loading dock. An overhead lamp missing one bulb illuminated a ramp. He stepped outside and Ingrid followed.

In the pale, yellow glow of the loading area, Kyle's wounds begged for attention. The gauze on his head bore a rust colored stain the size of a small dessert plate. His clothes were torn at the knees and elbows. The bandage on his left arm had fallen off leaving the stitched-up wound exposed. He massaged his jaw.

Ingrid looked him over in the pale, yellow light. "You look horrible."

"Thanks. I feel horrible."

"Come on. Follow me," Ingrid said. "I know where to go."

With no other options, Kyle followed her.

15

Ayumi was as patient and quiet as a snake. She eased her shoulders through the opening and slowly worked the duffle bag down to her waist. She lifted her hips and slid the bag out from under her backside and over her knees. Like a gymnast, her motions were deliberate and smooth. She lifted one leg out at a time and pushed the bag to the side. All without making a sound.

Her quarry was unprepared and thus, ready for the taking. She resisted the urge to move too fast. The slightest noise or movement of the vehicle and he was sure to turn around. Timing would be everything.

She felt the ring that had earlier saved her hand from being crushed in the hotel door and turned it 180 degrees until it faced backwards on the palm side of her right hand. She ran her thumb along its rough edge. The 3-carat diamond had broken sharply against the metal hotel room door and if pushed hard enough, the jagged rock would easily puncture skin.

She maneuvered herself into position. The man in the back seat leaned on the headrest, his head slightly tilted toward the roof of the car. His left hand rested on the seat clutching a flask.

His right arm was propped on the window frame. He flicked what was left of his cigarette out into the rain.

A distant car turned into the parking lot and a wave of light brushed across the man's face. His eyes were closed. Ayumi could see the remnant of their last encounter emblazoned upon his cheek. She readied herself. After the car had passed and the darkness returned, she raised her right hand above his head.

D mitri and Niko used the hospital's back door, exiting into the rear parking lot. The rain was coming down in cold hard pellets and the temperature was dropping. The SUV had been left at the far end of the dimly lit parking lot under a lamp that had refused to light.

On a night that reduced the city folk to phantoms, darting and dashing with heads down into doorways and under canopies, Dmitri and Niko walked with heads up and shoulders back. Clouds of condensation puffed in front of their faces as they marched through the parking lot. Dmitri carried the hospital sign-in clipboard and the chart from the foot of Kyle's hospital bed in one hand, a pilfered 9mm pistol in the other. Niko pinched the middle of his nose with his left hand trying to stop it from bleeding.

A security guard had confronted Niko as he was leaving the linen room. The distress on the Russian's face and the over-turned laundry cart no doubt cast suspicion on the scene. Niko deciphered the look on the security guard's face and before the man could access his shoulder mic and alert any fellow guards of his position and situation, Niko attacked.

Dmitri was impressed when he came upon the two. The security guard was every bit as big as Niko. The guard had him down and had rubbed his nose into the floor like a disobedient dog. But Dmitri would change the balance of power.

He took the security guard's gun and persuaded him to release his partner. Niko responded with a kick to the ribs as he stood up. The guard's cuffs were used to shackle his hands behind his back. An empty hospital room produced a roll of gauze and a blood pressure cuff and Niko knew just what to do. He shoved the roll of gauze into the guard's mouth and applied the blood pressure cuff to the man's neck. Niko pumped the bladder in his hand furiously until the guard's face and head turned purple.

A yumi slammed her hand down on Alex's right eye. The sharp diamond sunk deep and he cried out in agony as vitreous humor spat onto the palm of her hand. Before he could raise his hands in self-defense, Ayumi lifted his chin with her left hand and pressed the jagged diamond hard into his neck. She drew her hand slowly in a clockwise rotation, hoping to bisect his carotid artery in the process.

His left arm flailed and Ayumi ducked her head to protect her face as he reached back in desperation. She dug her knees into the back of his seat and continued to exert all of her strength as he clawed at her arm.

He managed to grab a bundle of her hair and he pulled it over the seat, trying to get her to release her grip. Her grip only grew tighter and her resolve stronger as the broken diamond drew a hideous red line across his neck. A long lock of black hair separated from her head.

A warm river of vengeance seeped between her fingers as Alex frantically arched and threw himself backward in an attempt to get out of her clutch. She moved with him until she found herself pinned against the back hatch of the SUV. Alex gurgled and gasped, kicking his legs wildly over the back seat.

The driver's door opened and the interior lights came on.

Alex yelled for help and both back doors opened immediately. Dmitri appeared in one, Niko the other. The Japanese woman was quite the artist. She had taken Alex's pale canvass and created an abstract in red. Alex's deflated eyeball made Niko wince.

Dmitri threw the clipboards on the front seat and checked the magazine in the gun stolen from the security guard. A full fifteen rounds. He reinserted the magazine.

Alex was still struggling with the woman in the back, cursing in Russian for Dmitri or Niko to do something. "Eyo strelyat'!" *Shoot her!* Alex yelled.

Dmitri switched off the safety and motioned for Niko to close his door. He pointed the gun in Ayumi's direction and instructed her to release Alex.

Ayumi closed her eyes and squeezed Alex tighter. "Nikogda!" She shouted. *Never!*

Dmitri fired the gun and a spray of warm liquid dotted Ayumi's face. Clumps of soft tissue and broken chips of bone landed on her bottom lip. She spit them away as Alex went limp in her arms. She tried to wipe the blood off her face but only managed to smear it.

Niko opened the door and gave Dmitri a desperate look after seeing the carnage. "What have you done?"

"Knock her out again and make it right this time." Dmitri ordered.

Niko hesitated, staring at Alex.

"Now!"

It was Alex who injected the woman back at the hotel. Being an addict, he was skilled at administering drugs via the needle to himself and others. Niko was less than enthusiastic about the process. He took a bag from the front seat and opened it. Inside were two syringes. One of the syringes had half as much agent in it as the other. He remembered that Alex had only used half of the one syringe back at the hotel. He took the full one, made sure there was no air captured in it and clamped it between his teeth.

Ayumi squirmed, but couldn't free herself from Alex's dead body. Niko reached for her over the back seat. She swatted at him to no effect. He grabbed her wrists and twisted them until he was able to restrain her with one hand. Then, with all the skill of a hack veterinarian, Niko plucked the syringe from his teeth and poked the needle into her neck.

16

The apartment was small yet airy. Caddy cornered furniture sat on a shag area rug that covered a real parquet floor. White walls. All of the knick-knacks were religious in theme save for an 8x10 family picture set upon a small end table and a little black sculpture of an overly rotund woman, posing on the coffee table. A miniature Botero. A too green, too full, fictitious plant adorned a corner shelf. On the kitchen's granite bar, a single, yellowing bamboo shoot begged for attention. Ambient lighting lent an understated appeal to the apartment. The place was clean, hardly lived in.

"Try not to touch anything," Ingrid said.

"Is this your place?" Kyle asked.

"No," Ingrid said. "It's my-*was* my parent's. My father left some clothes in the closet." She looked Kyle up and down. "They might fit you."

"Bathroom?" Kyle asked.

"Down the hall, first door on the left."

Kyle took off his boots and headed down the hall.

In the bathroom above the vanity, the medicine cabinet doubled as a mirror. In it, Kyle was able to assess the damage he sustained from his fall from the hotel for the first time. He caught a whiff of Old Spice as he peeled off the old man's sweatshirt, taking care around his throbbing elbow. He rinsed off the injured area to find that it wasn't as bad as he'd thought and the sutures were still intact. It might not have required stitches, but since the paramedics had already stitched his head, he figured they probably decided to do his elbow as well.

His head promised to be a different story. The gauze unwrapped easily from the sides and front of his head, but stuck in spots when it came to the rust colored stain.

The wound finally exposed, Kyle angled his head down and was surprised to see that his scalp hadn't been stitched, but stapled instead. He touched one with a finger. His head had needed it, but it too wasn't as bad as he feared. His head was shaved around the wound area only, leaving what looked like a divot from a nine iron in the middle of his head. Having been attended to by professional emergency medical technicians as opposed to professional barbers, this was understandable, however unbecoming.

I ngrid paced the master bedroom trying to piece together the details of what had transpired this evening. Who was the man in her bathroom and who were the men that had chased them? Two nurses were dead. Tobias Welke, also known as "The Chilean" was dead. An Asian woman was missing. Was any of this related? Everything had happened so fast.

"Despacito." Her phone.

She looked at her watch. Ten after nine. "Damn it, Edward."

She couldn't talk to him now. It was important that she was able to focus and think clearly when speaking with him. She was confident that he was hiding something from her, taunting her. He seemed unable to hide his delight while at the same time perpetuating a fraud. She only grew more suspicious of him by the day. Her phone continued to ring until it eventually went to voicemail.

K yle found a handheld mirror hanging from a hook on the side of the vanity. He leaned forward against the sink nearly pressing his face against the medicine cabinet mirror and ran his fingers over the bald, puckered red wound on his head and counted the staples.

Ingrid appeared in the bathroom and leaned against the door frame. She had her cell phone in hand and her arms were folded across her chest. "That looks painful."

Kyle eyed her in the mirror. "It's not that bad."

"Does it hurt?"

"No." He turned around to face her. "Do you have any razors?"

She wrinkled her eyebrows, "For?"

"You do shave your legs, don't you?"

"Yes, of course, I do." She was half offended. "They're under the sink."

Under the sink there was a small assortment of bathroom cleaning products, liquid drain cleaner, shaving creams, tampons, and a package of disposable razors. A mustache and beard trimmer set was stuffed in the back. He grabbed it and plugged it into the outlet next to the sink. "I overheard your conversation at the hospital," he said. Leaning in close to the medicine cabinet mirror, he set a depth of an eighth of an inch and put the trimmer to his head. "Edward is your boyfriend?"

Ingrid was still leaning against the door jamb. Arms still folded across her chest. "He is not my boyfriend."

He drew a clean line an inch and a half wide with the

trimmer from his widow's peak to the top of his head. "Does he know that?"

"He's been given no reason to think otherwise," she said.

He finished the line from the top of his head, down to his neck, tapped the clippers against the palm of his hand to get rid of the excess hair and began clearing a new row. "I'm sorry," he said. "It's none of my business."

Ingrid stood up straight. She wanted to respond, but couldn't find the right words. There was too much to unpack with regards to Edward VanRoy. It was probably best to say as little as possible. "No problem," she said. "I'll go get those clothes."

The apartment's one bedroom was at the end of the hall. An assortment of her father's clothes still hung in the closet. Clothes that her mother was most fond of and had refused to get rid of. Memories. Ingrid retrieved a pair of Chinos and a black sweater. The sweater was extra large and should accommodate Kyle's athletic physique.

The clothes were still covered in plastic from the cleaners. Ingrid removed the plastic and drew them in close. She inhaled deeply and, for a second, thought that she caught the distant scent of her father's cologne.

She wiped the beginnings of a tear from the corner of her eye and headed to the bathroom to drop off the clothes for Kyle. She was expecting him to still be trimming his hair, but to her surprise, he had finished and was stepping into the shower. His back was solid, legs strong.

Her cheeks got flushed.

"You've got to stop doing that." She instinctively turned away.

"Doing what?" He made no move to cover himself as he turned on the water.

She turned her back to him. "Taking your clothes off in front of me."

The shower head hissed, dribbled and then finally sprayed.

He covered himself with the curtain, more for her dignity than his. He was about to say something when he realized that he didn't even know her name. "I'm sorry, Ms.-," he started.

"Garcia. Ingrid Garcia."

"Ms. Garcia, I can't very well change into new clothes without taking off the old ones first. Nor, am I in the habit of taking a shower with my clothes on," he said. "It's not my fault that you can't stop peeping on me."

"I do not peep."

"Once is an accident. Twice, you're peeping."

Ingrid took a deep breath and turned around, maintained eye contact with him. "You may find this hard to believe..." She kept her eyes up, but couldn't think of anything else intelligent to say, so she blurted out, "...but you're not my type."

He let go of the shower curtain. "There's no need to get upset about it. You act as if I enjoy taking my clothes off in front of you."

Ingrid struggled to keep her eyes above his waist.

"So, if you wouldn't mind, I would like a little privacy." He turned around to face the warm water. He pushed the shower curtain, but it did not conceal the entire enclosure.

Before she left the bathroom, Ingrid peeped.

17

They were heading south on FDR Drive, Merylo cruising along at 45 miles an hour. The East River flowed with them on their left.

"Nuñez and Jackson from the hundred and fourteenth made it over to McCrees' house," Cavasano said.

Merylo kept his eyes glued to the road. "Good."

"That has to be the toughest part."

"What is?" Merylo asked.

"Having to tell the family that a loved one is dead," Cavasano said. "That's pretty tough."

"What, some dead guy that you never even met before?" Merylo huffed. "You think that telling his family that you also never even met before is the toughest part of being a cop?"

"Yeah, I think it's pretty difficult," Cavasano said. "Don't you?"

In the shadow of the Con Edison plant, Merylo slammed on the brakes. The sedan's best days were behind it and its worn tires refused to grip the road. The screeching halt that Merylo was looking to employ turned into a long drawn out whine. An old soda can rolled out from under the passenger's seat and tapped Cavasano on the heel. Cars honked as they sped by. A couple of motorists yelled obscenities. A car full of punks gave them the finger.

"No, I don't." Merylo glared. "You wanna know what the toughest part about being a cop is?" He didn't wait for Cavasano to answer. "Well, I'll tell you. It's having to tell the wife of your partner of seven years that her husband was dead because you had to go take a piss." His bottom lip quivered. "And as she's sitting there sobbing, their kids, their beautiful little kids come down from their bedrooms because they hear their mother crying. And they know right away. They know by the way their mother's crying, the way all cops' kids do, that their father isn't coming home anymore."

"It wasn't your fault, Frank." Cavasano could feel his partner's emotions bubbling to the surface. "You were on a stakeout in a rough situation, bad things happen."

Cars continued to honk mercilessly as they navigated around the stopped sedan.

"You don't know shit."

"Would you like to tell me about it?"

"You wouldn't understand what it's like to be on a stakeout at two forty-seven in the morning and you've got to take a leak 'cause you've had twenty ounces of coffee and three Cokes in the past four hours so that you wouldn't nod off.," Merylo said. "Your partner, he don't drink Cokes 'cause they aren't healthy for you and he's on some kind of a health kick after his wife was diagnosed with breast cancer. But you, you don't care because you don't got a wife because you're a miserable person to live with, so she divorced you three years ago. So, you can drink all the Cokes you want and nobody gives a shit."

Motorists continued to zip passed, honking and yelling and waving. Merylo ignored them. He went on, "So you get out of the car to go take a piss. You're in the south end of Brooklyn and for some dumb reason all of the street lights are working except the one you're parked under. But you can't whiz next to the car so this means you have to walk almost a block and a half to find a decent place to piss without being seen." The older detective was beginning to calm down. "You're on a stakeout, you don't wanna be seen, right?"

"Right." Cavasano nodded.

"Right. So, you duck behind a dumpster a block and a half away and do your business. It takes a few minutes, you know. It was three Cokes and a shitload of coffee."

Cavasano nodded again.

"So, you walk back to the car and get in and everything seems normal. You ask your partner if anything's changed and he don't answer you. His head is turned away and he looks like he's sleeping. That's when you think maybe he should have had some of your Cokes and he wouldn't have fallen asleep."

Another angry motorist drove by, called Merylo an asshole.

"So, what do you do? You try and give your partner a Coke to wake his ass up, right?"

Cavasano listened intently. The thought occurred to him that Merylo might not yet have had the opportunity to talk about what happened the night his partner was killed from a personal perspective. The older detective had gone from being angry to almost apologetic.

"But Benny didn't want any Coke, you wanna know why?"

Cavasano knew why. He braced himself for the answer anyway.

"Because he was dead, that's why." Merylo's voice cracked. "While I was away taking a piss, somebody shot him in the head. And there wasn't a damn thing I could do about it." Raw emotion spilled out of the old detective. "So, I got out of the car and yelled into the friggin' night for that son of a bitch to come back and shoot me, but he won't come. I wanted him to come back and shoot me so I didn't have to look into Benny's wife's face and tell her that her husband was murdered. While I was busy taking a piss. *That's* the toughest part about being a cop."

After letting the weight of the conversation settle down naturally, Cavasano spoke with an even and sincere tone. "Thank you for sharing that with me," he said.

"Yeah, well. I didn't want you to get any stupid ideas in your head."

Merylo's cell phone rang.

He answered, "This is Detective Merylo. Two? And Murdoch's not there? Do we have any idea where he might've gone?" He rubbed his forehead. "Of course, you don't. Shit. Alright, we're on our way."

Merylo stepped on the gas and the sedan lurched forward. A passing motorist honked rudely as the unmarked cut over a lane. The rain that was coming down in heavy drops had hardened and was falling with more intensity.

"What's happened?" Cavasano asked, happy to change the conversation to something that might be equally unpleasant.

"Two more dead bodies at the hospital," Merylo said. "And sleeping beauty has left the building."

18

Kyle wandered into the living room where he found Ingrid sitting on the sofa nursing a bottle of water. A second unopened bottle, sat on the coffee table in front of her. The clothes she had given him fit much better than the ones he had taken from the old man at the hospital. He took a seat on the edge of the sofa, far enough away so as not to invade her personal space. "Thanks for the clothes."

"De nada," she answered. "How's your head?"

"It's starting to throb." He ran a finger across his shaved head until he reached a staple. "But I found some aspirin in the bathroom."

Ingrid slid the bottled water in his direction.

"Thanks, again." He unscrewed the top and took a sip of the water and was instantly reminded that his bottom lip was split from the punch that he took from Ingrid in the laundry room.

She noticed him wince. "How's your lip?"

"Not as good as my head." He set the water down. "Where'd you learn to hit like that?"

"The Army taught me."

"I should have guessed. There was some pent-up frustration behind that punch."

Ingrid got up and walked to the living room window. She parted the curtains a little and attempted to look out. On most nights there was a good view looking north up First Avenue. Tonight, the window was blurred with rain.

Kyle could see her thinking. Her mind was working overtime. She seemed restless. "Can I ask what you were doing in my hospital room this evening?" He asked.

"I was looking for someone." She let the curtain fall back into place. "I thought you might be him."

"Who was it that you were looking for?"

"A bad guy."

"So, why my room?"

"Like I said, I thought you might be him." She continued to look out the rain-soaked window. "In reality, I think you are the one that fell on him. You and your colleague."

Kyle stood up and met her at the window. "You're talking about Tobias Welke?"

"Yes." She turned to face him at the mention of Welke's name.

"I overheard a couple of men, detectives I believe, mention him. He's from Chile?"

"That's what he wanted people to believe," Ingrid said. "He's really an American." She put the curtains all the way back. "He was using a false identity."

They moved away from the window and back to the middle of the apartment. Kyle tried to remember the details of the detective's conversation while they were in his hospital room. He took another sip of water. And then it came to him. "The Armsport," he said. "I heard the detectives mention that Welke was staying at the Armsport Apartments in Brooklyn."

"Do you know where that is?" Ingrid asked.

"Not exactly, but I'm sure we could find it with the GPS on my phone."

Ingrid's cell phone rang. It was Edward. Again.

"Perdón." She motioned to Kyle that she had to take the call.

He wandered around the living room while Ingrid tended to her call. He found a family photo on an end table and picked it up.

Ingrid did her best to keep an even demeanor. "Hi Edward."

"You're late." VanRoy's voice ended on a high note. There must be friends of his nearby. He was nothing if not discreet.

"I'm sorry, I got tied up at the hospital and-"

"With your friend?"

"A friend of the family, yes. And I just got home and-"

"I forgot to ask earlier, is this friend male or female?"

Ingrid glanced at Kyle. He returned to sitting on the sofa. He was looking at a family picture that was left behind by her mother. "Male." She said.

"Oh?" VanRoy sounded surprised, but not in a jealous way. "Tied up with your male friend? Sounds kinky. Is he good looking?"

"I'm really sorry, Edward. Could we please reschedule for some other time? My day has not been good."

"Hmm, an IOU."

"Call it what you like," she said. There was no enthusiasm in her voice. "Goodnight, Edward."

She ended the call and sat down next to Kyle on the sofa.

"Nice looking family," Kyle said. He handed her the picture.

"Gracias." She ran her hand over the glass. The photo was taken on the sidewalk in front of her father's flower shop on 21st Street in Chelsea by one of his customers. It was cold in New York that Valentine's Day, but it wasn't snowing and the sidewalks were alive with people. A number of whom ended up as extras in the family photo. It also happened to be the last time that Ingrid and her mother, father and sister, Juliana, were all together. She remembered when the photo was taken, but hadn't paid it much attention since she came back to her parent's apartment, until now.

"Interesting relationship you have with Edward," Kyle commented.

"Yes," she said. "It's, how would you say, pragmatic?" She was distracted by the picture. How happy everyone was at that moment, unaware of the despair that would soon engulf them. Their father would be dead less than a month later. A heart attack brought on by too many Bandeja Paisas made with chorizo and beef, her mother had said. Her niece Marlena, would go missing a month and a half later.

"Pragmatic to lie to him?" Kyle asked.

"He lies to me, too." Ingrid was too engrossed in the family photo to look up at Kyle. "Our relationship is based on lies," she said. In the photo, Ingrid and Juliana wore the same white knit hat with a ball tassel on top. And although she was almost three years younger, strangers often asked the sisters if they were twins. A pedestrian captured in the photo, standing on the side-walk several feet behind them and visible over Juliana's left shoulder, caught Ingrid's eye.

"Your relationship sounds very much cat and mouse," Kyle said.

"It very much is." Ingrid couldn't believe what she was seeing. How could she have missed it for so long. She held the family picture closer to get a better look. There, in the photo, standing behind her father and sister was a stranger in a blue pea coat. He had a cell phone to his ear and seemed to be aware of the moment the picture was taken. He met the photographer with a sideways glance, his lips were turned up in an arrogant grin. It was Edward VanRoy.

"If Edward isn't your boyfriend." Kyle worked the question over in his head before asking. "Then who is he?"

Ingrid set the picture down on her lap. Her heart rate picked up at the realization that Edward VanRoy had been that close to her family the whole time. She didn't hesitate to answer Kyle's question. "He's a monster."

19

Traffic was light. Maybe because the Yankees were in the Series. Maybe because of the freezing rain. Whatever the reason, for the moment, there were no cars behind them as Dmitri slowed the SUV to a stop on the lower level, eastbound, single outer lane of the Queensboro Bridge. He turned off the lights and motioned to Niko. "Hurry."

Niko got out and opened the rear hatch. The dome light illuminated the horror that had taken place earlier. Looking into the back, Dmitri spotted Alex's cellphone on the seat behind him. He grabbed it and put it in his coat pocket.

Dark blots of blood spattered the back window like a grotesque Rorschach Test. Alex was slumped unnaturally across the back of the SUV on top of the woman. His left eye was wide open, his right eye was missing along with a trough of skull. Disturbed by what he saw, Niko reached in and extinguished the dome light with his fist.

Limp as he was in death, Alex's drug use had left him a slight man. Niko had no trouble pulling him from the back of the SUV and propping him against the back wheel. He hurriedly situated the woman into a more natural position before closing the hatch and attending to his former partner in crime. With all the emotion of taking out the garbage, Niko hoisted Alex over his shoulder and threw the dead man over the railing of the dual level bridge. He watched long enough to see Alex hit the East River below.

Getting back into the vehicle, Niko noticed Dmitri looking at a picture of a little girl on his cell phone. Dmitri clicked off the image once Niko got settled into the passenger's seat.

"What is it?" Niko asked.

Dmitri turned the vehicle's lights back on and proceeded driving east. "Nothing." He paused. "I want to find that window cleaner."

"We don't have time to deal with a miserable window cleaner." Niko's voice rose with anger. "We leave tonight."

"I want to make sure." Dmitri squeezed the steering wheel, his fingers made little waves in the soft vinyl.

They took Jackson Avenue to 111th St. Both stared blankly through the windshield, mesmerized by the wipers and the falling rain.

Dmitri asked. "What is the peasant's address?"

Wedged between the front windshield and the dashboard were the two purloined clipboards from the hospital. Niko pressed the overhead map light and sorted through the items until he had the chart taken from the foot of the window washer's hospital bed.

They crossed over Newton Creek via the Pulaski Bridge leaving Queens and entering Kings County. A large green sign welcomed them to Brooklyn.

"Greenpoint," Niko said as he entered the window washer's address into the portable GPS.

"We are close."

Set in the northwest corner of Brooklyn, the neighborhood known as Greenpoint was a busy shipbuilding community in its former life. Settled by Polish immigrants at the turn of the century, Greenpoint's heritage is advertised by its churches, restaurants and community centers. The ethnic flavor did not go unnoticed.

"Little Warsaw," Dmitri said with disgust.

"I can smell the dirty bastards." Niko spat.

"Svin'ya." Dmitri agreed. *Pigs.*

"*Turn right in five hundred feet.*" The GPS assumed a woman's voice.

"Right here." Niko tapped the passenger window.

Dmitri listened to the woman and turned right down a narrower, less crowded, tree lined street.

"Over there." Niko pointed up ahead on the left-hand side of the street.

Dmitri slowed down and pulled the SUV to the curb. The street ran west, down to an abandoned shipyard on the East River. Large Sumac trees absorbed the light from the street lamps, limiting their glow to dim, compact, orange patches.

Dmitri pulled up out of the blush of the street lamp. The streets were clear. Only a couple of men sloshing around under the sidewalk awning outside of Jablonski's Tavern a half block away. He eyed them through the windshield. The ridiculous drunks wouldn't be a problem. He clenched his teeth and his jaw expanded. "What number?"

"Three zero two," Niko answered.

Dmitri held out his hand. "Give me your gun."

"Why?" Niko frowned.

"Because of the suppressor."

Niko made sure the safety lock was on and reluctantly gave Dmitri his firearm.

Dmitri reciprocated by handing Niko the gun stolen earlier from the security guard. "Here." He tucked the silenced pistol in his coat pocket. "I'm going up. Stay in the vehicle."

Rain pinged loudly off the roof of the SUV.

The Yankees scored.

Loud yelling from the inebriates down the street caused Niko to look over his shoulder.

"Hey." Dmitri flicked his throat with his index finger. "Pyany." *Drunk*.

The apartment building was an old brick structure. There were two lights on and neither one of them was on the third floor. The rain had cleared the streets of any pedestrians. Except for the drunks.

Niko continued to be preoccupied with the Polish bar.

"Leave them be." Dmitri warned.

Niko looked at his watch and nodded to the apartment building.

Dmitri got out and hurried across the street. He had to jump over a puddle to reach the sidewalk as he hustled for the front door of the small apartment complex. He didn't notice Alex's cellphone buzzing in his coat pocket as he crossed the street in the pouring rain.

The entrance to the old apartment complex was left unlocked and unattended and allowed him unfettered access. He climbed the stairs to the third floor and made a left. He put his ear to the door of apartment 302 and listened for a full minute for any movement or noise from inside. But any commotion would have been nearly impossible to detect due to the worsening weather conditions outside.

Dmitri stuck the barrel of his pistol where the latch bolt met the strike plate and fired. Wood splintered, metal clinked and the apartment door swung open with ease.

In the dim light that trickled in from the street, Kyle Murdoch's apartment was barren with the exception of a single chair, table and lamp. There were no knickknacks or other creature comforts in the tiny front room. Not even a television.

Dmitri crept down the hall to the dwelling's lone bedroom. The bed was made up tight and the closet was empty. A large rucksack leaned against the back wall. He was about to inspect it when a gunshot rang out from the street below.

Dmitri turned and ran out of the bedroom. As he rounded the corner from the hallway, Alex's cell phone fell out of his coat pocket. In the front room, he swiped the curtain back from the window and saw Niko standing outside on the street next to the SUV. He pulled the slide on his gun to make sure a round was chambered and ran out the door, leaving Alex's cell phone behind.

Outside on the street, there was more noise from down the block. Obnoxious cheering and carrying on from the drunken patrons. Three more had spilled out onto the sidewalk laughing and slapping hands with each other.

Dmitri arrived and scolded Niko. "Who did you shoot at?"

"I did not shoot at anyone," Niko said. "It was one of the pigs from the tavern."

"Get in the car," Dmitri ordered. "We must go."

How Niko wished one of them would stumble over in his direction. Before getting into the vehicle, he raised his left hand slowly and formed it into the shape of a pistol.

One by one, he shot them down.

20

The rain continued to come down hard and thick and was slowing traffic on the Williamsburg Bridge. At the time it was completed in 1903 at a cost of 24 million dollars, the bridge held the distinction of having the longest main span of any suspension bridge in the world, measuring an impressive 1,600 feet. Having taken the car that belonged to Ingrid's mother, they were now halfway across and had yet to utter a single word since leaving the parking garage.

Kyle was the first to break the silence. "How long have you lived in New York?"

Ingrid had been staring out into the East River below. She turned away from the window. "I don't live here."

"Oh." Kyle was somewhat surprised by her answer. "Where do you live?"

Ingrid turned back to the East River. "I'm from Medellín."

"Colombia?"

Ingrid turned back to face him. Her expression asked if there was any other Medellín.

"What brought you to New York?" He asked.

"My mother." She messaged her temples. "She wanted to

move back to Colombia, so I came here to help her. What about you?" She asked him before he could question her further.

"What about me?"

Kyle got off the Williamsburg Bridge and turned right onto Broadway. He followed Broadway back toward the East River where he made a right, cutting back under the Williamsburg Bridge. The freezing rain continued to make visibility difficult, but at least the city street was less slick than the bridge.

"How did you end up in this situation?" She asked.

"I was in the wrong place at the wrong time, I guess. I saw a woman being abducted from her hotel room and the next thing I know, all Hell broke loose and now these men are trying to kill me."

"What do you plan to do about it?"

"I don't know," he said. "Maybe I'll move." He thought for a moment. "Colombia sounds nice right about now."

K yle guided the car into a vacant parking space on the street. The brick buildings that lined both sides of the road were decorated in big puffy letters, artists in training. Bold, random, one-word statements. Urban hieroglyphics that were, at times, both comedic and threatening. A healthy Norway Maple sheltered them from above.

His apartment was up the street, but he parked Ingrid's car nearly a block away on purpose. Too many people looking for him. Approaching his apartment from a distance, he hoped to spot trouble before it spotted him.

All of the vehicles parked on the street were empty. The only action was taking place down the street at Jablonski's. The corner bar looked to be packed tonight. A couple of patrons were outside under the awning on the sidewalk smoking and carrying on.

"I'll be right back."

"Are we at the Armsport?" Ingrid looked around, but couldn't see out of the rain slicked windows.

"No. I've stopped here to pick up my things." He opened the door and got out.

"Wait." Ingrid got out of the car and ran after him. She held one hand over her head in a futile attempt to keep dry.

Kyle heard her and stopped. "I really hoped you would stay in the car."

"I'm coming with you."

They were getting wetter by the second.

"Alright." Kyle dropped his hands to his sides. "Follow me, then."

He led the way and they hurried down the sidewalk. Cutting through a narrow alley, he steered Ingrid between a group of beat up trash cans and a small mountain of overstuffed garbage bags that leaked trash, partially blocking the way between apartment complexes. The alley behind the apartments was confined and strewn with more litter.

"Third floor," Kyle said. He pulled one of the garbage cans over and used it to stand on. Jumping up, he was able to grab the ladder off the second-floor fire escape and pull it down. He held out a hand. "Ladies first."

Kyle followed Ingrid up the ladder and when they'd reached the landing, he made his way over to the window that led into his apartment and lifted it open. With the ease of an Olympic gymnast, he hoisted himself into the apartment while hardly grazing the window frame. Once inside, he leaned through the window with his arms outstretched and motioned with his fingers for Ingrid to come closer.

She was impressed at the ease with which Kyle operated. "Do you always go in that way?"

"No. Not always," he said. "Come on. I'll help you." He put

his hands on her waist and leaned toward her, his cheek brushed against hers. "Watch your head," he instructed. In one quick motion, Kyle lifted her by her hips and leaned back, tilted her horizontally and pulled her through the window over his shoulder.

The room was dark except for a sliver of light that filtered in from the back alley. Aside from the small, twin sized bed, the only other object in the room was a large army rucksack leaning against the far wall. Kyle reached under the mattress and pulled out a handgun. He paused for a moment to look it over and then held it out to Ingrid. "Are you okay to hold this?"

She took the gun from him without hesitation. "Army. And I lived through Medellín in the nineteen nineties. Of course, I'm okay." She rolled the weapon over in her hand and as a means of proving her knowledge and comfort in handling the weapon, she released the magazine and pulled back the slide. The magazine was empty, but there was a round in the chamber. "That's it?"

"I'm afraid so."

This struck her as odd and slightly out of character from what she'd seen of him so far. He struck her as the type to be on top of things, always ahead of the game. Maybe there was more than meets the eye. "How long have you lived here?"

Kyle retrieved a miniature flashlight from an outside pocket of the rucksack and turned it on. "Not long."

The flashlight danced around the tiny room with every movement he made, revealing more detail. An open bi-fold door on the opposite wall partly concealed an empty closet. There were a few cracks in the plaster walls and paint was missing in places. The floor was an old hardwood that hadn't been treated in decades. The bed was made up tight and without a wrinkle. Nice and tidy. Everything he owned was packed into the army rucksack. Except for the gun

"Do you like it here?" Ingrid asked.

Kyle didn't answer. He didn't know how to. "Let's take a look around."

Ingrid followed him down the hall past the small galley kitchen and into the cramped front room that would have been overcrowded had there been more than a chair, a table and a lamp. The door to the apartment was not completely closed.

Kyle pointed the flashlight at the door knob. Wood splintered out from a hole in the door between the knob and the jamb. He swung the beam of light passed Ingrid to the chair on the opposite wall. It too had a hole in it, and behind that was a hole in the plaster wall. "I don't think I'll be getting my security deposit back."

"Look," Ingrid said. She pointed to an object on the floor. "Somebody dropped their phone." She picked it up and handed it to Kyle. "Yours?"

"No. I keep my phone with me at all times." He patted his front pocket.

"Could be one of the men looking for you?"

"Could be," Kyle said. "I don't think my landlord would blow a hole in the door."

"They know where you live," she said.

"So, it would seem." Kyle clicked off the flashlight and brushed the curtain on the front window aside.

Ingrid thought about the men that had chased them and how they'd managed to escape despite Kyle's injuries. He didn't seem especially worried at all. She considered his physical abilities. The man was in perfect shape and had bounced back quickly after a devastating fall. There were no clothes in his closet and everything he owned was in that rucksack. Except for a gun that he had kept under his mattress. With one bullet.

"Who are you, really, Kyle Murdoch?" She asked.

"Me?" He was surprised by Ingrid's question. "I'm nobody special."

"I don't believe that."

Kyle looked down the street toward Jablonski's. The inebriates had all gone back into the bar. There was nobody out on the street. He let the curtain fall back into place.

"You must be somebody or those men would have killed you already."

"Well then, Ms. Garcia, consider me lucky."

If Ingrid only knew how close to the truth she was. That Kyle existed only if somebody else believed that he mattered. Before this afternoon, before the woman was abducted and before Carl was killed, his life was inconsequential. He had spent a lifetime training to defend the lives of others, but never ultimately having the ability keep the ones he loved safe from the hand of fate. It was only now that the despair and hopelessness seemed to subside. He'd found a reason to live.

"Why keep a gun with only one round in it?" Ingrid held up the firearm. "Who are you saving it for?"

Kyle didn't answer right away. He was caught off guard by her question. He finally answered, "Nobody special."

21

"Right here."

The cab pulled over to the curb and came to a stop. The driver slid open the partition that separated the front seat from the back. "Cash or credit?" He said.

The passenger in the back stuck a gloved hand through the opening and dropped a wad of cash on the front seat. "Fucking rip-off." He stepped out into the rain and slammed the door as the cab driver told him to go fuck himself.

He trudged up the street, protected from the elements by a dark gray trench coat. He had the hood up and the peak of which, flopped over his forehead and covered most of his face. As the rain fell harder, he picked up his pace. A dark phantom on the most miserable of nights.

His pulse quickened as he reached the steps of the Armsport Apartments. It had been a long while since he'd last been here and he was instantly aroused by memories of decadent encounters, taboo to the sophisticated world, that were perpetrated within its dingy brick walls. He didn't need an invitation. No secret code, knock or handshake required. He owned the building and had the key. So, he let himself in.

The building was just how he remembered it. In just enough working order to placate the Division of Building Standards and Codes, while not burdening his financial sheets. He cared less if the folks referred to his property management company as a slumlord. He rather liked the title, if he were to be honest. He always felt it more comfortable engaging in sordid behavior in the shadows. Humiliating the desperate in a sleazy environment that reeked of hopelessness. It added to the experience.

He was surprised to see that the building was quiet on this night. Only the faint whisper of the ballgame emanating out of one of the apartments. No one loitering in the vestibule or the hallway to escape the horrible weather. No one huddled up against the side of the building smoking, drinking or injecting. Most important and surprising of all, no police.

The carpeted stairs were worn to the wood in spots and plaster was missing in small chunks on the dirty walls. His heart pumped faster as he approached the small apartment on the second floor. But he hadn't come to revisit old memories. Nor had he come to give the property a much-needed wellness check. His reason for coming was more self-serving. He came this most miserable of nights to protect his reputation within the polite society.

Inside apartment 204, he closed the door and inhaled deeply. The aroma of past debauchery tickled his senses and caused a shudder down his spine. Memories. The room looked just as he remembered it. Dark and colorless. As if it were a picture drawn from an old newspaper. The tiny bed was were he remembered it. So was the cage on the far side of the room.

He looked through the drawers of the little bedside table. A pair of handcuffs, a chain and a ball gag with a leather strap. Toys from the past. How fun it would be to reminisce, but if he hoped to make future memories, he'd have to stick to the task at hand.

He glanced around the space for any evidence that would associate him with past dalliances in the room or with the man who'd most recently rented it. The room was as discreet as it was menacing. He checked the bathroom and found it empty, but for a few basic toiletries. A dresser opposite the bed housed a modest assortment of shirts, pants, socks and underwear.

He searched the kitchen cabinets only to find a stack of paper plates, an opened bag of potato chips and a half-depleted case of bottled water. A Styrofoam takeout container sat empty on top of the stove. In the pantry that housed the hot water tank, he found what he was looking for.

A sturdy titanium briefcase was tucked between the hot water tank and the wall. It wasn't the greatest of hiding places and to leave such potentially damaging information in such an easily accessed location was shocking, actually. As it was with most things in life, the longer the time without incidence, the less likely one is to be vigilant.

He picked up the briefcase and shook it, wondering what secrets were filed away inside. He had no doubt that its contents would be incriminating. Not just for himself, but for a number of other high-profile men. He'd shared in the liaisons with politicians, policemen, a celebrity chef and even a Royal, all of whom's identities were likely to be found within the confines of the shiny briefcase. A quid pro quo security measure that ensured its owner couldn't be hung out to dry on his own should the authorities start sniffing around.

He locked the apartment on his way out. A vacuum ran loudly in a room down the hall. In another apartment, a couple argued. On the first floor, the ballgame broadcast had been turned up a little louder.

The Yankees were winning.

He smiled to himself as he left the building and returned to the miserable weather that had plagued the great city on this night. He kept in the shadows of the sidewalk, sheltered from the glare of the street lights by decades old trees thriving in the tough urban landscape.

A single red four door sedan passed by as he continued up the block. He turned back to watch the vehicle do a U-turn and then pull up to the curb on the opposite side of the street. It wasn't the police, so he kept his walk at a leisurely pace.

A block later, he hailed a cab, set the briefcase on the back seat next to him and let out a sigh of relief. He was feeling much better about his situation. Now that he had possession of the single greatest threat to his reputation and security, all he needed to do was get rid of that Colombian pest, Ingrid Garcia.

22

K yle and Ingrid hurried down the street to where they'd left her car. Kyle's held a hand over his head, protecting it from the heavy, freezing drops of rain pelting them as they ran. Ingrid pulled up the hood on her jacket. The fake white fur outlining the hood was soggy and mingled with her dark hair. When they'd reached the car, Kyle tossed his rucksack in the back and then got in the driver's seat. The two of them closed their doors at the same time.

Ingrid wiped water from her face. She seemed to be energized by the freezing rain. "To Welke's place. Let's go," she said.

Kyle stuck the key in the ignition. "He's dead." He reminded her. "You're sure you really want to go?"

She wasn't ready to tell him why it was so important to her to visit Tobias Welke's residence. "I'm not leaving here without finding out all that I can about Tobias Welke. So, either you're going to take me there or get out and I'll go there myself."

"How are you planning to get in?"

"I'll think of something. I got in to see you, didn't I?"

Ingrid had a point and Kyle could tell that she wasn't going to let it go. She was serious about her desire to know all she could about Tobias Welke. She hadn't lost control of her emotion, but it was obvious that whatever her reasons, it was deeply personal. "Okay," Kyle said. "You're right. Let's go to Welke's"

He searched for the location using the GPS on his phone and found that the apartment complex was only a few blocks away. It should only take them a minute or so to get there. He started the car and pulled away from the curb.

Three blocks later he turned left down another tree lined street and drove west toward the East River. The weather had cleared the streets of its citizens, but for a lone walker shrouded in rain gear and heading eastward up the street.

"There they are." Kyle studied the apartments as they approached.

In the early 1900's, the apartments were used as part of a housing complex for the dockworkers and were owned by a prominent shipping company. A hundred years later and it had been reduced to nothing more than a set of cheap, single unit low-income apartments. A few of the rooms were rented out by the week. Of the six units on the East side of the complex, he noticed that four of them had their lights on. He could not see the west side. He did a U-turn and parked the car on the opposite side of the street, facing away from the apartments.

Kyle got out, opened the back door, grabbed his miniature flashlight and removed a tool kit from one of the pockets of his rucksack. He put the flashlight in his pocket and shoved the tool kit down the front of his waistband. Ingrid waited anxiously at the rear of the car.

"What are you doing?" She asked. She was impatient to get inside.

"I'm improving our chances of getting into Welke's apartment," he said. "Provided it's not already open and occupied by the police."

He closed the car door and the two of them hustled up the street dodging puddles. The freezing rain gathered as slush beneath their feet. Ingrid nearly slipped trying to avoid one.

They crossed the street to the apartment complex under the cover of a broken street light. Five fractured sandstone steps led to a small awning covering the entrance. A rusting white sign next to the doors advertised the Armsport as having furnished apartments. Kyle doubted it. The foyer was accessed through a pair of double glass doors. Kyle pulled one open and he and Ingrid stepped inside.

The small vestibule was illuminated by a single light set inside an outdated fixture. Various species of dead flies, gnats and mosquitos strangled the underpowered bulb and cast a jaundice hue throughout the room. In the murkiness, Kyle searched the mailbox name plates for one Tobias Welke.

No such luck.

However, all of the units with odd numbers on the west side of the building had names penciled in on their mailboxes. The word "Manager" was written in red on box 101. Of the even numbered units on the East side, three of the mailboxes were left unnamed. From what he could tell outside, two of those three had their lights on. That left unit 204 as most likely to be Tobias Welke's apartment.

He told Ingrid, "Keep your head down and don't look anyone in the eye. If any detectives or police show up, please let me know." He pulled the nylon bag holding a lock-picking kit from his waistband.

Ingrid identified it as a lock picking kit. "A window washer and a thief. What a convenient combination."

Kyle didn't feel the need to dignify the remark. "Just make sure to let me know if someone is coming."

The stairwell to the second floor came down on their right-hand side. Kyle climbed the steps two at a time, century old wood partially covered with dirty maroon carpet. When he reached the second floor, he stopped and tuned into the sounds emanating from behind closed doors. Room 201 to his left, the tenants had the ballgame on. In room 202 on his right, someone who was obviously not a baseball fan, ran an overworked vacuum cleaner that sounded like a South African vuvuzela.

He crept down the hall to room 204. If he had any thoughts of breaking the door in, the noise might be a welcome diversion, but at the moment, for what he wanted to do, the noise could present a problem. He knelt down in front of the door, opened his kit and laid out his tools. He slid on a pair of rubber latex gloves and tested the door knob to see if it was in fact, locked. It was. He grabbed a tension wrench and a feeler pick from his kit and stuck them in the lock. It was time to go to work.

23

F rank Merylo tapped a finger on the passenger's side window. "That's it over there on the right. Pull over, right here."

"Where?"

"Right there, The Armsport Apartments."

Cavasano pulled the unmarked over, rubbing the curb in the process and eliciting a stare from his partner.

"I know the car ain't much to look at, Cavasano," Merylo said. "But, do you mind?" He shook his head. "I knew I should've drove."

Cavasano didn't respond to the criticism. He had learned in his short time with Merylo that the old detective had a comment for everything. He was going to have to learn to live with it.

Merylo swiveled his head. "Christ, it's starting to snow, now. This has to be the worst October ever."

"That's global warming for you," Cavasano offered.

"It's snow, Cavasano. By definition that doesn't make any sense."

"Climate change, actually." Cavasano corrected.

Merylo squirmed in his seat, changed the subject. "This

Welke guy have anything else on his person? Pictures, anything?"

"No pictures. Just eight hundred odd dollars in cash, the apartment's address, and a plane ticket to South America. There was an up to date passport in his jacket. Bogus as hell as we now know. His cell phone was destroyed."

"That's it?"

"That's all."

"Alright. This should be easy then." Merylo unhooked his seatbelt. "Let's go in and take a peek, see if we can find anything before the Feds show up. Piss off the brass a little bit."

Cavasano nodded in agreement. He was learning.

Merylo grabbed the door handle. "Let's go."

Both men got out of the car. Cavasano put his head down and turned his coat collar up against the elements.

Merylo scowled and faced the wicked weather without bending. He scooped a bit of slush that had formed on the outer edge of the windshield and flung it on down at his feet. "Global warming, my ass."

K yle held the tension wrench in the keyhole with his left hand and turned it counterclockwise making sure to keep pressure on the plug. Five little pins, each of varying length, were the only barrier between himself and the inside of Tobias Welke's shit hole apartment.

It was the feeler pick's job to lift the pins out of the way. Having a good ear is helpful when picking a lock as it is the best way to tell when one of the pins has been successfully manipulated into place. The noise that filtered out into the hallway from the units on the second floor made this nearly impossible.

Kyle would have to rely on his fingertips and sense of touch to feel the slight click as the upper pins were pushed into the housing. He gently worked the feeler pick against the first pin, the one farthest in. Within a second, it had popped into place. "One down, four to go," he whispered to himself.

I ngrid shivered. Not because she was cold, but because she was anxious. Adrenaline did that sometimes. She bounced on the balls of her feet to trying to expend the energy building up inside her. She looked at her gaudy watch. Kyle had been gone a whole three minutes.

The vestibule was stuffy and she was starting to feel claustrophobic, as though she were suffocating on her own anxiety when suddenly, raucous cheering from one of the first-floor apartments startled her. Then she remembered that the Yankees were in the World Series. They must have scored. New Yorkers love their baseball. Ingrid didn't care. She needed fresh air. Now.

She pulled her hood up and stepped out onto the front steps of the apartment building and inhaled two lungs full of cold, damp, Brooklyn air. Leaning on the wobbly railing, she could see where Kyle had parked her car down the street. She inhaled some more, but almost choked when she saw a familiar, bristly gray haircut with matching mustache walking down the sidewalk toward the apartment complex.

W hat had started with so much promise had quickly devolved and become an exercise in patience. Kyle couldn't get the last two pins to slide into place. His fingers were sweating and slipping around inside the blue latex gloves. His left hand was beginning to cramp and he had difficulty working the pick with the finesse that was required.

Time was not his friend at the moment so, he decided to put the feeler pick back into the kit and pulled out a rake. This tool allowed for less precision and more force. Although not a stealthy instrument like the feeler pick, when employed, it is effectively five times faster.

Confident that the noise on the third floor would conceal the brief commotion, Kyle slid the rake deep into the keyhole, feeling the pins bounce around its uneven teeth. He kept even pressure on the tension wrench as he steadily pulled the rake back through the keyhole. It made a sound similar to a hacksaw biting into corrugated steel. Within seconds, the pins had sprung into place, the door knob twisted open, and Kyle was inside Tobias Welke's apartment.

"Evening ma'am." The tall detective greeted Ingrid as he walked up the apartment building steps.

She kept her back turned to him hoping he would figure her for some strung out junkie and leave her be. She didn't think she could explain herself if she tried.

Before he could say anything else, his partner elbowed him, holding out his hands and catching pellets of freezing rain. "First things first." He nodded to the front doors of the complex. The two detectives scurried into the building and shook themselves off like wet dogs.

Ingrid turned and watched them through the glass. When the tall detective craned his neck to get a look at her, she quickly spun herself around into the weather before he could see her face.

Kyle used his flashlight to look around the apartment, not wanting to risk turning on the lights. The single room units were no more than converted hotel rooms, containing a solitary bathroom and a small kitchen area. The room looked like a cave. Black foam acoustical tiles covered the walls from floor to ceiling. A large dog cage sat empty at the far end of the room. The wood floor was discolored and worn.

On the one wall, a twin-sized bed with a well-worn mattress and box spring that sagged in the middle. The covers were thin and the bed was unmade. Next to the bed on the right- hand side was a small, single drawer nightstand supporting an over-sized, square based lamp. Kyle made sure his gloves were on tight and opened the drawer. A pair of handcuffs and a ball gag used during sexual bondage and BDSM roleplay. An old dresser across the room held some of what he assumed were Welke's clothes.

He searched through the kitchen cabinets finding nothing of any significance. The closet adjacent to the kitchen housed the room's hot water tank and nothing else. The bathroom was empty with the exception of a few toiletries and a solitary towel. A piece of paper caught his eye in the bathroom trash bin. He picked it up and saw that it was a restaurant receipt. He hated to leave the apartment empty handed, but could find nothing else of importance and so, stuffed the receipt in his pocket.

He gave the apartment a quick once over to make sure he hadn't overlooked anything. Aside from the overall sexual creepiness of the room, there was nothing there. He had taken a big risk for nothing. His only concern now was getting out of Welke's apartment as discreetly as he had entered. After that, he planned to get as far away from the city as he could.

24

Ingrid's jacket had absorbed all the water it could hold. She was now thoroughly soaked from head to toe and shivering beyond control. Through the rain slicked doors she was still able to make out the figures of the two detectives inside. She moved closer to the glass to get a better look.

The detectives stood in the doorway of the first apartment on the left, just past the mailboxes. They were talking to a skinny man with an unhealthy gut. He was wearing dark pants and a white t-shirt. The shorter of the two detectives flashed his badge and the skinny man's hands flung out and landed on his bald head. The taller detective gestured and the man appeared to relax.

The t-shirted man left the two detectives for a moment only to return carrying an assortment of keys. It appeared as though he might be the apartment manager. He led the detectives to the stairway, stopping to talk for a second. When they'd started up the stairs and reached the first landing of the stairway out of sight, Ingrid raced into the building.

"Shit."

They couldn't be allowed to go upstairs. She needed to stop

them before they caught Kyle in Welke's apartment. The manager's apartment door was still open and The World Series broadcast spilled out into the hallway.

W hatever the reason was that Ingrid wanted to come here, Kyle was sorry that he'd obliged and even more regretful that he'd come away empty handed. He slipped quietly out of unit 204, closed the door and started down the hall toward the stairs. He was about to take the first step when he was greeted by the sound of jingling keys and a collection of male voices echoing up the stairwell.

At the other end of the hall there was a door with an exit sign over its frame. A second way out could prove to be valuable. Kyle waited to see if the men were coming up. He backed away when he caught a glimpse of one of their shoes. There wasn't enough time to make it to the end of the hall without being seen and re-entering Welke's apartment was out of the question. He needed a distraction.

When the scream came, it was loud, it was piercing and it was very distracting.

J oe Cavasano winced as the high-pitched wail threatened to pierce his eardrums. "What the-"

Before he knew it, Frank Merylo had already turned and headed back down the stairs. Cavasano raced after him, negotiating the steps two at a time. The apartment manager trailed behind, feebly trying to keep up.

. . .

Kyle froze when he heard the scream. The last time he heard a scream like that he had just dropped Ingrid through a laundry chute. This time though, it sounded contrived.

He leaned over the railing and looked to the landing. It was clear. Kyle descended halfway down from the second-floor landing until he was able to get a look at the first-floor lobby. Crouching, he saw Ingrid standing in front of an opened apartment, soaking wet and jumping up and down. Two men in overcoats and one in a t-shirt stood around her.

"The Yankees scored, the Yankees scored." Ingrid threw her arms around Cavasano, careful not to make eye contact or give him a good look at her face.

Cavasano smiled as Merylo gently pushed her off of him.

She continued her screaming, clapping and jumping up and down.

"Alright lady, enough is enough," Merylo warned.

"Who scored?" Cavasano asked.

Merylo shot him a look.

Ingrid wouldn't settle down. "The Yankees scored, the Yankees scored." She kept jumping and clapping and noticed Kyle crouched down on the stairway. He was pointing and mouthing something that she couldn't comprehend. Then he took off up the stairs.

The manager removed his hands from his ears and spoke up. "That's enough lady, didn't you hear the officer?" he shouted and slammed the door to his apartment cutting off the cause of her hysteria at the source.

As soon as the door was shut, Ingrid stopped screaming. She accidentally exchanged eye contact with older detective before tucking her head down and slinking back towards the front door.

"Get out of here," the manager said, giving her a helpful push out the door. "Damn vagrants."

"You have this problem a lot?" Cavasano asked.

"The damn security door lock is busted. They only come in when the weather's bad, like tonight. They come in to keep warm or dry."

"Or watch the Yankees game," Merylo added, clearly annoyed.

The manager called after her, "Go on, get out of here before I call the cops."

Cavasano gave the manager a look.

Merylo didn't acknowledge him. His eyes bounced between the front door and the tiled floor.

"Frank?"

Merylo shook his head and came out of his mini trance, "Yeah, right, let's go." He charged up the stairs.

Outside, Ingrid leaned against the wet brick building not sure what to do next. Her heart raced. She hoped Kyle was able to get something, anything that could help her find her niece. Emotionally, she was becoming overwhelmed. She was desperate to find Marlena and felt that this was her last best hope.

Running into the detectives again made her realize the severity of the situation. She was lucky that they didn't recognize her. If she was to get in trouble with the authorities in the U.S., her unit back home would be embarrassed and her career would be jeopardized. Her jacket rode up her back as she slid down the brick wall, unfazed as the sleet pelted her face.

She didn't see Kyle as he emerged from around the side of the building, but she felt him as he caught her before her back-side had a chance to hit the cold sandstone. He squatted down next to her and wrapped his arms around her, shielding her from the stinging sleet. She was trembling uncontrollably.

He tucked his head in close to hers. "Hey. Are you alright?"

Ingrid sat shivering and her teeth were beginning to chatter.

"Everything's going to be ok," he said. "I promise." He leaned into her. "But we've got to get out of here, first." He helped her to her feet.

"Did you find anything?" She asked.

He held her arm as they walked down the sandstone steps. "No." He knew that was only partly true. "The apartment was empty."

"That can't be," she said.

They started down the street in a fast walk.

"It's possible that I chose the wrong apartment," he conceded. "But I don't think so."

Kyle took a quick look back to make sure no one had followed them out of the apartment complex. As they got closer to Ingrid's car, they picked up their pace to a slow run.

When they were both in the car with the doors shut, Ingrid finally spoke, "He remembered me," she said.

"Who?"

"One of the detectives. The shorter one." She pushed away a strand of wet hair that was stuck to her cheek.

"He remembered you from where?" Kyle started the car.

"From the hospital," she said. "He saw me at the hospital."

Kyle positioned the rearview so that he could see Welke's apartment complex. At the moment everything was still. He wiped a water droplet off the stubble on his chin. "Alright," he said. "That makes the decision much easier."

"Where are we going?"

"We've got to get out of the city," he said. "We're going to go somewhere safe."

. . .

Tobias Welke's apartment had been left unlocked, and besides the dog cage and acoustical tiles on the walls, there was nothing else to talk about. The few residents that Merylo and Cavasano spoke to all gave the same response when asked about Welke. They either didn't know him, or had seen him, but never spoke to him. Cavasano made a phone call and enlisted the assistance of the nearest patrol officer to stand watch over the apartment until a forensics team could get there and sweep for fingerprints.

Merylo stood in the vestibule of the apartment building looking through the rain slicked glass. He replayed the events of the past thirty minutes over in his mind, a technique that he often relied on before leaving a crime scene or interview in order to make sure he didn't miss the details. Cavasano finished the formalities with the manager and met Merylo by the entrance. It was at that instant that Merylo recalled the woman in the hallway. He had seen her before.

Tonight. At the hospital.

"Shit." Merlo pushed the glass doors open and walked out into the freezing rain.

Cavasano followed, noticing the determined look on his partner's face. "What's the matter, Frank?"

"Where's that red car that was parked over there across the street?"

"What red car?" Cavasano asked.

"The red car that was parked down the street when we drove up," Merylo barked.

"Who knows?" Cavasano chased after Merylo who was now speed walking back to the unmarked. "Why, what's up?"

This time, Merylo went to the driver's side. "Give me the keys."

"Would you like to tell me what's going on?" He tossed Merylo the keys.

"I want that list from the hospital. I want to know everyone who came into that hospital tonight." Merylo opened the door and got in the unmarked.

"We're on it, Frank, but it's gonna take a while. There are a thousand people on that list." Cavasano climbed in the passenger's side.

Merylo ran his hand through his hair, sending droplets of water flying. "The woman that was jumping on you, yelling about the Yanks."

"Yeah?"

"She's turned up twice tonight," Merylo said. "Once at the hospital earlier and now here at Welke's apartment."

Cavasano didn't reply. He just stared.

"Jesus, Cavasano." Merylo shook his head. He pulled away from the curb. "What kind of detective are you?"

25

The street had come to an end and Dmitri pulled the SUV to the curb out of the gaze of any overhead lighting. The freezing rain had turned to snow which was now coming down in large wet flakes. In front of them, fenced in and brightly lit against the dark night sky, were large multicolored, steel boxes that indicated the site was a container terminal for cargo ships.

There had been nobody home at the window cleaner's address. In fact, the apartment had hardly seemed lived in. Dmitri had left the apartment in the Polish neighborhood quickly knowing that they were behind schedule and that Niko couldn't be trusted in that situation for very long.

Dmitri grabbed his leather attaché bag and met Niko at the back of the SUV. He gestured for the big man to pick up the soiled bag. Niko tried to grab the bag delicately, not wanting to get stained with Alex's blood.

Dmitri prodded him with a quick jab to the ribs. "Don't worry about it." He chided. "You can clean up later."

Irritated from the poke to the ribs, Niko grabbed the bag and slung the straps over his shoulder. He gave Dmitri a forceful stare before stepping away so that his partner could close the door.

A ten-foot fence topped with razor wire provided the shipping terminal with ruthless protection. Multiple 400-watt lights lit up the yard as if it were day time and served to accentuate the intensity and volume of precipitation falling from the blackened sky. The main gate was padlocked and attended to by security personnel housed in a shed a few meters away.

When Dmitri and Niko reached the gate, the security guard eased himself out of the shed and walked slowly over to meet them. The guard looked to be in his late sixties, was noticeably out of shape and outfitted in a crisp gray uniform. Both of his thumbs were tucked in his belt.

"What can I do for you guys?" He asked.

Dmitri spoke. "We are looking for a ship. The Revolyutsiya. I am told it is docked here."

"That's right. It's over on pier eight," the guard said. He removed one thumb from his belt and hooked it backward.

"We need to get on that ship." Dmitri said.

"What do you think those big colored boxes are, someone's luggage? This is a container terminal, pal. It means we only handle cargo ships. Passenger terminal is on the other side." The security guard pointed westward and started back to his shed.

"It is very important that we get aboard that ship." Dmitri gave his best attempt at a smile.

The guard's brow wrinkled and eyes narrowed. "What kind of accent is that? Are you guys Russians or something?"

"We are."

"Well, they aren't hiring." The old man spat. "We've got enough of you communists working here as it is."

Veins appeared on Niko's forehead like vines grabbing a foothold on a masonry wall. His temples bulged.

"We don't want to work here," Dmitri said. He made sure his voice remained easy, nonthreatening.

The security guard squinted and leaned in close to the fence. His eyes darted back and forth between Dmitri and Niko. "You guys ever see Rocky four?"

Dmitri shook his head. Niko frowned.

"True story," the guard continued. "Not like the first three."

Niko spoke up barely able to contain his anger. "We need to be on that ship."

The security guard considered Niko and his oversized bag. "Goin' home with that, are you?"

Dmitri put a light hand on Niko and stepped in front of him slightly. "Yes."

"Big bag. What have you got the rest of your family in there?" The guard chuckled at his attempt at humor.

Niko's frown deepened.

Dmitri faked a chuckle along with the guard. "Maybe," he said.

"Well I wish more of you would go." The guard hissed. "And take those damn Chinese with you."

The snow was picking up and the bag was beginning to slip from Niko's shoulder. He considered his options. There was a four-inch clearance between the two sections of locked gate, more than enough room to reach an arm through. A set of keys hung from the guard's belt loop. One of them must unlock the gate. He could easily pull the guard up against the fence with one hand and put a bullet through his head with the other and be done with this nonsense.

"Have you been through registration yet?" The guard asked.

"What is that?" Dmitri asked.

The guard pointed to a building down along the chain link fence to their left. "The building that says registration on it."

"No, we have not."

"Well then, I'm afraid I can't help you. Nothing or nobody gets in here without proper registration."

Niko hefted the slumping bag high onto his right shoulder and slid his right hand into his jacket until he felt the cold, textured handle of his gun. He threw his left hand toward the opening in the gates. His hand was greeted by the wet smack of Dmitri's palm. Surprised, Niko looked at Dmitri who gave him a barely detectable shake of his head. The security guard had missed the entire exchange.

Dmitri tried a new tone of voice. "Maybe this will change your mind." Out of his coat pocket came a roll of bills held together with a rubber band. He passed it between the gates to the guard.

"What's this?" The guard peeled off the rubber band and counted the money, a total of $1,000.

"It is a gift," Dmitri said. "Since we are returning to Russia for good, what use is American money to us?" He turned on the charm. "I would rather leave it with an honorable American security guard."

The guard rolled the money between his fingers. "It's not like I'm letting you *into* the country, I'm actually letting you *out*."

"That's right. It's a good thing," Dmitri agreed. "Only communist countries don't let people out."

The guard looked around the yard, curious if anyone had seen the transaction. "They're going to close this place down anyways," he said. "They're going to make it into another cruise ship terminal or something." He selected a key from his key ring and inserted it into the heavy lock. "Can you imagine, another fucking cruise ship terminal in Brooklyn?"

The guard opened the gate and let the two men inside. Dmitri stopped, but Niko walked briskly by.

"It was nice doing business with you guys," the guard said.

Niko yelled over his shoulder, "Yob tvayu mat'."

"What did he say?" the guard asked.

"He said it was nice doing business with you also," Dmitri said.

When they had made it some way past the guard shed, Dmitri cynically scolded Niko, "That's not a nice thing to tell someone to do with their mother."

26

D mitri and Niko walked north through the lot surrounded by a maze of containers. The stacks of different colored metal boxes littered the dockyard like giant Legos. The yard smelled of a mixture of fuel oil and seawater. As they neared the water's edge, the two cranes of the *Revolyutsiya* towered above the docks as if standing guard, ready to do their masters bidding. She was a new ship. Seawater had not yet tarnished her paint, nor had it dried out any of her lines. The three-hundred-foot cargo vessel was moored with her port rail dockside. Her four-story bridge was awash in lights illuminating a pearly finish. The deck was filled to capacity with containers.

The two stopped where the gangway met the dock at the stern of the ship. At the top of the stairs, a man in dirty bib overalls called out to them, motioning for them to come aboard.

Niko hitched up the bag and followed Dmitri up the steel, non-slip stairs. When they reached the top, the deckhand pushed a bottle of vodka into Dmitri's chest. "Zdarova muzhiki!" *Hello peasants!* The sailor said.

Dmitri grabbed the bottle and took a long swig, swallowed

and then dabbed at his lips with his shirt sleeve. Without warning, he slapped the sailor across the face. The blow was unexpected and hard enough to knock the man to the deck. Dmitri stood over him. "You were supposed to meet us at the gate. Instead, you are drunk."

"You were late," the sailor said. "You were supposed to be here two hours ago." The sailor wiped his lip and a streak of red stained the back of his hand. "I wasn't sure you would show at all."

"Nonsense. You just cost me my dignity and one thousand American dollars."

The sailor started to get to his feet, but was persuaded against it as Niko crowded him from behind, stepping on his arm.

"Where is the captain?" Dmitri asked.

"Up on the bridge." The sailor's words came out with difficulty as Niko exerted more force on his arm.

"And the accommodations?"

"Second deck stateroom," the deckhand moaned. "There are two. You can take whichever you like."

"Thank you, Stevan." Dmitri swung open a heavy steel door that led to an enclosed stairwell that would take them to the bridge. "Niko, see that our possessions are put away and then meet me on the bridge."

Niko nodded and stepped over the prone sailor, grinding the heel of his shoe into Stevan's arm before following Dmitri through the doorway.

The quality of the stateroom on the second deck was well above that of container ships past and came furnished with its own bathroom and shower. A full-sized bed occupied the middle of the room. A cherry stained dresser topped with marble was placed on the opposite wall, a matching night-stand next to the bed. A flat screen television hung over the dresser and a mirror was attached to the same wall nearest the stateroom door. Two small wall mounted fixtures on either side of the bed lit the room. A wall light near the dresser and a ceiling fan with lamp in the middle of the room remained dark. All of the furniture was bolted down into a teak hard-wood floor.

Niko set the duffle bag gently on the bed. He unzipped it and opened it as wide as it would allow. The woman was still limp and in the fetal position. He unfolded her arms and eased her head and torso out onto the bed, careful not to scratch her with the teeth of the zipper. After he had her completely removed from the bag, he slid her head onto the pillow, turned down a corner of the bed and eased her legs under the covers.

The big Russian brushed a strand of hair from her face and crossed her arms over her chest. He refastened the top button on her blouse that had come undone and straightened her shirt collar. He noticed the tiny spot on her neck where he rudely delivered the anesthetic.

He tapped her cheek lightly to see if she would respond. Satisfied that she was still unconscious, Niko pulled the blankets up to her chest and switched off the light over her side of the bed. Halfway out of the stateroom, he gave her one last long look before shutting the door and heading to the bridge.

U p on the bridge, Dmitri met Captain Drogzvic. The Captain was a trunk of a man, sloppy around the middle, but wide in the shoulders. His face was almost completely hidden behind a spectacular exhibit of black facial hair. Ruby lips, a hawkish nose and dark eyes poked out from the mass of hair.

Dmitri held out his newly acquired bottle of vodka to the Captain.

Drogzvic waved him off. "No thank you. The weather insists that I don't."

Dmitri said, "I appreciate your willingness to wait Captain."

The Captain stared straight ahead through the snow dotted glass. "I had hoped to depart without you, actually. Your presence onboard my ship does not make me comfortable."

"There will be no trouble. Once you've reached Kaliningrad, you will forget all about us."

"You are very optimistic," Drogzvic replied.

Niko entered the bridge and the Captain took a moment to size him up before stating, "I am informed that there is contraband."

Dmitri nodded. "That is true."

The Captain shifted his stance, folding his hands behind his back. "I must insist on a fee for the transport of contraband."

Dmitri said, "I will not be traveling with you, but when the ship docks in Kaliningrad, Niko will pay you the fee."

Niko stepped forward giving the Captain a good look at his size.

"I must insist that the fee be paid upfront. Kaliningrad is a six-day voyage."

"I'm confident that your voyage will be uneventful," Dmitri said.

"Your optimism is boundless. I'm beginning to question if you really are Russian," the Captain said. "I insist on the fee upfront."

"Okay," Dmitri said. "How much?"

"Thirteen thousand rubles," Drogzvic said. "If you don't wish to pay, I will ask you to leave my ship." He did not back away from Niko.

Dmitri removed a wad of the Russian currency from his coat

pocket, counted out the amount asked for and handed it over to Drogzvic.

The Captain put the money in his jacket pocket and shifted his weight to his left leg. "Now, do you have time for a quick meal?"

"Yes," Dmitri answered.

"Good. Then please join me in my stateroom. Mr. Ling, the cook, has made an excellent pelmeni." Before leaving the bridge, Captain Drogzvic cleared the ship for departure and called for the first mate to take up the helm.

When they reached the Captain's stateroom on the third level of the superstructure, Niko excused himself. He couldn't risk the woman coming to on her own. There was no need for an unnecessary disturbance before they were even out of port.

When he'd reached the entrance to the stateroom on the second level, he noticed the door was ajar. He eased the door open an inch at a time until he had a full view of the mirror. There was someone was in the room. In the mirror's reflection he saw the back of a pair of bib overalls.

Stevan stood at the side of the bed, his back to the cabin door. The covers had been pulled back on the bed and the woman's body was exposed down to her knees. Her panties were still on, but her blouse had been parted. The drunken sailor had slid a dirty hand under her bra, while his other hand was shoved in his overalls.

Niko crept up behind Stevan, his fists clenched. When he was close enough to hear his faint, labored breathing, Niko attacked. He threw his arm around the unsuspecting sailor's neck and squeezed. Stevan drew himself up on his tiptoes and spastically tried to claw his attacker's face. Niko squeezed tighter. Stevan let loose another spasm of self-defense as his neck was on the verge of collapse. Niko ended the drama with a quick, powerful squeeze. Once he felt the hyoid bone in Stevan's neck crack, he loosened his grasp and let the dead sailor fall to the floor face first with a dull thud.

He emptied the deckhand's pockets and was rewarded with a full pack of cigarettes, two hundred and forty-two American dollars and twenty-three hundred Russian rubles. He stuffed the bounty into his pocket and then kicked the sailor over onto his back.

He turned off the lights in the stateroom and went out into the hall. There was a door adjacent to the stateroom that led to an uncovered set of stairs on the outside of the superstructure. He opened it and looked out. The only sailors on deck were forward of the bridge and busy rolling line.

He went back to the stateroom and hefted Stevan over his shoulder and hurried through the hall and out onto the stairway. When he'd descended to the aft deck he shuffled past a row of double stacked wooden crates and a pair of safety rafts enclosed in their fiberglass capsules. Reaching the stern rail, he let the dead sailor slide slowly down his chest and over the rail until he held the man by his ankles. Niko lowered Stevan's lifeless body as far as he could, keeping him close up against the hull of the ship. When he let go, Stevan hardly made a ripple as he dropped head first into the cold and black of the East River. By the time Stevan would reappear, the *Revolyutsiya* would be well out to sea.

Back in the stateroom, Niko turned on the lights and was relieved to see the woman still sleeping. Her shirt was still opened and as he approached, he was able to get a good look at her.

Visible through her unbuttoned shirt and covering her upper torso was a canvas of colorful, intricately designed tattoos. Niko opened her shirt more to get a better look at the fusion of fish, serpents, dragons and swords. Colored ink covered both arms down to her wrists and her shoulders up to her neck.

Under her bra, both breasts were covered with the exception of a bare, unmarked strip that ran down the center of her chest. A suit-coat made of ink.

He sat on the edge of the bed next to her, fixed her bra and re-buttoned her blouse. He knew what the ink meant, and what she was capable of, recalling the horrific scene in the back of the SUV with Alex. He pulled the covers back up to her chin, tucking her in like a child. Before he turned off the lights and closed the door to the stateroom, he gave her one last long look.

The Japanese woman was beautiful.

And very dangerous.

27

The bright lights from the city disappeared in the rear-view mirror. "Where did you say we were going?" These were the first words Ingrid had spoken in half an hour.

"I didn't," Kyle answered.

Ingrid accepted the answer without objection. At this point she didn't care. She was warm and felt safe in his presence. She watched him as he drove. He was focused and she could tell he was thinking. Not just about the crazy night that they had been through, but something else. There was something going on deep inside him. She thought about his apartment, how he said that it wasn't where he lived, rather just where he was staying. As if he wasn't living at all. She thought about his gun and the one bullet.

"I know that life can feel desperate sometimes," she said.

Kyle kept his eyes fixed on the road ahead with only a brief glance down at his hands as if he considered replying, but he did not.

"We all feel that way at different times in our lives, but you must not give up hope. A better tomorrow is right around the corner." She leaned her seat back just enough to get comfortable.

"How can you be so sure?" He asked.

"I lived it," she said. "When I was growing up, Medellín was the most dangerous city in the world. Everyone that lived there personally knew someone who had been killed due to the violence that was taking place." She turned in her seat toward Kyle. "My mother met my father and ran away to the United States because she had lost hope," she said. "I wanted to stay and help Medellín become what it was always meant to be." She rubbed the charm that hung around her neck between her fingers.

"So, you joined the Army?"

"You remembered." Ingrid smiled. "Yes. I joined the Army. And today, Medellín is the most beautiful city in the world."

Kyle returned her smile.

"Mi abuela, my grandmother, taught me that if you are afraid of the dark, it's best not to sit idly by waiting for the sunlight to save you. She said that if you run toward the darkness, you'll reach the sunlight more quickly on the other side."

"Smart woman," Kyle said. "Is she still alive, your grandmother?"

"No." Ingrid turned to the window. "As I said, everybody knew somebody personally."

Kyle didn't know what to say. An apology was fast to appear on the tip of his tongue, but he swallowed and it was gone as quickly as it had come.

"Don't go trying to kill yourself on purpose, Mr. Kyle Murdoch," Ingrid said. "There are plenty of people in this world who would be happy to do it for you."

They continued on in silence the rest of the way. The only audible noise was the wet road beneath them and the hypnotic dancing of windshield wiper blades. Kyle kept the car at a steady 65 mph. No need to push his luck speeding.

Every now and then he'd steal a glance at Ingrid who was curled up on her side facing him. Her hands were pressed together under her head and at this angle she looked like a woman at peace and deep in prayer.

An hour later under heavy eyelids, Kyle steered Ingrid's car onto the cobblestone driveway of a two-story carriage house. He left the car running while he got out and keyed in the access code for the garage door. Inside, the three-car garage hosted a five-year old, white Ford Mustang and a newer model, blacked-out, matte finish, Indian motorcycle.

A procession of cabinets spanned the entire length of the back wall of the garage along with an impressive set of mechanic's tool chests. The door into the house was on the left, flanked on one side by a refrigerator and the other by a utility sink.

Kyle pulled Ingrid's car into a vacant spot on the left, got out and closed the garage door. From inside the back of the refrigerator, he took a set of house keys from an empty box of baking soda, unlocked the door to the house and quickly punched his birthday into another keypad that chirped as it disarmed the home security system.

Drunk with exhaustion, Ingrid held onto Kyle as she shuffled into the house. A mudroom with washer, dryer and shower separated the garage from the kitchen and the rest of the house. Kyle kicked off his shoes and then lifted Ingrid up onto the washing machine and helped her out of her wet shoes and jacket.

"Where are we?" Ingrid asked.

"Somewhere safe."

Ingrid was still half asleep and spoke with her eyes closed against the light of the mudroom. "Where's that?"

"Montauk."

"Why did you take my shoes off?"

"House rules," Kyle replied. "Come on. I'll show you to your room."

He swept her off the washing machine and carried her through the center of the house and up a wide flight of stairs. At the top, he made a left down a long hall turning into the first door on his right. A four-post, king sized bed occupied the center of the left-hand wall. A stone finished fireplace took up the opposite wall. A bay window with cushioned seating allowed for a full view of the back of the property. A guest bathroom was accessed from a door next to the bed. The room was huge.

He laid Ingrid on the bed and draped her with the unused portion of the comforter. She grabbed hold of a corner and wrapped herself up in the warm blanket.

Downstairs, Kyle retrieved his rucksack from Ingrid's car and brought it into the house. He changed out of the borrowed clothes and into a pair of gray sweatpants and t-shirt. He found a heavy wool blanket in a basket next to the fireplace and spread it out on the oversized leather sofa.

The house was cold and quiet. Two characteristics the home accepted on the day his mother died. It still amazed him how one woman could create such warmth and joy all on her own. He missed her dearly.

Fortunately, the home was paid for and the money that was left in his mother's estate allowed for property taxes, utilities and lawn and pool maintenance. Kyle paid for a bi-monthly Thursday visit from the cleaning lady, Ms. Craft, who'd kept the same schedule for the past twenty-three years.

Growing up, his family made good use of the great room with its massive fireplace. Open to the kitchen, it was the place where friends and relatives gathered to relax, laugh and enjoy each other's company. And there was always a fire burning in the fireplace. He needed one now. He needed a fire from long ago to take him back to those days when all was right with the world.

There was still almost a full cord of wood on the firewood rack on the back deck, unused and dried for many years, now. He recalled his father's fire building instruction from when he was a young boy and decided to put his memory to the test.

He brought in six logs altogether and positioned three of them in the center of the fireplace, the three others he set on the hearth for later. He opened the damper and retrieved a starter log from the end of the hearth, placing it under the firewood. A bucket full of old newspapers were crumpled into loose balls and stuffed in and around the logs. A box of fireplace matches on the mantle would seal the deal. He took one, struck it and touched it to the paper. The room lit up immediately with the familiar, warm, soothing, orange glow.

He eased onto the sofa and pulled part of the blanket over him, propping his feet on the sturdy coffee table. Memories flowed from the burning fire. Flame tips danced and laughter mingled with the crackle of burning wood.

He didn't see Ingrid initially as she descended the staircase. She had the comforter wrapped around her as she shuffled across the floor to the sofa. Kyle looked up at her when she got near and gathered a section of blanket to make room for her on the couch next to him.

They didn't talk as she curled up on a vacant plot of leather. Warm and comfortable in front of the fire, Ingrid let her head rest on Kyle's shoulder, the religious pendant firmly in her hand.

Both were lost in their own thoughts, mesmerized by the dancing flames and crackling wood and before long, both had closed their eyes and fallen asleep.

28

East River Park, New York

C avasano pulled the car off of the road and onto the snow-covered grass.

"What the hell are you doing?" Merylo barked.

"I didn't think you wanted to walk that far," Cavasano shot back.

"They just redid this park. The Mayor would have our balls if he saw you." Merylo ran his fingers through his hair. "Just pull over next to the ball field for Christ's sake."

"Over here?"

"Yes. Right there."

Cavasano steered the unmarked back onto an asphalt walkway next to a sodden baseball field.

As they got out of the car, Merylo stepped into a puddle of slush. "Global warming my ass," he grumbled.

Ahead, on the banks of the East River, a group of onlookers formed a half circle. Merylo pushed his way through the crowd eliciting a number of angry glares which he was more than happy to return. When he and Cavasano had finally reached the center of activity, it was clear what had drawn the crowd.

It wasn't the fact that the man was dead. New Yorkers aren't new to seeing dead bodies, but every once in a while, the City throws seekers of the macabre a treat. At 7:45 this morning, that treat had gotten stuck on the banks by the East River Park. Word had spread quickly that this dead man was a sight to see.

At the moment, he was lying on a blue tarp, a black body bag next to him. His skin was an unnatural gray-green and part of his head had been gouged out as it was blown off above his right eye.

Merylo kept his distance while Cindy Yu, the coroner's assistant, finished photographing the body. Three uniformed officers kept the crowd back while a fourth scribbled information on a notepad. Two men that worked for the coroner's office stood ready to zip and ship the body.

When Yu started packing her camera, Merylo approached her. "How you doing Cindy?"

She looked up. "Oh, hi Frank. Good morning. So, you're the lucky one who gets this case."

"That'd be us. This is my new partner, Detective Cavasano."

Cavasano stuck out his hand. "Nice to meet you."

Cindy Yu offered her hand and gave Cavasano a professional smile. "Pleased to meet you."

Merylo pulled out a pair of blue latex gloves from his coat pocket. "Do you mind if I poke around a little?"

"Be my guest," she answered. "I was just getting ready to head back to the office."

"Were you able to pull any ID?"

"I got it under wraps in the van."

"Driver's license?"

"Passport."

"Really?" Merylo glanced over at Cavasano. "Country?"

"Finland," she said.

"Huh." Merylo frowned. About how long has our friend here been dead, ballpark estimate only?"

The assistant coroner thought for a moment. "This is just a rough guess, I'll know more later-"

Merylo cut her off. "It's okay. I'm not going to hold you to anything. I'm just looking for a best guess."

"Off the record, not long in my opinion. He's probably not been dead twenty-four hours yet," she said.

Merylo knelt down next to the dead man on the tarp.

"I'm sure Dr. Shah will be able to narrow it down to at least a four to six-hour window," she offered. "I'll have him call you as soon as he knows something."

"That'd be great. Thanks Cindy." Merylo gave her a wave and then turned his attention to his partner. "Come here and check this out."

"Do I need to put on some gloves?" Cavasano asked.

"No, just kneel down here."

Merylo turned what was left of the dead man's head to its left side. Wrapping around his neck was a blue-black snake tattoo.

"He was a drug addict," Merylo said. He pulled open the man's shirt, exposing more tattoos. "That's Cyrillic. Look familiar?" Merylo asked.

"Russian?" Cavasano asked.

"You better believe it. See this here." Merylo pointed to a dagger tattoo that appeared to stab the man through his neck. "The dagger through the neck means that he killed someone in prison and he's available for hire."

"Wonderful." It was beginning to dawn on Cavasano that his partner was enjoying the moment.

Merylo grabbed the dead man's right hand. A small skull was tattooed on the middle finger, a cross on his index finger. "A murderer and a thief," he said. "Cyrillic lettering. If he's Finnish then I'm Chinese."

"Like those two from the hospital," Cavasano said.

"Exactly."

"Are you thinking that he's one of the two? Or do you think there's more than two?"

"What? You think one guy offs the other guy and that's it? Not a chance." Merylo stood up and Cavasano followed suit.

The two detectives were interrupted by one of the coroner workers. "Are you finished here detective?" The man asked.

"Yeah, yeah. I'm good, thanks." Merylo snapped off the rubber gloves. He turned back to Cavasano. "Where was I?"

"You don't think that one guy killed the other," Cavasano said.

"Right," Merylo went on. "I think that's highly unlikely."

"Do you think he's connected to the other two?"

"I do," Merylo said. "You don't find too many beauties like this guy walking around much anymore. He's totally legit."

"You think he's from out of the country?"

"Definitely," Merylo said. Look at that ink job. It's prison quality shit."

"So, you think he's related to the other two from the hospital?"

"Most likely."

"You're thinking they killed one of their own?" Cavasano brushed snow off of his knee. "That seems a bit desperate."

"Desperate? I don't know," Merylo said. "This guy is a murderer, a thief and a fuckup. Maybe he was becoming a problem, so they fixed it. These bastards will shoot you just to see if the gun is loaded." He stared out across the East River into Brooklyn on the other side. "Maybe the Bratski Krug is nervous."

"Who is the Bratski Krug?" Cavasano asked.

"The Brother's Circle," Merylo said. "The top of the Russian criminal food chain."

Merylo's phone rang. He answered, "Merylo."

Cavasano pushed snow around with his shoe while his partner took the call.

"Hi, Frank. Matt Reed, here," the caller said. "Wanted to give you a head's up that Detective Carballo and I got a dead body in an apartment on East forty ninth that might be related to the Millennium Hotel case you're working on."

"How so?"

"It looks like our DB knows the woman that's gone missing from the hotel. Found her name and hotel itinerary on the deceased, Mr. Hinata Sakai's desk," Reed said.

"No, shit." Merylo glanced at Cavasano.

"Yeah, shit. We might want to combine our notes on this sooner rather than later," Reed said. "On account of the missing woman."

"Absolutely. Thanks, Matt," Merlo said. "We'll meet you this afternoon, put our heads together and see what we can come up with."

"Sounds good, Frank. See you later."

Merylo hung up and turned to Cavasano. "Reed and Carballo found another piece of the puzzle in an apartment on forty-ninth," he said. "Dead guy, knew the missing woman from the Millennium Hotel."

"Are they going to share?" Cavasano asked.

"Yeah. We'll meet up with them this afternoon. After we pay a visit to an old friend."

A concerned look crossed Cavasano's face. "Detective Merylo, we're Homicide. You're talking about organized criminals. That belongs to the Criminal Enterprise Division. No disrespect, but you're not supposed to be poking around in that arena."

"This is a homicide," Merylo protested, pointing to the Coroner's van. "I can't help it if it happens to be the homicide of a criminal, organized or not. I'm just going where the case is leading. And right now, it's leading me to Brighton Beach."

"Frank, you have to report it, *I have to report it*. Let the station decide what to do from here."

"And let O'Leary and Esposito get all the credit? No way," Merylo said. He slapped his younger partner on the back. "C'mon, I got someone I'd like you to meet."

29

Atlantic Ocean

Ayumi woke up, but had yet to open her eyes. The room smelled of freshly baked bread and coffee, cigarettes and seawater. The aroma of the coffee and bread stirred her stomach. The cigarettes and seawater stung her nose. She opened her eyes and sat up slowly, propping herself up on her elbows for support. The light was painful. When she'd gathered the strength, she maneuvered herself so that she was sitting up with her back against the wall behind her.

A man in gray sweats sat in a chair across the room, a wrinkled copy of Pravda in his hand. He folded it up and placed it on the dresser when he noticed her slowly coming to. Once she was fully awake, he met her at the side of the bed with a plastic cup filled with water. Ayumi pulled the bed covers up as far as they would go. She remembered him as the one that almost killed her in the hotel room.

When she didn't respond to the cup of water, the man left it on the bedside table and returned with a small plate of dark bread and a cup of black coffee. These too he set on the bedside table. Offering her food and drink was a good sign that he had no intention to try and kill her again. At least not yet.

Before leaving the room, he pulled out a gray hooded sweatshirt and a pair of matching sweatpants from one of the dresser drawers and tossed them on the bed. He made note of a black rain jacket that hung on the back of the door leading Ayumi to understand that leaving the room was not out of order.

After he'd left and shut the door behind him, Ayumi washed her face and hands in the stateroom's bathroom and then changed into the oversized sweats. Her legs were still wobbly and weak. She sipped some water, tasted the bread and coffee and slowly felt her strength begin to return. Several minutes later, hydrated and with a little food in her stomach, she was ready to try out her sea legs. She took the raincoat from the back of the door and walked out of the room.

Outside, the morning sun failed to appear, overmatched on this day by the thick, endless, gray clouds that blanketed the sky. Ayumi found the man that had given her the food and water close by, leaning against the deck railing smoking a cigarette and staring out into the dark waters of the Atlantic. She leaned on the rail next to him and peered out into the ocean trying to see if she could find what he was looking for. Silently, he offered her a cigarette. She declined, but thanked him for the food and drink.

"Where are we going?" she asked him.

He continued to stare out to sea.

The North Atlantic shipping lanes are some of the busiest in the world. Routes established long ago to take advantage of the trade winds and ocean currents still provide the most efficient mode of transporting goods across the globe. The twenty-foot-long, steel containers that occupied almost every available square inch of storage space on the *Revolyutsiya* were loaded with various American exports such as automobiles, agricultural machinery, oil and natural gas recovery equipment and meat and poultry. Most of the items in the containers on board were accounted for and were being transported legally. Others had been stolen. As it was with the cargo, so it was with the passengers.

"Kaliningrad," he finally said.

"Ah, yes. Of course," Ayumi said. "Another territory stolen by Russia."

Kaliningrad, once called Königsberg, was annexed by the Soviet Union after World War II. Its German residents were expelled and replaced with Russian settlers. Often referred to by the Soviets as the "West," Kaliningrad became a strategic military outpost during the Cold War. Now thriving culturally and economically, the Baltic Sea port is also used by organized criminals as a transshipment point for illegal contraband into Eastern Europe.

"A gift," Niko corrected. "From the President of the United States and the Prime Minister of Great Britain to Russia as appreciation for winning the Great Patriotic War. Just like the Kuril Islands." The last comment was made to sting the Japanese woman.

"You mean the Norther Territories," she said.

Niko spat into the sea.

"And Crimea." She added. "You Russians think you can take whatever you want."

Niko laughed. "The Russian Federation has nothing to do with it, with you." He flicked the half-smoked cigarette over the railing. "Someone wanted your friend dead for personal reasons, not political ones." He stared her down. "Russia couldn't care less about Mr. Sakai or you," he said. "Your troubles have sprung up from your own garden."

"What have you done to Mr. Sakai?" She asked.

"I didn't do anything, but watch him bleed," Niko said.

"Death will come for your partners Mr. Murdoch and Ms. Garcia as well. I only wish I were there to see it myself."

Ayumi didn't have any partners. Her captor was confused. She thought about correcting him, but felt it could be advantageous for him to believe something that wasn't true. "So, what do you want with me?" She asked.

"What is there to want from a yukuza whore?" He said. "If it was up to me, I'd have thrown you into the sea already. But I just do what I'm told." He pushed away from the railing and turned his big frame toward her. "Fortunately for you, I've been told to keep you alive." He gently tapped the side of her face and she winced and pulled away at his touch. "I'll let you know when the situation changes." He straightened up and walked away toward the ship's bow, disappearing into the maze of steel containers.

The rain was coming down as mist and water beaded into droplets on the black rain coat. Ayumi looked over the rail and stared blankly into the Atlantic. Her heart sank at the thought of Mr. Sakai. She became short of breath and her legs felt weak again. She had come to the United States at his urgent request and the information that he shared, that she now carried, was the reason that he had been killed. She could hardly believe that it was true.

She understood Mr. Sakai's reasoning for contacting her. Her father was a difficult man to track down. His reputation had become as inflated as his bank account, and he had finally caught the attention of the National Police. So, although this wasn't the first time that Ayumi agreed to be a conduit through which to reach her father, the information she received had never been so significant and the potential consequences never so great.

Until now, only three people had ever seen her tattoos. The Horishi, or tattoo artist, a deceased lover, and her father. All knew what they represented. Her father could have disavowed her on the spot because of this, but he didn't. She was his only daughter. Because of this, and despite their differences, she had remained fiercely loyal to him and her family.

The *Revolyutsiya* cut through choppy, four and five-foot waves, spraying cold seawater back into the ocean as it slapped off its hull. It was at least ten feet if not more from the bottom rung of the railing to the surface of the frigid water. Against the darkened sky, the ocean appeared black and bottomless.

Ayumi had to get off the ship. She owed it to Mr. Sakai to transmit his message. She knew that they would eventually come for her father and she was determined to get to her family before they did.

A fine spray of seawater blew upon her. She could taste the salt on her lips and feel the chill against the exposed skin on her hands and face. She knew the North Atlantic shipping lanes were busy. And even though she had yet to see another vessel, the probability remained high that one would eventually pass by. It was time to consider all of her options.

30

Northern Honshū, Japan

W ind and rain lashed the deck of the *Orso* as the last of ten giant casks was lowered into the cargo hold by the harbor crane. Brilliant floodlights illuminated the vessel while also displaying the intensity of the current weather situation against the menacingly dark background. A team of men in bright yellow, high visibility rain gear worked frantically against the rain and wind to uncouple the cask from the crane's rigging. Another team worked to secure it to the hold. It was nearly midnight and this was the last of the ships that would be loaded or unloaded until the weather calmed down.

At almost 350 feet long, the vessel was built in Italy in 1997 for NEPC, a Japanese utility company. Designed to resist impact and with enhanced buoyancy, it had two separate hulls to prevent the ship from sinking. Navigation, communications and other essential systems were duplicated and separated. The *Orso* was equipped with twin engines and propellers as well as extra firefighting equipment, refrigeration and a flood holding system.

Extra precautions taken to prevent a catastrophe in the event that an incident arose. With good reason.

The *Orso* was constructed with the intent to transport High Level Nuclear waste from Japan to third party countries where the still radioactive material would be reprocessed and then returned for final waste disposal or storage. The ship had sat idle since 2003 and was then sent to auction five years later during the Asian financial crisis when the utility company went bankrupt. The vessel was last purchased at a discount by Siberian Energy Enterprises, a Russian oil and natural gas conglomerate based in Vladivostok.

Untethered from the cask's trunnions, the crane operator was given the "thumbs up" hand signal to raise the hoist out of the *Orso's* hold. Laid out below deck were the ten massive steel casks. The casks were cylindrical and looked like giant thermoses. Each was made from ten-inch thick, forged steel and weighed over 200,000 pounds. Inside each cask was more than 15,000 pounds of spent nuclear fuel. A portion of which was still viable plutonium.

When the phone rang in the administration building's only office, Toshi was leaning back in his chair with his feet on the wooden desk, sucking on a cigarette. A cold cup of coffee was just out of reach next to a single, underpowered lamp. "Moshi, Moshi." *Hello.*

"Good evening, Toshi." The caller spoke in Japanese with an obvious American accent.

Toshimitsu Sato knew who it was immediately. He sat forward and planted his feet on the floor. "Good evening, Koba." He spoke up in order to be heard over the wind and rain that was driving against the roof of the building.

"Everything on schedule?" The caller asked.

"Yes, sir." Toshi leaned forward and wiped at the fogged office window overlooking the docks. Water streamed down the glass making it impossible to see the *Orso* clearly. But through the rain streaked window, he could see the arm of the crane in the white blast of floodlights moving out of and away from the center of the ship. "The last cask has been loaded."

"Any issues with Customs or the Port Authority?"

"No, sir," Toshi said. "The port has been running a very light crew for the last few days due to the typhoon. Most vessels have stayed out at sea."

"Good. And her itinerary?"

"Next port-of-call is Vladivostok." Toshi hesitated, then said, "But it will be delayed due to weather."

"Delayed for how long?"

"It's hard to tell. We have no control over the weather?"

"I'm on a very tight schedule, Toshi. There is a lot at stake and it's imperative that the Orso disembark for Russia as soon as possible. Do you understand?"

"I do, but the weather..."

"I don't give a damn about the weather. I want that ship out of your port first thing in the morning." With that, the caller hung up.

Toshi hung up as well and stubbed out his cigarette. He pulled out his wallet and removed a wrinkled piece of paper and smoothed it out on top of the desk. A phone number was scrawled on the paper in red ink.

But before he could call the number written out on the paper, a male voice from behind startled him. "Was that Koba?" The voice asked. "The man who commissioned the *Orso*?"

Toshi turned around in his chair. "Yes. I was just about to contact you, sir," he said. "I didn't hear you come in."

A man wearing a long hooded rain coat, still beaded with rain water, stood in the shadows of the small administration office. A small puddle had formed at his feet. He stepped forward into to the dim light. "I understand that he hired a team of men to kill my friend, Mr. Hinata Sakai."

"I had no idea," Toshi said.

"Russians." The man stole a cigarette from an open pack on the desk. Toshi handed him a lighter. "One of them called to say that they were going to kill my daughter as well. A snitch named Alex."

"Sir." Toshi stood up. He was ready to do whatever was asked of him without question.

"They've been convinced that harming Ayumi would be a bad idea." He took a draw on his cigarette. "But we are still without word that they've let her go."

"Tell me what you'd like me to do."

The man exhaled a long plume of blue smoke that threatened to choke out the room's single, dimly lit light bulb. "I want you to make sure that the *Orso* doesn't leave this dock," he said. "I'll take care of the rest."

According to the latest census numbers from the Russian Federation, there are fewer than 2,000 Japanese nationals living inside the country. One of them, a man named Tomo, had acquired a very bad reputation. Daichi Kagawa pulled his cell phone from his coat pocket and called him. When the man answered, Ayumi's father got straight to the point. "Good afternoon, Tomo."

"Good evening."

"With regard to our earlier conversation."

"Yes."

"My patience has expired."

31

I t's been said that people who are bilingual dream in their native language. So, when the unusual ring of an unfamiliar cell phone woke her up, it was not surprising that the first words out of Ingrid Garcia's mouth this morning were in Spanish. "Que hora?" She asked.

"It's eight o'clock," Kyle answered.

"Donde estoy?"

"You're at my family's home."

Ingrid rubbed her eyes and didn't seem to find the fact that Kyle understood Spanish the least bit interesting. She slid out from under the blanket and shuffled to the kitchen. A breakfast bar overhung the back of the kitchen counter and extended into the great room. Ingrid took up a seat on the end. She blindly fixed her hair with her fingers and rubbed the sleep from her eyes while Kyle rummaged through cabinets and drawers looking for nourishment of some kind.

He checked the refrigerator and then the freezer for something, anything, that might be appropriate at this hour of the day. The refrigerator housed a can of coffee, the freezer, a container of concentrated orange juice. Both employed a box of baking soda to protect their integrity. "Coffee or orange juice?" He asked.

"Coffee please," Ingrid answered. She finished manipulating the last strands of hair.

Kyle filled the coffee maker with water. "We should be able to catch our breath here for the moment," he said. The filters were in an overhead cabinet. He placed one in the coffee maker and filled it with grounds, closed the lid. "We can figure out a plan on where we go from here."

She noticed the cell phone that they'd found in his apartment last night on the counter in front of him. "Have you discovered who that belongs to?" She covered her mouth and tried not to yawn.

"I haven't," he said. "But it just received a call a minute ago."

"I heard."

"The call came from a country code seven, area code four nine-nine. There are some texts in Russian. I used a translating app to decipher some of them. It appears as though the owner of the phone was planning to board a ship."

"Taking a cruise, I'm sure," Ingrid said.

"My thoughts, exactly."

Ingrid removed her cell phone from her back pocket and saw that she had a missed call from Edward VanRoy.

When Kyle saw that she might dial her phone, he slammed his hand on top of hers. "I wouldn't do that," he said. The forcefulness of his action startled her. "I wouldn't use your phone. Not until we figure out what we're going to do."

"Okay."

"There's a desktop computer in the office that you can use if you need it." He pointed to the room next to the staircase. "The password is Zeus, with a capital Z," he said. He flashed her a disarming smile. "Zeus was our family's dog." He let go of her hand.

"Zeus. El perro," Ingrid repeated. "That must be a picture of him over there on the wall." She motioned to a section of wall just outside of the kitchen.

Kyle had swung around to the great room to retrieve his army bag. "That's him, indeed."

While the coffee brewed, Ingrid surveyed her surroundings. Lots of natural light. The house was spacious and incorporated generous amounts of real wood and stone, but there was enough soft furniture, deep area rugs and flowing curtains to blunt most of the home's sharp edges.

Kyle dropped the rucksack by the breakfast bar and placed his cell phone next to Ingrid's on the granite counter. Each had the exact same model in the exact same color.

"Well, at least we have that in common," she remarked.

Kyle dug out the crumpled receipt from Welke's apartment and handed it to her. "I found this in Welke's apartment last night," he said. "It's not much and I'm not sure it's of any value. I didn't want you to go away totally empty handed." His tone of voice was gentle, as if he were making up for startling her moments earlier. He returned to the kitchen to attend to the coffee.

Ingrid folded up the receipt and put it in her pocket for the moment. "Tell me something," she said.

"What's that?"

"Why the little apartment in the city?"

Kyle thought for a moment before answering. "It seemed fitting."

"By that, you mean that you didn't want to kill yourself some-where nice, like this house?"

He gathered the rest of the coffee paraphernalia. "Cream and sugar?"

"Sugar, please." Ingrid gave him a pass for not answering the question. "How does a window washer afford *this* house?" She asked. "Are you sure you're not a thief?"

"I'm sure." Kyle made her coffee to order and pushed a mug in her direction.

"Gracias." Ingrid wrapped her hands around the warm mug. "Do you have any siblings?" She asked.

"No." He waved his hand, gesturing to the house. "*This* is one of the few benefits of being an only child. Once your parents pass away, there's no competition for their estate."

"I'm sorry to hear that." Ingrid said. "How did they pass?"

"My mother died of cancer two years ago," he said. "This is the first I've been here since."

Ingrid waited for Kyle to acknowledge his father's cause of death, but he said nothing. So, she asked, "And your father?"

He took a therapeutic sip of coffee. "My father died in a hotel room in Bucharest when I was young." His answer was very matter of fact and interesting in its lack of cause of death.

Ingrid couldn't help herself. "How, may I ask?" The question was instinctual and she was almost sorry that she'd asked as soon as the words escaped her mouth.

He took another sip before answering. "The official report says he was poisoned."

The sheer uniqueness of his answer only begged for more questions considering that nearly twice as many people die each year from the measles as do from some sort of poisoning. The manner in which he disclosed this fact, his inflection, led Ingrid to believe that his father didn't accidentally ingest a household cleaning agent, but she decided not to press him.

"What about you?" he asked.

"What about me?"

"You mentioned when you gave me the clothes that they *were* your father's."

"My father died of a heart attack eight months ago," she said.

"He was a lifelong New Yorker. My mother was just a girl from Medellín. They met when he visited Colombia to find a supplier for his flower shop. She's gone back home to be with my sister and our family."

Kyle looked past Ingrid and into the great room. A picture of his parents was set over the fireplace, a large framed black and white photo of two young newlyweds staring deeply into each other's eyes.

Ingrid could see a flicker of emotion in Kyle's eyes. It was impossible to tell if it was pain or anger, but it was real and it was raw. She was about to ask him more before he cut in mid thought.

"Are you hungry? He asked. "There isn't anything to eat in this house," he said. "But I know a little bakery nearby."

"That sounds wonderful." Ingrid raised her coffee mug. "Some food would be nice."

"Good." He swung around and met Ingrid on the other side of the counter where he'd dropped his rucksack. "Please remember not to use your phone."

"Right."

He took the gun that he'd given her the night before from his rucksack and placed it on the counter. Digging through the well-worn bag, he pulled out an assortment of t-shirts and jeans and found an old hooded sweatshirt to go with his sweatpants.

Ingrid picked up the gun and rolled it over in her hand. She released the magazine, inspected it. It was still empty. She pushed it back into the well and set the gun on the counter. "Does this bakery sell ammunition?"

"No." Kyle smirked. "Wouldn't that be something, though?" He said. "Bagels and bullets."

"I like it." Ingrid chuckled. "It sounds very *American*."

They both laughed at the thought.

"Please make yourself at home," Kyle said. "I'm not quite

sure what we have here, but feel free to look around."

"I will. Thank you," Ingrid replied.

Kyle grabbed the keys to the Mustang off of a hook in the mudroom, closed the door and stood in the garage. An anxiety washed over him. The house was located on a cul-de-sac one street off of the main drag, mere minutes from the bakery. Still, the thought of leaving Ingrid alone for any length of time bothered him. Combat was sometimes like that. Friendships were made quickly and sometimes the epoch was short lived. But that didn't make them any less significant. He would just have to hurry.

Ingrid grabbed the gun out of habit and went upstairs to the spare bedroom where Kyle had laid her down the night before. Attached to the bedroom was a large guest bathroom decorated in clean, gray tile. Toiletries were set out on the vanity and fresh towels were folded on a shelf next to the shower waiting to be used by guests.

She set the gun on the counter and changed out of her clothes, deciding to take advantage of the opportunity. The large stone tile shower was inviting and the warm water soothing. The filth of the previous night was scrubbed off and rinsed down the drain.

After her shower, Ingrid wrapped herself in a towel and discovered an impressive collection of women's clothes stored inside the massive walk-in closet. Brand names and designer label dresses, jackets and shirts as well as an assortment of hats and scarves. She flipped through them, checking the tag on a few. Most of the clothes were her size. Casual clothes were tucked away in a row of drawers. Jeans, sweats and yoga pants, all stylish and in good condition.

While admiring a pair of expensive designer jeans, she froze at the sound of the front door. Someone had entered the house. She assumed it was Kyle, but he had gone out through the garage. She tiptoed across the hall to a bedroom that faced the front of the property. Looking out the window into the yard below, she saw a black pickup truck parked in the driveway.

She didn't remember seeing a pickup truck last night, but she was half asleep when they'd got home and could have missed it. Holding the towel that covered her tight, she hurried across the hall back into the spare bedroom to retrieve the gun. Heavy footsteps echoed up the stairway from the kitchen down below. She made sure her towel was wrapped tight and inched down the hallway, keeping against the wall until the kitchen came into view from the top of the stairs. One bullet. She unlocked off the safety on the hand gun. When Kyle left the house he was wearing a pair of gray sweatpants. Whoever it was in the kitchen downstairs was not.

C ustomer traffic inside the little bakery was light, but unfortunately, all of the customers were of the older and slower variety. A well-dressed group of six octogenarians took turns changing their minds about what they wanted and squabbling over whose turn it was to pay for it. Kyle could only smile and wait.

Once he'd finally received his order, Kyle pulled out of the bakery's parking lot with a dozen doughnuts and an urge to speed. The trip had taken longer than he'd expected and he was anxious to get home. It had been a while since he felt compelled to rush home to someone for any reason, but he kept his speed under control, made a left off of route 27 and headed north on E. Lake Drive. Lake Montauk filled the view out the driver's side window. When he'd made it to his street, he put a little pressure on the gas pedal. Coming around a bend, the carriage house was visible. A black pickup truck was now parked in the driveway. He pushed the pedal to the floor.

32

K yle left the Mustang parked in the street two houses down. A line of conifers acted as a privacy fence between the neighbors yards and offered him cover as he approached the house through the adjacent property. The truck in the driveway looked to be unoccupied, but he needed to verify before entering the house. It was a newer model pickup with an extended cab and a short bed, expensive and more white collar than blue. It was empty.

He went around the side of the house and entered the garage through the man door. The overhead would make too much noise. Inside, he opened the tool chest and grabbed the largest wrench he could find. He put his ear to the door that led into the house via the mudroom. The door was solid wood and through it, he could hear nothing.

He gripped the knob with his left hand and pushed the door open, making sure he shielded himself with the heavy slab of pine. He exposed just enough of the interior of the house to get a partial view of the kitchen and breakfast bar that extended out into the great room. From this vantage point through the mudroom, he could make out the back of a lone man seated at the bar, an ankle holster poked out from the bottom of his right pant leg. There was no sign of Ingrid.

Without taking his eyes off of the intruder, he slipped out of his shoes and socks and tiptoed across the tile floor through the mudroom. The man seated at his breakfast counter was broad shouldered and wore dark blue jeans, a sturdy, black work jacket, and a black wool knit cap that was pulled down over the tips of his ears. Slivers of gray hair forked out from underneath.

The right move would be to crack the man with the wrench now and ask questions later. He raised the wrench, intent on doing just that.

At the same time, Ingrid stepped off the main staircase. She was in the final act of pulling on a sweater and saw what Kyle was about to do. "No!" She yelled.

Kyle took his eyes off of the intruder and turned to Ingrid.

That was all the opportunity that the man in the black cap needed. He shot up off of the bar stool and used a forearm to chop the wrench out of Kyle's hand. Lunging backward, he threw an elbow, but Kyle was able to turn his chin in time and suffer only a grazing.

Kyle countered by wrapping his left arm around the man's neck and clasping it with his right hand. His opponent was able to drop his chin in time to avoid a complete choke hold. The man forced Kyle backward, slamming into the pantry door. His head throbbed on impact and he felt as though one of the staples had let loose. He didn't have time to think about that too long before an elbow to the ribs forced him to exhale a lung full of air. Ingrid screamed. The man laughed. Kyle winced.

Kyle was in a bad position. A second elbow followed, but he was able to turn at the waist to protect his ribs and to not give his opponent a square target. He held on with the hope that his assailant would make a mistake. With both men locked in a stalemate, the intruder shimmied into the open space of the kitchen and in a desperate maneuver, attempted to flip Kyle over his head.

But before his feet tumbled over his head, Kyle let go of the intruder's neck and dove head first toward the ceramic tile floor. On his way down, he was able to latch on to the man's legs with his arms and apply a scissor hold with his own legs around the man's neck. He squeezed. The result was immediate and effective. The move thwarted the intruder's attack, immobilized him and rendered the man powerless to inflict damage. Kyle squeezed harder and an audible gasp escaped his assailant's lips. The man's face looked ready to burst.

Unable to pry Kyle's legs from around his neck, the intruder was becoming desperate. He moved forward in short, choppy steps, as though his shoes were tied together at the laces. When he was clear of the kitchen counter and facing the great room, he bent at the waist and dove forward into a somersault. After completing one full rotation, Kyle was thrown from his opponent into the back of the sofa.

The intruder was on his feet and stood over top of Kyle who lay in the prone position. He balled a fist and cocked his arm, ready to deliver a knockout punch.

Without taking his eye off his opponent, Kyle raised the pistol that moments earlier had been in the man's ankle holster. "Missing something?" He asked.

The intruder unballed his fist, stuck out his hand and helped Kyle off the floor.

"I could have killed you," Kyle said.

"You wouldn't dare."

"Gentlemen." Ingrid tried to interrupt.

"It's been a hell of a weekend," Kyle continued. "I wouldn't tempt me, if I were you."

"Well, I didn't expect anyone to be here." He gave Kyle's head a long look. "And I didn't recognize you with your fancy haircut."

"I didn't recognize you, either. What are those jeans, size thirty eight?"

"Thirty six."

"Gentlemen, please." Ingrid stepped in between the two men. "Your uncle Rick has already introduced himself."

"He's not my uncle," Kyle replied. "We're not even related." He still had the gun raised.

"It's a term of endearment. I'm a friend of the family," Rick said. "I've known Kyle his whole life." He turned to Kyle. "This is the first time he's pulled a gun on me, however."

Kyle lowered the weapon. "Keep sneaking around like that and it won't be the last."

"Are you two always this nice to each other when you get together?" Ingrid asked.

Both men looked at Ingrid and answered in unison, "Yes."

33

Over doughnuts and coffee, Kyle recounted the events from the previous night. Uncle Rick sat silently as Kyle described how he observed the abduction of the woman from the UN Millennium Hotel, the death of his coworker, Carl McCree, and his subsequent fall from the side of the hotel. Ingrid contributed details about the events at the hospital and the men who pursued them. She avoided any mention of why she was there.

While the two of them spoke, Dunn stole a glance at the picture above the fireplace. He couldn't help be struck by the similarities between Kyle and the man in the picture. It wasn't that the father and son were so much alike in appearance. Anyone who knew them agreed that Kyle took after his mother in this regard. In remembering his friend however, it was the mannerisms, the body language, and his voice that drew particular parallels between Kyle and his father. As Kyle continued, Dunn wondered silently if a winner had yet been declared in the timeworn dispute between nature and nurture. "Sounds like you two had an exciting evening," he said.

Kyle turned and lifted the coffee pot from the burner. "You

could say that." He offered more coffee. Ingrid declined. Dunn accepted. Kyle topped off his own mug. "You haven't said what brought *you* here."

"I always stop by this time of year," Dunn said. "Even when your mother was alive. I turn off the water to the outside spigots before winter so the pipes don't freeze. Set the thermostat for Mrs. Craft so that she doesn't freeze either." He sipped his coffee. "I came by earlier than normal this year because of the cold front." He took another sip of coffee, swallowed.

"And the pickup truck?" Kyle asked. "I didn't recognize it as yours."

"Borrowed it from old Jimmy down at the Montauk Airport."

"You flew here?"

"Yep. Just me and Miss Mandy," Dunn said. "Everyone was grounded yesterday, but this morning wasn't too bad."

Small talk wasn't Dunn's strength. So, he decided to steer the conversation back to relevancy. "You know, whoever it is that's looking for you will eventually catch up with you here." He glanced over at Ingrid.

"Right. So, while we've got a little time here, maybe you can help us," Kyle said.

Dunn had raised his coffee mug to his lips for another sip, but put it down without drinking after Kyle's proposition. "Oh. How might I do that?"

"I want to find the woman."

"The one from the hotel?" Dunn asked.

"Yes."

Ingrid followed the exchange with her eyes. First to Dunn, then to Kyle.

"I don't know how I could possibly help you find her, son," Dunn said.

"I may have a lead," Kyle said. He handed Dunn the phone that they found in his apartment the night before. "Last night, someone broke into my apartment in Brooklyn. I believe it was one of the men who tried to kill me at the Millennium Hotel. The same men that killed Carl and abducted the woman. They used a gun to get into the apartment and they accidentally left this behind."

"Why were you renting an apartment in Brooklyn?" Dunn asked.

"I wanted some time away."

Dunn knew better than to push the issue. He cleared his throat. "So, what did you find on here?" Dunn turned the phone over in his hand.

"I found a text message string in Cyrillic. Russian, I believe. There's also mention of a boat or a ship," Kyle said. "The text mentions the woman, but not her name."

Dunn furrowed his brow. "So, how is it that you think that I can help you?"

"I'm sure you have a world of resources to call on from your days with the Agency," Kyle said.

The statement was posed as a question. Dunn had winced at the reference to his time at the Agency with Spa Group, his mind immediately drifting to the thought of his friend, Kyle's father, dead in a hotel room in Bucharest. He rubbed the corner of his eye, stole another glance at the portrait above the fireplace.

"Probably even more so from your time afterwards."

Kyle was right. In his post-Cold War career as a freelance "security advisor," he had acquired a host of contacts from around the world. None of them mattered as much as the team from Spa Group, however. This was intentional. And although some were loyalists, many just owed him favors.

"It's been quite some time," Dunn said. "And I'm fully retired, now." He sipped some coffee. "Add to that, we wouldn't have much to go on. Presuming that what you believe to be true, is in fact, true. That is, an Asian woman was kidnapped by three Eastern European men of suspected Russian origin. It hasn't risen to the level of international incident at this point." Dunn was apologetic in his answer. "I wouldn't know where to start."

"Come on, Rick. I'm sure we could get a good start with some of this information. You've got great instinct."

Dunn had a masterful sense of intuition sharpened by years of observing human behavior, particularly criminal behavior, displayed and perpetrated en masse in the Eastern Bloc states of the former Soviet Union. His talent lying in the ability to predict in advance the probable actions of a particular group or individuals based on their beliefs, culture and politics.

Large groups, governments or organizations he found rather easy to predict given the typical public display of ideology. The actions of small groups or individuals were more difficult to anticipate and so once all was learned that could be learned about a particular subject, all that remained was pure intuition or as Kyle had said, instinct.

"Instinct without information is like a spear without a point," Dunn said.

"You've still got quite a sharp point," Kyle said. "You more than held your own a few minutes ago. Besides, if there were ever a man of more consequence than Richard Dunn, I've never met him."

"And I'm also old enough to know when someone's blowing smoke up my ass," Dunn said.

Ingrid turned to Uncle Rick. "What is it that you do that has such consequence?"

"Did." Dunn corrected her. "Officially, I was in the security business."

"Unofficially?" Ingrid asked.

Dunn sipped his coffee. "Unofficially, I hunted down bad guys."

Ingrid was intrigued. "What do you mean by hunted?"

"It's the past tense of hunt, ma'am," Dunn said with more than a hint of sarcasm. "Technically, it means to chase or search for the purpose of catching or killing."

"Where did you hunt these men?"

He took another sip of his coffee. "You name it," he said. "Darfur, Jakarta, Mexico City for God's sake."

"Colombia?"

Dunn finally recognized her accent, but didn't answer the question. "The world is full of bad guys, ma'am."

"Yes, I know. Was it your plan to kill every bad guy on the planet."

"Of course not," Dunn answered. "You only need to kill one, to terrify a thousand." Dunn raised his mug. "You gotta love Sun Tzu."

"You think that's a reasonable way to go about it?" Ingrid asked.

"I'm not sure that it is," Dunne replied. "But you want to know what's absolutely unreasonable?" Dunn swung his stool toward Ingrid so that his entire body faced hers. "It's unreasonable to think that the blue helmets from the U.N. could actually stop Islamic warlords from murdering Christians in the Sudan. That a bumper sticker would stop the flow of illegal drugs across our borders. Or that an infomercial by some Hollywood celebutards would actually prevent the abduction and sale of young boys and girls in Asia, South America, Africa and Eastern Europe."

"So, you think *you* had the answer?"

"I had *an* answer," Dunn said. He reached into his pocket and pulled out a brass 5.56mm bullet. He slapped it on the counter.

"A bullet?"

"Preventative maintenance."

While Ingrid and Uncle Rick continued with their back and forth, Kyle turned on the small flat-panel tv at the far end of the counter. He kept the volume at a polite level and tuned in to a 24-hour cable news channel.

"I'm not trying to agitate you, Mr. Dunn," Ingrid said. "We used the same tactics in my country with great success." She attempted to disarm him with her smile. "May I ask, who were your clients?"

"I'm sorry, Ms.-"

"Garcia."

"Ms. Garcia, you'll forgive me for not disclosing the contents of my portfolio."

"Hypothetically." Ingrid leaned in. "Who would have been likely to pay...who would hire you?"

Dunn paused, but he knew he wasn't going to be let off the hook. "Hypothetically, it might have been a non-profit whose revenue for the year was surplus to requirements. Lots of money, but very little in terms of results. Sometimes a well-placed piece of metal makes a difference in terms of morale and the bottom line."

"You expect me to believe that these organizations were in the killing business and hired you as their contractor?" Her eyebrows narrowed.

"Well, when you say it like that."

"Who else?" She asked. "Governments?"

"Sometimes."

"Why didn't they just do it themselves?"

"Like Colombia?" Dunn said. "A lot of governments do. But for some, it could make life difficult politically, if it were known that a certain state was actively involved in the assassination business. Hell, even our CIA shies away when the discussion arises about the mere possibility of targeted killings unless it involves Al Queda or ISIS or some other terrorist groups. But we had the best contacts in the world. All targets were thoroughly researched. Most requests were turned down."

"And requests from individuals?"

"Never."

"Why not?"

"Obvious reasons."

"Did you ever not kill someone?" She asked.

"Meaning?"

"Were you ever hired to just...find someone?"

"Find them and not kill them? No," Dunn said. "Was never hired for that. Not that I'd have been opposed to it. Finding someone is often times the hardest part. Killing them is rather easy."

"Killing someone is easy?"

Dunn raised the bullet to Ingrid's eye level, nodded and then placed it in his shirt pocket. "Did you have someone in mind that you'd like me to find and *not* kill, Ms. Garcia?"

Ingrid's lips parted in what was about to be the formulation of a question. She wanted to ask him if he could help her find her niece, but she couldn't find the right words. Her eyes dipped momentarily to the floor. Dunn was about to turn away from her when she lifted her head, "The woman from the hotel. You haven't said if you would agree to help Kyle find her?"

"Let me give you some free advice," Dunn said. "Four of the five most important words in the English language are, I-need-your-help."

Ingrid took the bait. "And what is the fifth, Mr. Dunn?"

Richard Dunn paused for effect. "No." Then, "This person would have to be awfully significant to employ the resources needed to find and rescue her, if what you believe happened is true."

"Would you consider this significant?" Kyle was tuned in to a news story on the small kitchen television. A picture of a

Japanese man with a caption indicating that he was an employee with the IAEA for the United Nations in New York City. The details stated that his death was being investigated in relation to another Japanese national that went missing from the Millennium Hotel the night before.

Dunn focused on the picture of the man plastered across the flat screen television until the cable channel changed to a story about the weather. He turned to Kyle. "Oh, hell," he said. "Okay, soldier. Grab your bag. Let me see what I can do."

34

Brighton Beach, New York

Dmitri took the contaminated Suburban to the Brighton Beach neighborhood in south Brooklyn. A crook named Andrily had agreed to provide Dmitri with a new car in exchange for the SUV and some cash, of course.

"Little Odessa," as it is affectionately called, offered Dmitri a moment of familiarity. Over the last quarter century, Brighton Beach has become home to over 100,000 emigrants from the former Soviet Union. The petite grocery stores, restaurants and watering holes could have easily been lifted out of the old communist empire and dropped neatly into New York's southern borough. Many of the signs on the avenues and businesses are written in Cyrillic and English is often a second language. One could be excused for thinking they were no longer in America.

As Dmitri stood on the street corner outside of a crumbling brick garage smoking a cigarette, two women approached from the adjacent street corner, one old and one much younger. They appeared to be mother and daughter or possibly grandmother and granddaughter. The old woman pushed a wobbly wire grocery cart while cursing the younger woman in what Dmitri recognized as Ukrainian. He made eye contact with the younger woman but no pleasantries were exchanged either in words, body language or facial expression. The old woman looked at Dmitri with disdain and he was instantly reminded of home.

Little remains of the country that Dmitri grew up in. Nearly half of the population that was once part of the Soviet Union can now thumb their noses at The Russian Federation without fear of retribution as they hide behind the banner of the Commonwealth of Independent States. Dmitri's generation was weak his father liked to say, and the reason for the union's collapse.

The old woman continued her verbal assault on her young companion as they crossed the street. As they passed by, Dmitri eyeballed the old woman. She stared back defiantly and cursed at him, calling him a criminal in her native tongue. He gestured back with his thumb pressed between his index and middle finger. The young woman flashed him a brief, but knowing smile. Dmitri smiled back. He imagined his young daughter, Valentina, might one day look just like the young woman when she grows up. His thoughts drifted to her picture. Then to the thought of the call he received at the hotel. If she grows up. His smile faded

The rusted metal door to the garage opened behind him and Andrily called out from the doorway, "Your car is ready."

Dmitri crushed the expired cigarette beneath the heel of his shoe and followed the man into the garage. Inside, the air of the weakly lit garage was heavy with the scent of freshly sprayed paint and thinner.

Andrily waited while Dmitri inspected the vehicle, an over produced Japanese model with a gray interior. It was an older model year than the SUV and didn't come standard with a navigation system. As Dmitri walked around surveying the car, a man picked tape from its headlights. The formerly red, two door Honda was now painted a forgettable silver. And although the paint job was less than excellent, he knew the car would go virtually unnoticed throughout the streets of the city. Dmitri nodded to the worker pulling tape as he came back around to the front of the car. At the back of the garage a second man was busy adjusting the pneumatic tool on the end of an air hose.

"How much?" Dmitri asked.

Andrily threw his chin out, "Two thousand, American."

Dmitri half smiled. "We agreed to one thousand dollars and including the other vehicle."

Andrily nodded to the Suburban parked at the other end of the garage where the man with the air hose worked at removing the wheels with an impact ratchet. "It's very badly soiled. It will take some time to clean that up."

Dmitri took a step forward and stroked his chin, giving Andrily a good look at the four skulls that were tattooed on the knuckles of his right hand. He countered, "And your painting job is shit."

Andrily considered the tattoos and swallowed hard. "Fifteen hundred," he said.

The man pulling tape had watched the exchange with interest, but pretended not to notice when Dmitri looked his way. Men like Dmitri and Andrily were bound to and united by a code of honor. Vory v Zakone. It didn't matter if one was a member of the Kazan criminal enterprise in St. Petersburg, the Luchanskiy syndicate in Moscow or the Kostenaya gang from Vladivostok, one Russian Mafiya member did not try to undermine another. Andrily had just tried to break the code and the significance was not lost on the man who was now just pretending to pick tape off of the Honda's headlight. The air tool in the background stopped and the man operating it watched the others out of the corner of his eye. Dmitri turned away from Andrily and walked over to the silver sedan.

The man who had been pulling tape stood up as Dmitri approached. He was wearing black denim overalls and a gray thermal long sleeve shirt. He smelled strongly of lacquer thinner and paint. He wiped his hands off on his pants.

"You are trying to steal money from me because you are a capitalist." Dmitri spoke to Andrily without facing him. "So, I have changed my mind," Dmitri said. "I will take my business elsewhere."

A frown snaked across Andrily's face.

Dmitri turned to Andrily, "That is what capitalism is all about, right? Freedom of choice," he said. "I am going to give my money to this man, because I believe that he is more trustworthy." Dmitri pulled out a roll of money from his coat pocket and counted out $1,500 slowly, deliberately. When the tape puller reached for the money, Dmitri grabbed his hand and turned it over revealing a cross tattooed on the man's right middle finger. "Am I correct?" he asked. "That you are more trustworthy?"

The man nodded that he was.

"What is your name?" Dmitri asked.

"Ilya," the man replied.

Dmitri turned to face Andrily. "You see. Ilya, is a true Vor. A thief within the law."

"He is nothing, but a Shestyorka, an errand boy." Andrily spat out the words as if they threatened to poison his tongue. It was an attempt to belittle the man and invalidate the transaction.

"Was," Dmitri said. "Ilya *was* just a Shestyorka. *I* have made him a Vor." Dmitri turned to the newly minted criminal and spoke softly. "Make him unrecognizable."

Ilya snapped his fingers loudly. In the back of the garage, the mechanic had abandoned the wheels of the SUV. He now concerned himself with changing the tool on the end of the air hose. Off came the impact ratchet and in its place a shiny new air chisel.

Dmitri asked. "Where can I get some privacy?"

Ilya pointed to a small room in the front corner of the garage that served as a makeshift office. Dmitri patted Andrily on the shoulder as he walked by.

Dmitri entered the office and closed the door. His cell phone had gone off while he was out in the garage schooling Andrily on the sensibility of capitalism as well as the rules of the Vory v Zakone. He checked his phone and saw that the call had again come from Russia as noted by the +7 country code and applicable Moscow area code. He called the number back.

When someone on the other end picked up, Dmitri got straight to the point. "Where is Valentina?"

"Where is Alex?" A man responded. It was the same male voice that had called him before. This time, Dmitri noticed a slight Japanese accent.

"Fuck Alex," Dmitri said. "What have you done with my daughter, you fucking *Xiao Riben*?"

"A Chinese slur leveled against a Japanese man. I'm impressed. I wasn't aware that you spoke Mandarin," the caller said. "Birds of a feather, I suppose." He chuckled. "Little Valentina is right here in front of me. She won't be harmed as long as I have proof that the woman has not been harmed."

"The woman has not been harmed," Dmitri said. He paced around the little office. "Let me speak to my daughter, now."

"As you wish," the caller said.

Dmitri's heart pounded as he heard muffled talk in the background. Then, a tiny, scared little voice. "Tata." *Daddy.* These were the only words the girl was allowed to speak.

"Valentina," Dmitri said.

The man came back on the phone. "I'll be expecting to hear from the woman soon."

"Let my daughter go," Dmitri barked.

"If not, I'll have no choice, but to assume she has been terminated and I'll be forced to apply the same fate to Valentina."

"Dmitri!" Hearing his ex-wife's voice yell in the background stung. He felt small and worthless in her presence. He had failed to provide for her in even the smallest of things and knew that she was right to have left him.

He cleared his throat and spoke with an air of confidence in the chance that his ex-wife could hear him. "Give me your name so that when I am finished here, I can return to Moscow and pay you a visit."

"Oh, you wish for fair play." The caller laughed. "My name is Tomo," he said. Seriousness quickly returned to his tone of voice. "But I must warn you, Mr. Korychnevy, I'm not very much fun to play with."

"You leave my daughter alone."

"You have one hour," Tomo said and hung up the phone.

Playing both sides of the same coin was a dangerous gamble. Whether the woman lived or died did not matter to him, but he could not say the same about Valentina. Her life meant everything to him and he was not about to gamble with it over some woman he cared nothing about. But he was still confident that he could leverage the woman on both accounts and make money both ways.

Niko could be reached via the *Revolyutsyia's* internet system and would prove to Tomo, the caller from Moscow, that the woman was alive as instructed. From there, Dmitri would negotiate the terms of her release as he worked to get close to the man that had taken his daughter.

Koba, on the other hand, expected the Japanese woman to be terminated vis-à-vis, Mr. Sakai. Since there was no proof that she was in fact, alive, Dmitri believed that he could convince Koba of her death, thus retrieving his payment.

He removed the hospital guest sign-in log from his pocket and unfolded it on the table in front of him. The last name on the list, an Ingrid Garcia, had indicated a check-in time of 7:55 pm, shortly before Dmitri and Niko had arrived at the hospital. Ms. Garcia was the only visitor that evening not to have entered a check-out time and so it was clear to him that she was the one with the window washer, Kyle Murdoch. Out in the garage, the air compressor kicked on and rumbled loudly.

Dmitri gave the mouse attached to the desktop PC a little shake and the monitor came to life. Using a map program, he typed in Ingrid Garcia's address as written on the hospital guest log. He grabbed a stray pen from the desk drawer and wrote down the directions on the back of a torn envelope. The directions put her at the apartment complex on the corner of 23rd and 1st Streets, not far from where they had pursued her at the hospital. Dmitri was sure that Ms. Garcia would lead him to the window washer, whom he suspected could lead him to the man who kidnapped his ex-wife and daughter.

Shouting from inside the garage intensified and caught Dmitri's attention. He turned his ear to the door to hear Andrily pleading and cursing all at the same time in Russian. Pathetic promises to his tormentors that would be impossible to keep.

Out in the garage, Andrily's screams threatened to rise above the din of the air compressor until they were muted by the insertion into his mouth of a balled-up rag that had been used just moments before to wipe down the inside of the soiled SUV. He was tied to a chair in the far corner of the garage with his arms strapped vertically by his side. Blood dripped from his finger-tips, all of which had been clipped off by a pair of yellow handled tin snips. Tears streamed down his cheeks and his eyes darted wildly between Ilya and his associate who was approaching his face with the air chisel.

Andrily was no longer trying to talk his way out of his unfortunate circumstance. As his teeth were knocked out one at a time by the air powered industrial chisel, he had resorted to screaming like a man resigned to his fate yet holding on to the truth that as long as he could still make noise, he was not yet dead.

35

Cavasano locked his cell phone and dropped it into his coat pocket. "We got the okay to track Murdoch's cell phone," he said.

"In real time or after the fact?" Merylo asked.

"Real time."

"How'd you manage that?"

"Said it was an emergency, that Murdoch's life was in danger. I got Moses lookin' after it."

"Great. We'll take care of that once we're finished here," Merylo said. "That's it, right there." He pointed to a corner brick storefront across the street. Large, black Cyrillic letters jumped off a dirty white sign anchored above the door.

Cavasano brought the unmarked to a stop a half a block away in front of another store that advertised Black Sea Shoes. Before he shut off the ignition he asked, "This is the sixtieth's precinct. You think maybe we should let them know?"

"Let them know what?" Merylo's eyebrows wrinkled. "You're a detective now, Cavasano. You can go wherever you damn well please. You don't need permission and nobody has to know. Understand?"

"Sure."

"Good. Now let's go see what this commie bastard knows."

"How do we know he's a communist?" Cavasano asked.

Merylo jabbed a finger at his partner. "Once a communist, always a communist. I don't care what they call themselves now, a social democracy or whatever. I don't care if they change their name to The Little Sisters of the Poor, they're still communists to me." He opened the glove compartment and pulled out a black leather pouch with a pull cord closure. "Next lesson. Fifty cent pieces," he said. "Benny put them in there a while ago."

"What for?"

Merylo smiled. "Communists love them."

The two detectives got out of the car. Merylo stuffed the leather bag in his coat pocket. They marched across the street under a heavy gray sky made darker by the transit rails that ran overhead. When they'd reached the sidewalk on the other side, Cavasano nodded to the sign above them, "What is this place?" he asked.

"Joe's Market," Merylo answered.

"You can read that?"

Merylo opened a battered, paint peeled door and held it for his partner. "No, I can't." He followed Cavasano into the store.

Inside, the brick walls of the store were white washed. Thick layers of high gloss paint nearly smoothed out the mortar lines. The paint was chipped near the door, revealing a history of blue, green and pink décor. Cavasano picked at it as he walked by.

The store's aisles were cramped. The shelves were stocked with fruit preserves, jams and syrup. Everywhere there were jars of pickled vegetables and mushrooms. Canned fish and pasta also appeared to be very popular. In the back of the store were two old, oversized freezers. Merylo waited with his hands folded behind his back as an old woman rummaged through stacks of frozen meat and fish. She looked up at him, her face was weather beaten and wrinkled. Wispy little hairs wavered from the end of her trembling chin. She looked an unkindly woman and the detective didn't waste his energy on a smile. He just stared blankly back at her.

Cavasano was uncomfortable, but he stood silently, watching, taking his cue from his partner. He watched as the old woman gave up her search for whatever it was she was looking for and shuffled away.

Merylo attacked the freezer with purpose. In a matter of seconds he held in his hands what appeared to be a black frozen sausage. With eyes.

"What the hell is that?" Cavasano asked. He kept his voice low, not wanting to draw attention to the situation.

"It's an eel," Merylo said. "Don't worry. I'm not going to ask you to eat it."

At the worn laminate counter they were greeted by a steely faced woman in a lime green sweatshirt and a twenty something male with dark rings under his eyes. The punk was wearing a dirty white and blue Nike soccer jersey with an advertisement for Gazprom embossing the front of the shirt. The logo over his left breast was for a team from St. Petersburg. Merylo had seen his type before. The punk was a raver, a meth freak. Merylo dropped the frozen eel onto the counter with a thud. Shards of ice splayed out and quickly melted into little pools of water.

"I'd like to speak to Josef," Merylo said. The request was made in perfect Russian.

The drug addict turned away from the counter and exited through a door in the rear of the store. Cavasano was tempted to ask where the punk was going, but was confident he wouldn't return with a gift bag. The eel had been meant to be sold fresh, but was now past its selling date by more than a year. The store clerks knew that Merylo wasn't here to buy it.

Merylo was content to stare down the woman behind the

counter until a sturdy man entered the store from the rear door. The lines on his face suggested he was at least in his fifties. He wore a pair of light brown overalls with a white long-sleeved shirt rolled up to the elbows. A frayed denim apron with dark stains on it hung around his neck.

He sniffed as he made his way to the front and a thick black mustache twitched under his wide nose. When he got to the counter in front of the detectives, he looked down at the thawing eel before lifting his head up to meet Merylo. The man nodded to Cavasano, "Who is he?" His voice was heavy with a thick Eastern European accent.

"This is Detective Cavasano," Merylo said. "He's my new partner."

"What happened to the other one?" The grocer stared at Merylo, unblinking. The beginnings of a sinister grin began to form upon his face.

The question stung Merylo, but he did not respond.

The grocery store owner sniffed and then raised one of his thick eyebrows. If he cared about the answer, he didn't let on. He took the eel off the counter and started on his way to the door in the back of the store. Merylo and Cavasano followed.

Cavasano discreetly tapped Merylo's shoulder. "Hey," he said.

"What?"

"I thought you said that you didn't speak Russian?"

"I said I couldn't *read* it."

Walking passed the freezer from where Merylo had taken the eel, Josef callously tossed it back in among the other frozen meats.

The back door was a heavy, steel, bulwark of a structure. Cavasano rapped on it with his knuckles as he passed by. A thick layer of foam weather stripping lined the inside frame of the door. The long narrow room was dry walled and an obvious addition that was not part of the original building. The walls were painted a pale yellow, made all the more drab by a pair of weak industrial type fluorescent lights. Foam acoustical tiles nearly covered the whole of the ceiling, an obvious attempt at soundproofing. A second door exited the far end of the room.

The detectives were offered a seat in the form of a pair of wooden folding chairs leaning against the dirty, marked up wall. Merylo declined the invitation just as Cavasano reached for a chair. The new detective understood the implication and took up a flanking position near the door.

Their host waved his hand in response to Merylo's snub and sat down heavily next to a beat up metal desk. Half of an unlit cigar balanced in an ashtray. He rescued it and lit the end.

"How long has it been Josef?" Merylo asked. There was a hint of venom in his voice.

"I don't know." Josef stroked his mustache. A river of bluish smoke rose lazily from between his lips. "You tell me," he said.

"About as long as that tube fish has been sitting in your freezer." Merylo inched closer. The act was almost imperceptible, but its effect was obvious. Josef squirmed in his chair. "Are we supposed to believe that somebody actually eats that shit?"

"It's actually quite good with a little mustard." Josef blew a puff of smoke in Merylo's face. The detective didn't flinch.

"What is it you want?" Josef asked.

Merylo planted himself on the edge of the desk and rudely plucked the cigar out of Josef's mouth and stubbed it out in the ashtray. "The same thing everybody wants who comes in here, Joe," he said. "And it ain't your shitty food. I want information."

Josef's face went red. He was still simmering about the cigar when Merylo pulled the leather drawstring bag from his coat pocket and dropped it on the desk in front of him.

"I understand you guys are fond of President Kennedy," Merylo said.

Josef said nothing.

Cavasano cocked his ear to the door, kept his eyes on Josef. He transferred his weight to his other leg.

"No?" Merylo opened the sack and pulled out a handful of large silver coins. "What about this? You like these? They got President Kennedy's mug on them, see?" He stuck his hand out.

Josef eyed the sack and then the detective.

Merylo went on, "There's over a hundred of them in this bag. You know how much that is? Of course not. You communists aren't any good at math, that's why your little empire kept running out of money."

"It was anything, but little," Josef smirked. "What are your questions?"

"You *do* like them," Merylo said. "How about that, Cavasano? Benny was right."

The way Merylo was acting made Cavasano nervous. He shifted his stance again.

The veteran detective faked a smile and put the loose coins back into the sack. "I had a face to face with one of your Mafiya brothers a little while ago." He leaned in toward Josef. "The coroner's office fished him out of the East River this morning. Only problem was," Merylo paused for dramatic effect. "He didn't have a face."

Josef was unmoved.

Merylo went on, "Ever seen someone without a face?"

"I have not," Josef said.

"You don't want to," Merylo said. "His name was Alex Kashvili. You know him?" He asked.

Josef eyed the money sack, but remained silent.

"I'm betting that he's a Torpedo, you know the type. So, I asked myself, where would I go if I wanted information on a Russian contract killer on the loose in New York?" Merylo gestured with his arms. "Here I am."

Merylo pushed the sack inches closer to the Russian.

"But I could really care less about him. I want to know who he works for." Merylo leaned in until his nose was only inches from Josef's. "I want to know what's going down? Who's his Krestnii otets?"

Josef didn't move. Didn't even blink.

Cavasano was transfixed by the moment. He had forgotten about the store beyond the metal door. He had forgotten that somewhere there was another young man and an old woman that would be interested in the circumstance of the store's namesake. For an instant, Cavasano forgot that he was a police officer and that he had a loaded gun under his left arm.

Josef stole a glance at Cavasano who blinked and momentarily shifted his eyes. Staring menacingly back at Merylo, Josef said, "Detective Merylo, if I knew who his Krestnii otets was and I told you, I would then have to kill you."

Merylo grasped the sack of coins tightly in his right hand. "Well, Joe. That's a risk that I'm willing to take."

36

The commute from Montauk airport on Long Island to the Falmouth Airpark in Massachusetts took roughly 45 minutes. Before they had left the Murdoch residence, Dunn secured the services of one Lawrence Ames of the United States Coast Guard.

With a steel gray sky for a backdrop, Dunn eased the plane down on the tarmac. The Falmouth Airpark had a single 700-meter asphalt landing strip and enough hangar space to house the 50 or so aircraft that called the public use airport their home.

The plane bobbed gently as it rolled down the runway. A lone member of the airpark's ground crew appeared and guided *Miss Mandy* with his marshaling wands off the main runway and directed him toward a hangar at the far end of the strip. Dunn eased the plane to a stop a few meters before the hangar, removed his head set and placed it on the cockpit floor next to the pilot's seat. Kyle did likewise. Both men climbed out of the plane and Kyle came around to the pilot's side where Dunn was retrieving their bags from the modest cargo hold.

"You sure your friend can help us?" Kyle asked.

"I don't know, but he's our best chance at the moment," Dunn said.

"He owes you a favor, does he?"

"Something like that," Dunn replied. He handed Kyle his bag.

Kyle paused. "What did you do, kill someone for him?"

"No. I did not kill anyone for him." Dunn winced. "It was something much worse than that, actually."

"Oh, yeah. What was that?" Kyle asked.

"I introduced him to his wife."

Kyle chuckled. "A matchmaker and an assassin," he said. "Quite the resumé."

Dunn left that statement alone. He had introduced Kyle's father and mother to each other many years before as well. Watching from the sidelines, Dunn had always wondered if Kyle resented him for what had happened to his father and the pain it had caused his mother. He wouldn't blame Kyle if he did. Dunn carried with him the burden of Thomas Murdoch's death. And if anyone ever bothered to ask him, he'd admit that he has never gotten over it himself.

The rhythmic chatter of an unseen helicopter pulsated in the distance growing louder each second before finally cascading over a line of mature maple and pin oak trees from the north. Dunn peeked in that direction and less than five minutes after the *Miss Mandy* had landed at the Falmouth Airpark, Captain Lawrence Ames of the United States Coast Guard was ushering the two men into the back of a Sikorsky Jayhawk helicopter. He handed out Coast Guard issued, white and orange helmets to the two men as well as headsets and then instructed them to turn them on.

Lawrence Ames was a large man by anyone's standards. At a

sturdy six and a half feet tall, there was hardly a vehicle made that didn't cause him fits. Dunn believed that that must be the reason for the permanently etched scowl on his face.

As the helicopter lifted off the ground, Captain Ames decided to lay down the ground rules. He stressed the fact that his was the only Coast Guard Aviation facility in the northeast. With an area of responsibility that stretched from New York City to the Canadian border, his hands were full. Ames made it perfectly clear to Dunn that only his pilots flew and that he would have to abort this mission at any time, under any circumstance if he got a call that needed his attention elsewhere, even if that meant having to rescue some drunken socialite from Martha's Vineyard who'd fallen off his yacht. Both passengers understood.

The flight from the little airpark to Air Station Cape Cod took just under five minutes and after explaining his possible need to opt out, Ames used the rest of the flight time to brief the two men on the situation thus far.

"Alright gentlemen, here's what I know." Ames's voice boomed through the headsets. "I called down to the New York Port Authority and spoke to a contact, we'll call him *Leo*." Ames paused for effect. "After a little prodding, *Leo* checked the logs for the last two days. There's only one ship that I think would interest you. Its name is the *Revolyutsiya*. That's Russian for revolution in case anyone gives a shit," he said. "The *Revolyutsiya* is a three-year-old, three-hundred-foot-long container ship out of St. Petersburg, Russia. It's carrying a crew of ten, not including any potential VIP's"

"Any idea what kind of cargo she's carrying?" Kyle asked.

"Mostly likely, American made cars," Ames said. "Know anybody that's had theirs stolen recently and there's a good chance you'd find it on board as well."

"Destination?" Dunn asked.

"Kaliningrad," Ames said. He turned towards Kyle. "The world's largest used car lot. For the reasons just mentioned." Lawrence Ames continued, "A ship that size would be traveling at an average cruising speed of about fifteen to eighteen knots, and if she left at the time specified in Leo's log book, she'd probably be anywhere from seventy to eighty nautical miles south southwest of Nantucket Island, depending on the seas." Ames looked at his watch. "Right about now."

"Thanks, Lawrence," Dunn said.

"Don't thank me just yet Rick, because I've got some bad news to go along with the good."

"Let's hear it," Kyle said.

"The good news is, the ship is within reach of our Ocean Sentry. If we can get up and running immediately, I'm confident we can catch her wake soon enough. We'll have one of our Jayhawk helicopters follow behind." He looked at Kyle, "You know how to jump?"

Kyle paused. It had been a while. He wondered what altitude they'd be at.

Ames knew what the hesitation meant. "We still do it feet first," Ames said. "Makes life a lot less painful." Ames continued, "I'm putting my ass on the line here fellas." He shot Dunn a look that communicated his displeasure at returning a favor at this moment and in this manner.

"How's the missus?" Dunn attempted to brighten his mood.

"We're divorced, Rick."

"Sorry I asked," Dunn said. "And the bad news?" He was desperate to get back on topic.

"The bad news is, the Jayhawks have a limited range," Ames said. "That means if you take too long, you'll miss your extraction and we won't be able to bring you back. At that point you'll be on your own."

"That's bullshit, Lawrence," Dunn said.

"That's the way it's going to be, Rick," Ames countered.

"We're not going to just leave him out there."

"It's okay," Kyle said. "We'll worry about that if and when the time comes. Just get me to that ship."

37

Kyle, Richard Dunn and Lawrence Ames sat together in the Coast Guard's HC-144 Ocean Sentry as it cruised at a brisk 215 knots out over the Atlantic. A 20 knot tailwind graced the back of the plane as it cruised at an altitude of 1500 feet. The 21,000 pound aircraft features an 84 foot wingspan and rear service ramp. Its 1,800 mile range and endurance of nearly 10 hours makes it the ideal aircraft for search and rescue missions.

They had been in the air just twenty minutes when the co-pilot, a lifelong blueblood named Doyle, suggested over the coastguard headset that now would be the time to start looking out for the container ship *Revolyutsiya*. Sidwell, the pilot, had drawn a course that had taken them over the main New York to Europe shipping lane.

Ames had given instructions not to drop altitude until they were at least 70 miles south of Nantucket Island. The idea was to approach any vessels headed east from the stern and get a look as the passed by. Having surpassed the 70 mile benchmark, Sidwell eased the plane down to 1000 feet and lowered its speed down to a mere 180 knots.

"Here." Ames handed Kyle a pair of Swarovski binoculars. "You can use these."

Doyle's voice cracked over the headsets, "Potential target an estimated five miles ahead, we'll be passing on her port side."

A minute later the ship came into full view. Through the view finder, Kyle was able to clearly make out the details of the 300-foot-long cargo ship. The ship was pearl white topside with dark green hull paint that rose just above the water line. Stretched across the stern in bold white letters was the name *Revolyutsiya*.

"That's her," Kyle said. The Ocean Sentry zipped past the vessel. He handed the binoculars back to Ames and pulled a high impact floatation vest over his tactical operations dry suit. He slipped a parachute on last.

Ames called out directions over the headsets. "Sidwell, circle back and make another pass." The 70 foot plane leaned to its left and rose noticeably into the overcast sky. Ames turned to Kyle. "Okay son, we're going to kick you out two miles ahead of that ship. By the time you get settled, you should have less than five minutes before she's on top of you. Make sure you get a good bead on her path on your way down. I don't think I have to tell you that you've only got one shot or you'll be sitting out there until support arrives."

Kyle adjusted his earpiece and lowered a pair of goggles over his eyes. "I know." He made a last-minute check of the equipment. A pair of tactical suction cups dangled from his waist belt on his left hip, a survival knife was sheathed on his right. He slipped his cell phone into one of the waterproof pockets of his tactical dry suit.

Ames noticed, "You plan on ordering a pizza?"

"No sir," Kyle said. "I just take it wherever I go."

Ames wasn't impressed. "You might want this instead." He

reached into his flight bag and extended his hand to Kyle. In it was a 9mm handgun. "I take *it* wherever I go."

Kyle considered the gun. "I appreciate the offer, but no thank you, Captain."

"Have it your way." Ames put the gun away. "Nobody tells me how to do my job either." He put the incident behind him and concentrated on the present. "Okay, here's how this is going to work."

Ames explained that they would take the plane up to approximately 2000 feet and utilize the aircraft's cargo service ramp. It would be a no-frills insertion. Sidwell swung the jet back to its original flight path and was now closing back in on the *Revolyutsiya*. He gave the crew a command, "Time to get into position."

Ames lowered the service ramp and Kyle got into position in the center of the cargo hold. He held on temporarily to a stainless steel rail that ran overhead. The cabin pressure changed noticeably as the ramp lowered and the air gusting in through the opening in raised the decibel level in the aircraft.

Ames spoke up. "Sidwell will put you on a direct path with that ship. The son-of-a-bitch used to be one of those aerial acrobats with the air show," Ames said. "Anyways, when I give you the signal." Ames gave a thumbs up. "That's when I want you to go. I've got a Jayhawk helicopter that will be entering the arena shortly to pick you up." Ames checked his watch. "In about thirty minutes, so don't procrastinate. With or without the...woman, you'll need to get yourself to the highest open area that you can. Obviously, that would be on top of the super structure. Any questions?"

"No sir."

"Thirty minutes." Ames repeated the time frame for emphasis.

While Kyle waited for the service ramp to open fully and

Sidwell to get in line with the container ship, he started to fiddle with the cord for the earpiece and micro phone, attempting to tuck it into the neck of his dry suit.

"Don't worry about that son," Ames said. "All our shit's waterproof." A few seconds later, Ames gave Kyle the thumbs up.

When Kyle had fully slipped past the Sentry's open hatch, it was only a matter of running the few remaining feet to clear the aircraft's cargo ramp. He turned back and gave Dunn a nod who reciprocated the gesture. Ames just raised his eyebrows in what was an obvious sign to get moving. It had been what seemed an eternity since Kyle's last jump. His heart raced and he could feel the sweat on the palm of his hands. Even so, there was a burning desire to get on with it and get on that ship. Ames tipped his head to the open cargo ramp. Kyle ran.

There are very few things in the world that stimulate the secretion of epinephrine in the human body quite like jumping out of an airplane. And the sudden realization that he was free falling from 2,000 feet at nearly 20 feet per second was all it took to remind Kyle of the proper technique and procedures with which to execute a successful jump. He spread his arms and legs wide and arched his back into a stable free fall position. With the plane already a fair distance away, the only noise he heard was the wind whistling passed his dry suit and his heart thumping to some far-off allegro symphony. His blood was filled with adrenaline.

When he felt his acceleration level off, he knew that he was now falling at a constant rate of speed of approximately 120 miles an hour.

Hello gravity.

He counted to five as he turned his body north into the wind and released the pilot chute. The bridles followed and popped the deployment bag from the container. Once the risers had released and fully extended, the immediate tension pulled the parachute out of the deployment bag.

The chute opened without incident. Sidwell had guided him into a perfect path east and directly ahead of the *Revolyutsiya*. He only had to make slight adjustments with the toggles to account for the wind and he was able to keep himself in line with the cargo ship. As long as the freighter kept its course, in time, it would run right over him.

As the dark waters of the Atlantic Ocean rose up to meet him, Kyle gave the toggles one last pull, slowing his descent and settling him down upon the crest of a three-foot wave. He unhooked his parachute, gathered it into a ball, and kicked it into the deep to keep it out of view.

The drop had been executed to perfection. Kyle bobbed in the water slightly north of the cargo ship's path. Aided by the wind, it would take little effort to maneuver himself into a direct line with the vessel. Ames' voice crackled through his earpiece.

"This is Guardian Angel to Mako, do you read me?"

Guardian Angel? Mako? They hadn't discussed code names and Kyle was wondering why he was given the name of a type of shark.

"This is Mako," he answered reluctantly. "I hear you Guardian Angel."

"How's the water?"

Kyle licked seawater from his lips. "Cold and salty."

"Sounds like my ex-wife." Any ounce of humor in Ames' voice didn't filter through Kyle's earpiece. "Have you got a bead on the ship?"

"Affirmative."

"Good. The Jayhawk should be in the area in about twenty-five minutes. Get the girl and make yourself tall." Ames went on, "We'll be in radio contact with you throughout the duration. You're going to be just fine."

Kyle wished he shared the captain's confidence. Although he had been trained for this type of operation, it had been many years ago with the key word being training. The parched deserts of the Middle East hadn't exactly kept his amphibious assault skills sharp.

Kyle kicked his legs to keep his chin just above water as an unruly wave slapped him in the face. He adjusted his mic and spit out the splash of saltwater that pooled under his tongue.

"Hey captain," Kyle said.

"Yes."

"Why Mako?"

Silence.

"Captain?"

"I figure you're just like the Mako shark right now. Fast and mean."

The bullshit was coming through Kyle's earpiece loud and clear.

"You saw one didn't you?"

More silence.

"Captain?"

"Alright, it was about seven feet long and looked about five hundred pounds. Jumped ten feet clear out of the water. I spotted her as I was closing the service ramp. Don't worry, she's about one and a half miles east northeast of your position, but I would suggest making good on your first attempt to board that ship," Ames said. "Oh, and...try not to bleed."

38

"C'mon Frank, that's enough," Cavasano pleaded. Josef's left eye had begun to swell shut. Blood ran freely from his nose and dripped off his thick mustache. Still, he sat upright in his chair, hanging his head and breathing heavily through his mouth.

"Would you look at that." Merylo shook the bag of coins in the store owner's face. "Another Russian beat down by JFK."

"C'mon Frank, he don't know anything. Let's just get back to the station," Cavasano said. "We shouldn't be here."

"Bullshit. This son-of-a-bitch knows who killed Benny," Merylo spat.

He struck another blow to Josef's head.

Cavasano couldn't take anymore. He lunged forward and grabbed his partner from behind. "That's enough Frank," Cavasano said. "This ain't gonna bring Benny back."

Merylo struggled, but could not free himself from the bigger detective. "He knows who did it. He knows who killed Benny," he shouted.

Cavasano held Merylo tight. His partner was out of control. Overcome by his emotions, Merylo had stepped over the boundaries of law enforcement. Cavasano knew the consequences of such actions would be severe. His second day on the job as a Detective I and he was sure to be reprimanded along with his partner. He wouldn't let go.

"He knows who killed Benny, Cavasano," Merylo continued to struggle free. "Let me at the motherfucker! I'll kill him!"

"That's right," Josef huffed. A wicked smiled curled one side of his mouth. "I know who killed your partner, Benny."

"I told you, Cavasano. Now let me go, goddammit!"

The store owner lifted his head. "I did," he said proudly. "And now I am going to kill you."

Before either detective had a chance to respond, the back door swung open and hit the adjacent wall with a thud.

It was the punk.

With a shotgun.

Cavasano let Merylo go.

Before the bleary eyed, grocer's son could get his sights set, Merylo pulled the Beretta from his waist and put two shots into the kid's shoulder. The punk dropped the weapon and fell backward into the doorway.

The heavy steel door coming from the grocery store crashed open and struck Cavasano in the back of the head sending him down onto one knee. Just above him, a Czech made semi-automatic pistol at the end of a lime green shirt sleeve pointed in Merylo's direction.

The wife.

Two shots.

Two hits.

Tiny fibers of polyester and nylon burst from Merylo's coat. He fell down. Blood smeared on the wall behind him.

Cavasano chopped down hard on the green sleeve with his left hand, knocking the woman's gun to the ground. He pulled out his Italian, department issued firearm with his right.

Merylo sat up and emptied three slugs into the woman's chest. She fell face first in front of Cavasano.

Josef reached under the desk.

Cavasano aimed his gun at him. "Don't move," he shouted.

The grocer ignored him.

Cavasano pulled the trigger, but he hadn't taken the safety off. "Shit!"

Joseph lifted his arm.

Cavasano flicked the safety and pulled the trigger. Josef's left eye exploded. He dropped his gun and slumped over in his chair.

Cavasano shuffled on one knee over to his partner. "You okay, Frank," he asked.

Merylo squirmed. He didn't answer, just grunted.

"Frank?"

Merylo finally answered, "I hear you." His voice was raspy.

"Shit Frank, you're bleeding like a stuffed pig." Cavasano took a handkerchief from his coat pocket, pulled open Merylo's jacket and shirt and pressed the cloth onto his partner's wounds. He kept one hand on his gun. "Jesus, Frank."

"Get your phone," Merylo sputtered.

"Right," Cavasano said. He took his partner's hand and put it on the handkerchief to hold it in place. Kneeling in a gathering pool of blood that ran out from under Josef's wife, the young detective dug in his coat pocket searching for his cell phone.

"The other pocket," Merylo said. He tried to sit up straighter, squinted in pain and then decided against it. "Find it?"

"I got it," Cavasano said. He switched hands with his gun and found his cell phone in his right coat pocket. He pulled it out and fumbled to get it in position to dial. His hand was trembling and his fingers slipped and smeared blood across the face of his phone causing him to misdial. "Dammit!" He wiped his fingers off on his pant leg and tried again.

There was movement from across the room. The punk in the soccer jersey sat up in the doorway. A large red stain had blossomed on the left shoulder of his white shirt. He picked up the shotgun that lay at his side. The punk's aim wasn't steady, but it was a shotgun and it was pointed in the right direction.

"Got it," Cavasano announced as he hit the call button. When he looked up, he saw the punk with the shotgun aimed in his direction.

"Shit, Frank, get down!" Cavasano dropped his phone and pulled Merylo toward him onto the floor. Shooting with his weaker hand, the junior detective managed to put two of his three shots on target, the first into the punk's cheek and the second one into his neck. The third bullet sped out the door and into the side of a brick building across the street. This time the punk would not get up.

Cavasano sat Merylo upright against the wall. The room was silent but for a cough that fizzled into a wheeze from Merylo. There was blood on his phone and this he wiped off on the side of his suit pant leg. The big detective rose to his feet, slipping a little on the spilt blood. A spent shell rolled off of the table and clinked on the tile floor.

The red polka dots that speckled his forehead smeared as he wiped it with the back of his hand. He cleaned his phone off again, this time on his jacket. He tucked in his shirt and adjusted his tie. His hand wasn't trembling anymore. He scrolled through his contacts and punched in the number for the station. He asked for backup and an ambulance.

39

The *Revolyutsiya* was bearing down on him. Kyle knew it was important to attack the ship head on at its bow. If he were to attempt to latch on to either the port or starboard side, the wake would toss him aside like flotsam and he would miss his chance to get onboard. When the ship was just a few feet away he raised his arms, a tactical suction cup in each fist and at the last moment, thrust himself as far out of the water as he could. The cargo ship's bow hit him.

Hard.

His elbows and forearms bore the brunt of the impact and his already injured left elbow caught fire once again. He let out a short grunt.

Kyle pushed the burning sensation in his arm to the far reaches of his mind. He had a new problem now. He had only managed to thrust himself out of the water as far as his mid-thigh. Even at a little over twenty knots, the drag pulling at his legs threatened to rip him from his perch.

He couldn't board the ship from this position. It was best to attack the vessel from the stern. Using his right thumb, Kyle depressed the button on the end of the cup's handle. It released from the hull with a pop. Kyle waited for the cup to reset and then reached out as far and as high as he could before slapping the cup against the steel hull. He repeated this process with both hands until he had managed to draw himself up and away from the turbulent waters on the ship's port side.

Ames' voice crackled over his earpiece. "Guardian Angel to Mako."

Kyle shimmied another three feet across the side of the ship. He did not pause to answer. "Go ahead Guardian Angel."

"Have you made contact with the vessel?"

"Contact is too nice of a word."

"What's a matter, soldier? Getting hit by fifteen thousand tons of steel head on isn't all it's cracked up to be?" Ames asked. "Anything broken?"

"Negative."

"Good. You're going to have to get to the ship's stern," Ames said.

Kyle looked down the length of hull. It seemed an impossible distance. Nearly three hundred feet of steel would challenge his endurance. "I know," he said. The stress in his voice was now unmistakable.

"You hang in there, son. If you need anything, you just let me know. Understood?"

There was a new sentiment in Ames' voice, a tone that Kyle hadn't expected from the captain. In one moment, he had gone from soldier to son. The weather beaten old salt had just given him permission to fail. Kyle recognized it as the reason he retired and it was surely the reason Ames transitioned to the Coast Guard. People had become more important than the mission.

People.

That is exactly how Kyle ended up in this position, hanging from the hull of a cargo ship steaming eastward through the cold Atlantic Ocean, all to save one woman's life. A single, solitary life. If there was a bigger picture, at this moment he didn't know what it was. He had spent his whole adult life believing in and fighting for the bigger picture, pushing the individual to the side. The goal was always to complete the mission regardless of individual consequences. Kyle appreciated the captain's offer. "I understand," he said.

Hanging by outstretched arms with his chest and thighs flat up against the cold painted steel, he craned his neck in both directions, trying to catch a glimpse of the unseen Coast Guard aircraft.

"Hey Captain."

"Yes?"

"When'd you say that chopper was going to be here," Kyle asked.

"About thirty minutes."

"Just make sure he's on time."

"I'll do my best."

Lactic acid coursed through his arms and Kyle thought that his biceps might burst at any second, but he was making good progress and had moved down the port side of the *Revolyutsiya's* hull quicker than he had anticipated. Four agonizing feet at a time he would release and reattach the suction cups, left hand then right, inching upward along the way. Summoning the strength to pull himself topside would be the next challenge.

He dangled from the ship's stern on white knuckles and bulging veins. His arms beginning to quiver and he knew if he didn't get onboard now, he might never make it. The deck of the ship was less than three feet above, but with the little strength he had left it might as well be a mile. If he could cut that distance in half it would make boarding the ship easier.

He depressed the button on the suction cup in his right hand and was surprised when the tool that weighed less than a pound pulled his arm down almost lifelessly to his side. In his haste, Kyle lifted and slapped the suction cup against the stern before it had reset. The cup bounced off the stern, and tumbled into the foaming sea below. The sudden transfer of body weight nearly threw him off the back of the ship. A fall from his position above the ship's enormous prop could easily turn him into ground beef.

Kyle buried his head in his shoulder as he contemplated what had just happened. He had been sloppy and in this type of situation, it's the little mistakes that get you killed.

He composed himself and avoided looking down. With both hands draped over the handle of one suction cup, climbing up to the deck would require that much more strength. He readied himself, took three quick deep breaths and focused on the rail four feet above him. Kyle would aim for the rail and settle for the deck. He counted down in his head: 3-2-1. Just as he made a powerful lurch toward the rail, the single suction cup slipped, negating most of his upward momentum.

Kyle clawed in the air and held on tight when his wrist slammed down on the textured deck of the cargo ship. He let go of the cup with his left hand and brought it up as well to the cold, rough deck.

At this point, he didn't care if he was seen. That would be a situation that he would be glad to deal with. He reached up and grabbed a hold of the rail, swung his legs over the stern and onto the deck.

He rolled on his stomach out from under the stern rail and found cover behind a large loading crane. Forward of him, the *Revolyutsiya's* massive superstructure stood like a castle wall, spanning all but a few meters on each side of the ship's beam. To his left, near the underside of a stairwell that snaked down from above, one of the ship's crew members stood with his back to him.

The crewman didn't look to be anything other than an ordinary seaman. Dressed in tan coveralls over a gray sweatshirt, the sailor had no visible tattoos of the kind that Kyle had seen on the men at the hotel. He appeared to be just another hard working merchant marine that was unaware of the potential trouble aboard and the trouble he was about to be in.

Inching forward in a crouched position, Kyle played out how he would take care of this first obstacle. There were three crates buried under the stairwell, one stacked on top of the other two. It was a nice out of the way spot for the crewman to take a little nap. A quick grab around the neck with the right application of pressure would stop blood flow to the brain and cause a sudden loss of consciousness. *Painless and effective.*

When he was in position, a step behind the crewman, Kyle rose up and began to reach around the man's neck. He was about to deliver the submission hold when the cell phone in his pocket inexplicably went off. The crewman turned and saw Kyle. They shared a look of disbelief as the phone rang out a muffled rendition of "Despacito."

40

T he phone kept ringing, but she didn't pick up. The dynamic of their relationship had changed. She was becoming isolated and that meant the she would soon be uncontrollable.

She must know.

He was curious to know if she had found him out. It's possible that he didn't give the South Americans enough respect with regard to their investigative abilities. He believed that all Latin American countries were naturally corrupt and that they had no real interest in the wellbeing of their citizens. Because they didn't have the resources to burn, the pursuit of justice was usually a short lived endeavor. Apparently, he was wrong. Even so, he had the most important and potentially incriminating piece of evidence in his possession.

Tobias Welke's briefcase.

It was hard to believe that such sensitive information would be carried in such an unsophisticated piece of equipment as a briefcase with two, three dial rotary combination locks. Perhaps, it was better not to draw attention that way.

With the briefcase in his lap, he started with the three-number combination to the left of the briefcase's handle. He applied outward pressure on the left opening mechanism, aligned each of the three dials to zero, and then began rolling the third dial farthest to the right beginning with the number one and proceeding until he reached zero.

Next, he rolled the second dial from the right to the number one so that he had ultimately tested out ten combinations. Beginning again with the dial farthest to the right, he once again rolled in ascending succession until returning to zero where-upon, he rolled the second dial from the right to the number two. Having tested twenty combinations, the strategy was repeated, keeping pressure on the opening mechanism all the while.

On the fifty sixth combination, the latch sprung open. The same number code was applied to the set of three dials to the right of the briefcase handle. Zero, five, six. The lock sprung open on this side as well. The whole process had taken less than two minutes.

The briefcase opened without incident and the inside was unexpectedly neat. Business like. Impressive, even. A pair of designer pens, one made of an exotic wood from the Amazon, the other of ivory from Africa, were secured tightly over a pocket that contained passports from three different countries. In addition to his fraudulent Chilean national status, Welke would also have one believe that he was a citizen of Denmark and South Africa. A United States passport completed the trifecta.

He pulled out a bundle of folders held down by an adjustable strap, and fanned them out on the floor. Each folder contained a picture of a different man and that of a young child. Some contained multiple children. He looked through each folder, interested to know who else had found Mr. Welke's services to their liking.

Some of the men he knew personally and was not surprised

to find their pictures among the folders, other men he had at least heard of and confirmed some of the rumors that had made the rounds with the cocktail crowd. Most, if not all of the men were extremely wealthy and well connected. There was a famous athlete as well as a politician. One surprised him so much, he had to look at the man's picture twice. All were royalty in one form or another.

When he got to his folder, he took his time. He liked the photograph that was chosen. It was taken a few years ago when he was younger and in better shape. Welke snapped the photo of him without his knowledge a few moments before they met for the first time. He smiled at the thought. "That little bastard."

Underneath was a picture of the little girl. She was wearing a bright yellow dress that was made all the more extraordinary by the dark green mountains in the distance behind her. She wore white tennis shoes and smiled broadly as she looked up at her mother holding her by her left hand. Her "tia," or aunty, held her right hand and was dressed in green camouflaged military fatigues that tucked neatly into her boots. She wore her dark hair pinned up and sported a serious pair of aviators.

He ran his fingers over the picture. The smile of a few moments ago had vanished. His eyes narrowed and darted back and forth as he plotted his next move. He had Welke's briefcase now and was beginning to feel invincible.

The fun and games are over, tia.

Cruising down route 27, Ingrid struggled to keep her speed under 75 miles per hour. She appreciated Kyle's hospitality and offer to stay at his home as long as she liked, but she wasn't really one to sit around. In the interest of satisfy his generosity, she'd gone ahead and borrowed his car.

The crumpled receipt that Kyle had retrieved from Tobias Welke's apartment had given her the chills. The receipt was from a restaurant that Edward had invited her to have dinner with him. A dinner date that she had turned down, but that he said he intended to keep. The date and time stamp on Welke's receipt would have placed him in the restaurant at the same time and on the same day as Edward.

By way of the computer in Kyle's office, she used an email retrieval service to see if her colleague, Carlos, had gotten back to her with any information on Tobias Welke, aka, Richard Allen Sawyer. He had.

It wasn't much, but Carlos had discovered that Tobias Welke had been arrested the year before for causing a mild disturbance while intoxicated at a Colombiamoda event. He'd spent the night in a Medellín jail and was released the following morning. He was picked up at the station by one Edward VanRoy.

That was just too much coincidence between these two men for Ingrid to ignore. Add in the family picture that VanRoy had photo bombed and there was no way, at this point, to convince her that Tobias Welke and Edward VanRoy were not conspiring together one way or the other.

She was just outside of Islip when her mind finally slowed down enough to make sense of the events of the last twenty-four hours. A freak accident and chance encounter had led her here and given her hope that a family torn apart by tragedy would soon begin the road to discovery and recovery. She began to have hope that Marlena would be found and reunited with her family.

Ingrid glanced at the speedometer on the Mustang. Eighty miles an hour. She eased up on the gas. Almost a half a year had passed since she last saw her niece and the emotions that bubbled under the surface were as strong today as they were when she first learned that Marlena went missing.

She wasn't happy that Welke was dead. There were a lot of questions that she would have liked to have asked him. Edward VanRoy was still very much alive and she believed more than ever now that he held the key.

Ingrid had played his game long enough. She knew she was close to getting to the truth. Going to the police first however, would not be the best option. With VanRoy's wealth and celebrity status, she was sure that her allegation would fall on deaf ears. She wanted answers. Kyle's gun sat on the seat next to her. It was time to deliver that raincheck she'd promised him.

41

"It's for you." Kyle held the cell phone out to the startled crewman. "Despacito" was still playing out of the phone's tiny speaker. Without thinking, the crewman reached for the phone. With his free hand, Kyle grabbed the sailor's arm and jerked him forward, lowered his head and delivered a knockout blow to the crewman's chin.

One down.

If Ames's source at the port authority was correct, there could be as many as nine more men aboard, not including a few special guests.

Kyle took two of the half dozen life vests from their position on the bulkhead and secured them on the unconscious sailor. Using a length of one-inch thick nylon line that he found coiled up under the stairwell, Kyle fastened one end to the limp sailor and the other to the ship's bottom transom rail. He carried the crewman over his shoulder to the stern and heaved him overboard. The sailor hit the water hard, but the life vests did their job righting his body and keeping his head above water. A hundred feet later, when the slack in the line was finally taken up, the sailor spun around so that he was being towed backward.

Seawater rolled over his shoulders and formed an eddy under his chin. The crewman would live, but it would be a while before anyone knew he was missing.

Ducking behind the crates for cover, Kyle pulled out his cell phone and checked the home screen.

Missed Call: Edward

Shit.

Dunn's voice crackled through Kyle's earpiece, "Everything okay?"

"So far, yes. It seems I've taken Ms. Garcia's cell phone by mistake, that's all." Kyle said.

"Have you encountered any resistance yet?" Dunn asked.

"I ran into sailor who was eager to dance," Kyle said. "You know how those Navy boys are."

"Very funny, soldier." Ames voice boomed through Kyle's headset.

"Did you take care of him?" Dunn asked.

Kyle looked out over the stern rail to check on the sailor. The unconscious crewman was still upright and attached to the line. "Affirmative," Kyle said. "I sent him for a little swim."

"Alright, well the chopper is still on schedule, look for the woman and get up high where they can see you."

"Roger, that," Kyle said.

He wiped off Ingrid's phone and put it back in his watertight pocket. A gust of wind whipped over the stern bringing with it droplets of sea water that gathered on Kyle's face. Cool, wet, salty beads that ran down his cheeks like tears. He brushed them off. If this ship was indeed carrying the woman abducted at the hotel, he doubted he would find her out here on the open deck. It was more than likely she was concealed away in a cargo hold in the belly of the ship like contraband. Or, she was holed up within the ship's superstructure that towered above him.

Cavasano's help wasn't necessary to push the gurney, but he wasn't about to take his hand off it. His partner was in bad shape. An oxygen mask covered part of his face. An IV tube snaked out of his hand. Frank Merylo suddenly looked very old.

A small group of onlookers gathered across the street from the storefront. A couple of boys in their teens hovered around the ambulance craning their necks as the paramedics got ready to load Merylo into the back.

Three more gurneys exited the grocery store, one at a time. With these, there were no oxygen masks and no IV's. The occupants were zipped up in heavy duty, 15 mil, blue vinyl, reinforced PVC body bags. When the teenage boys saw this, they hurried over to get a better look.

Before he was loaded into the ambulance, Merylo pulled his oxygen mask aside and lifted his head up. "You did good, Joe."

Cavasano patted his partner's leg. It was the first time his partner had called him by his first name. "You going soft on me now, Frank?"

"Hell no," Merylo said. "Go get those bastards." The exertion made him cough and before he could say anymore, one of the paramedics quickly placed the oxygen mask back over his mouth.

"Don't you dare die on me you, miserable son-of-a-bitch," Cavasano said.

Merylo furrowed his brow and mumbled something indiscernible through his oxygen mask.

"I'm gonna follow you to the hospital, Frank. I'll be right behind you." Cavasano stood almost paralyzed as the medics loaded Merylo into the ambulance and closed the door. In the course of twenty-four hours he had lost the first partner to which he'd been assigned as a detective, at least temporarily. He couldn't imagine the pain that Merylo felt in losing a longtime partner forever to the likes of a scumbag like Josef. The ambulance siren echoed off of concrete and steel as it pulled away from the curb.

The transit rattled overhead coming to a stop at the 3rd Street entrance. NYPD pushed back a growing crowd gathering around the three dead bodies that were being loaded into the waiting ambulances. Cavasano looked down at his hands. Dried blood crusted on the soft flesh between his thumb and index finger. His cell phone rang.

"Cavasano," he answered. He tugged at his slacks. A dark wet stain at the knee was sticking to his skin.

It was Moses from the station. "Hey Joe," he said. "We've got a real-time track on Kyle Murdoch's cell phone like you asked. He's just outside Amityville, traveling west on the Sunrise Highway. Looks like he's coming back from out on Long Island. If he stays on this route, he could be back in the city in a little over an hour."

Cavasano looked at his watch. "Okay. Thanks, Moses," he said. "I'll keep in touch with you." He hung up. The ambulance carrying Merylo made a left turn and disappeared from view.

The real time tracking on Kyle Murdoch's cell phone had been successful. Moses was keeping an eye on it. There was nowhere in the greater New York area and vicinity that Kyle's cell phone could go without Moses knowing about it.

42

Kyle worked his way around to the starboard side of the superstructure. Another stairwell snaked down from above and he crouched beneath it. Not yet ready to get out in the open spaces of the cargo ship, he paused and pondered his next move. It would be difficult under the circumstances to proceed undetected. Without the cover of darkness, his dry suit would stick out like a sore thumb even in the relative blanket of gray mist. He did not relish the thought of being seen through the scope of a rifle as he blindly searched for someone who might not even be aboard the ship. Fortunately, it wouldn't come to that.

From above, the steel steps pinged. Whoever it was coming down the steps did so in pain or with caution or both. As the footsteps grew nearer, Kyle could tell the person was a man, descending the stairs with caution. He was coming down sideways, one rain slicked step at a time. This was not just another crew member, however. This man had on dark gray pants with a wide blue stripe. It was the captain. Just the person he was hoping to see.

He crouched down and got as far under the stairway as he

could. The pair of black boots were three steps from the deck. As the captain's left foot came down on the second step, Kyle made his move. He sprung both hands through the opening in the metal stairs and grabbed hold of the black boot. With all his strength he yanked the man's foot out from underneath him, sending the sailor crashing to the deck.

Before the captain could get his bearings, Kyle was out from behind the stairs with his knife at the man's throat. "Don't make a sound," he warned. He dragged the captain back under the stairs.

"My hip, I think it's broken," the man cried as he clutched the side of his left leg.

Kyle pushed the knife into the loose skin under the man's chin. "I guess you didn't hear me."

The captain swallowed hard.

"I'm going to ask you some questions and I only want you to nod your head for yes or shake your head for no. Do you understand?"

The man nodded his head.

"Good." Kyle poked his head out from under the stairs and scanned for any crewmen in the vicinity. The coast was clear. He turned back to his subject. "Are you the captain of this vessel?"

"I am-"

Kyle pushed the knife harder into the man's neck. "We're having trouble following orders, captain," he said. "One more time. Are you the captain of this vessel?"

The captain nodded.

"That's better," Kyle said. "Is this vessel headed for Russia?"

"Da."

Kyle put more pressure on the knife. "Just nod, please."

The captain nodded frantically.

"Good. Did you take on any passengers while you were at dock last night? Any non-crew members?"

The captain nodded that yes, he had.

"How many?"

With this question, the captain was confused. He had already been instructed rather forcefully to answer only yes or no to Kyle's questions. Not wishing to feel the sharp edge of the knife again, he remained silent as his eyes grew wide.

Again, Kyle persuaded him with the knife.

"Two," the captain yelped.

"Was one of those passengers a woman?"

He returned to nodding.

"A Japanese woman?"

The captain shrugged.

Kyle applied pressure to the knife. "Take a guess."

The captain again nodded furiously.

"Good." The two men exchanged stares as Kyle stood up. He checked the walkway to make sure there were no crewmen in the vicinity. Still clear. "Where were you going before our little meeting, here?"

The captain looked silently at the American.

Kyle stepped on the captain's injured hip. "New rule captain, answer my question, but speak softly."

The captain moaned in pain, barely able to spit out the words. "To the galley."

"Lunch time?" Kyle kept his foot on the captain's leg. "Since when does a captain fetch his own food?"

"Not for me. For the Mafiya," he sputtered.

"Mafiya? Kyle asked. "How many Mafiya?"

"One."

Kyle remembered seeing three at the hotel and then two at the hospital. "Where are the others?"

"I don't know."

Kyle leaned on the captain's leg.

"I swear it," the captain winced. "Two came aboard, but only one stayed."

"Where would I find the Mafiya on this ship?"

"Second level stateroom." Drogzvic nodded in the direction of the stairs, his face was a mask of agony.

"And the girl?"

"The same."

Kyle hesitated before asking his next question. "She's still alive?"

"Yes," the captain said. "I want them both off my ship."

"I think I can help out with that," Kyle said. "You just listen to me or you're going to have more than a broken hip."

Drogzvic nodded his understanding.

Kyle sheathed his knife and pulled the captain up by his coat lapels. The *Revolyutsiya's* captain groaned and sighed as he leaned against the bulkhead for support.

Kyle said, "What's your name, captain?"

The weathered sailor stood as tall as he could. Feebly, he rolled his shoulders back trying to project even the smallest amount of confidence. "My name is Captain Drogzvic."

"Well, Captain Drogzvic, I'd like to assist you with that lunch request," Kyle said. "Why don't you show me to the galley."

A yumi spat on him. Over the last several hours she had become increasingly hostile. Niko wiped her saliva from the side of his nose and took three long steps back. She swore at him in his native tongue and out right challenged him to kill her.

He just stood and stared at her, captivated by her beauty and at the same time enraged by her actions. He wanted to be able to hold her beautiful head in his hands and break her neck. For that, he would have to wait until he was given an order. All he could do until then was fantasize.

In the meantime, Niko had directed his frustrations at the *Revolyutsiya's* captain, a traitor who works for a free market capitalist pig. Wealthy Russian capitalists and those who worked for them always amused Niko. For no matter how large their portfolios were and how hefty their bank accounts, business in Russia did not move unless men like Niko allowed it to move. At the end of the day, the captain and his employer had to ask for permission or protection from people like Niko.

To prove his point, Niko sent the pathetic Captain Drogzvic to get him some food. Convinced him was more like it. Niko took pleasure in the expression on the fat pig's face once he had a nine-millimeter stuck in his ear. The captain had almost wet himself on the spot. The big Russian chuckled at the thought.

The woman had finally calmed down. She now sat on the edge of the bed, arms wrapped around her, hugging herself. Her eyes were filled with rage. Niko smiled. Seconds later, a heavy knock sounded on the stateroom door. Instinctively, Niko unlocked the safety on his gun before going and unlocking the metal stateroom door.

He stepped back into the middle of the room and fingered the lock on his gun one more time just to be sure it was off. He hid the gun behind his back and answered, "The door is open."

The door opened and Captain Drogzvic stood in the doorway holding a wooden folding tray. Behind him, a cook in a white t-shirt, apron and hat held a large silver serving platter with a covered plate, a bowl of borscht and a loaf of bread. The cook's t-shirt was tight and his apron marked messily with food extracts. "Your meal," Drogzvic said.

Niko nodded for the men to come inside. He was impressed with the captain's expediency. Then again, capitalist pigs were always aiming to please. No doubt that if this vessel were owned by the state, he'd be lucky to see his meal before sunset. He motioned to Drogzvic to set up the folding tray close to the bed in front of the woman. The captain moved with a noticeable limp.

The cook followed, partially obstructed from Niko's view by the Captain. He craned his neck to get a good look as the cook hurried by and felt an uneasy familiarity about the man. The cook's uniform looked a couple sizes too small, enhancing his athletic physique, but it wasn't his build that gave Niko pause. It was something else. He thought he saw something or rather felt something when the cook first walked in the room. It was fleeting and it put him on alert, until Drogzvic opened his mouth.

"I will send a bottle of vodka," the Captain said.

"I want one of *your* bottles," Niko said. "Not one of the shit bottles you give to the crew."

While Niko and Drogzvic continued their conversation, the cook took the bowl of borscht and loaf of black bread from the serving tray and placed them off to the side on the wood tray table. Next, he set the covered plate in the middle and lifted the lid revealing a plate of beef pelmeni topped with vinegar and dill. A fork and spoon were wrapped in a napkin and tied with a red nylon ribbon.

Ayumi initially regarded the captain and cook with equal disdain. Particularly the captain. Having been brought up in a family whose work revolved around seafaring vessels, she knew what the captain's responsibilities were and knew that they didn't change regardless of ship size. This captain had compromised his duties. The cook however, was a different story.

She thought that she'd seen him wink at her when he entered the room. As he brought the platter of food, his eyes were fixed to hers and so she maintained a defiant eye contact.

Once he set the food down, she noticed his eyes were welcoming and reassuring.

The cook then untied the ribbon that held the silverware together and unwrapped the napkin. In tiny letters written inside was the singular word, *Tora?* She had seen these eyes before. On the window washer from the hotel.

43

The cook or window washer, whoever he was, gestured to her with his eyes, rolling them toward the doorway and she realized that she hadn't misread him. She glanced at her captor to see if he'd noticed the exchange, but he was busy with the Captain. Turning back to the cook, she held his gaze, trying to communicate non-verbally while the others began to argue.

"What do you mean you have no caviar," Niko said. "This is a capitalist owned vessel."

"This is not a cruise ship," Drogzvic replied.

While the two debated the free market and sturgeon eggs, Kyle pretended to fiddle with the newly arrived food, arranging the dishes under the false pretense of culinary snobbery, he even went so far as to wipe the edge of the plate with a napkin, all the while communicating with Ayumi without uttering a word. She followed his eyes as he glanced down at the steaming bowl of borscht and understood his intentions when he turned his head and eyes ever so slightly in the direction of the big Russian.

Kyle patted the wooden tray with the middle three fingers of his right hand and waited for a sign that the woman understood what he meant. She indicated that she did with a barely perceptible dip of her head. Kyle then placed his index finger on the tray to signal the number one. Waiting a second, he indicated the count of two with his middle finger. The woman wrapped her right hand around the bowl of borscht and shifted her weight forward on the edge of the bed, ready to spring off it and toward the door.

Just then, two crewmen appeared in the stateroom doorway. One of the men was soaking wet and smelled of seawater. The other was animated and described how he just rescued his colleague from the sea after being tied to the stern of the ship.

It could have been the woman's slight movement or simply that he realized that while he was engaged in the conversation between Captain Drogzvic and his crew members, he had almost forgotten about the cook and the woman. Whatever it was, something drew Niko's attention their way. The woman was leaning forward on the edge of the bed looking up at him with intention. He noticed she had one hand wrapped around the bowl of borscht while her other hand held a fork.

Looking closer, Niko saw that the cook was wearing dive shoes and he detected the possibility of a wet suit under his white culinary uniform. A thin black wire snaked up the man's neck and into his right ear.

At the same time, the drenched crewman in the stateroom doorway pointed to the cook and shouted, "Vot on!" *There he is!*

Kyle turned and saw the crewman that he had earlier thrown over the back of the ship. "Uh, oh." He shouted, "Three!"

Before Niko had a chance to raise the gun from his side, he was hit broadside in the face with a scalding hot bowl of beet root soup. Ayumi flipped the wood tray table out of her way and landed a solid kick that knocked the gun from Niko's hand.

The two crewmen bolted from the doorway and charged into

the room, shoving Captain Drogzvic out of the way. Kyle threw the silver serving tray backhand like a disc, striking the first sailor between the eyes and knocking him to the floor.

Ayumi launched forward and attacked the big Russian who was wiping borscht from his face, plunging the fork deep into his left breast just below his shoulder. She took a step back to give herself some space then landed a perfectly positioned forward jump kick to Niko's jaw, sending him flailing backward where he tumbled over one of the already prone crewmen.

The second sailor, dripping wet from having been tossed overboard, clicked open a switchblade and lunged at the imposter cook. Kyle fended off the crewman's slashes and jabs with the knife by using the plate cover as a shield, but the sailor kept coming, forcing Kyle backwards onto the bed. Ayumi cut the seaman down with hard kick to his knee. Kyle rendered him unconscious with a kick to the side of his head.

Kyle sprung off of the bed and grabbed Ayumi's hand. "Come on." Together, they bolted across the stateroom, knocking Drogzvic into the pile of bodies on their way out the door.

Kyle led them up the steel steps to the top of the cargo ship's superstructure. The outside observation deck formed an upper-case "T" and allowed for easy viewing of the entire ship. Every square meter of the *Revolyutsiya's* deck was covered by shipping containers. A variety of colors stacked on top of one another. But the location offered nothing in the way of refuge.

Kyle slipped out of the apron and hat, crumpled them into a ball and threw them across the observation deck. "I've got a heli-copter coming," he said. He took off the cook's white t shirt and pants.

The wind had picked up and at this altitude, shouting became a requirement. "They'll catch us up here," Ayumi said. She clawed at strands of black hair that whipped across her face.

She was right. At the moment, there was nowhere to run. Kyle scanned the horizon in all directions looking for signs that the coast guard helicopter was close at hand. Visibility was low, and if the helicopter was nearby, he couldn't see it.

Ayumi got down on both knees. The height of the super-structure combined with the wind to have a debilitating effect on her senses. The railing surrounding the perimeter gave her no comfort. She remained motionless with her arms spread wide and her hair thrashing across her face.

Kyle knelt down beside her. "Guardian Angel, this is Mako. Can you hear me?" Kyle called.

There was a long moment of silence. Kyle tried again. "Guardian Angel, this is Mako. Come in?"

This time Ames' voice filtered through his earpiece. His voice was even lower than usual. "Go ahead, soldier."

Kyle sensed a problem. "I've got her, Captain," he said. "How far away is that bird of yours?"

"I'm afraid that chopper isn't going to make it anytime soon." Ames's words were strung together with regret.

"Come again."

"There's been an emergency back at the Vineyard. The chopper had to turn back." Ames apologized. "I promise you I'll find a way to get you out of there, but you'll have to hold tight."

"Hold tight?" Ayumi was shivering. Kyle instinctively put an arm around her. "We don't have the luxury," he said. "Rick?" He called out for his father's lifelong friend.

"The ship should have some inflatable life rafts," Dunn said. "May be best to use one of them for now It'll buy you some time."

"Rick is right, Kyle. We can make a recovery from the raft with the Jayhawk when one becomes available," Ames chimed in. "The life raft is your best hope."

"Roger, that," Kyle answered.

The *Revolyutsiya's* superstructure was like a four-story steel apartment building connected by a network of stairs positioned on the port and starboard sides that accessed each floor before eventually leading down to the main deck. Kyle helped Ayumi up and together they ran for the stairs to exit the observation deck on its port side. Kyle hurried down the stairs first, Ayumi followed slowly behind.

As they passed by the second story landing, they heard gunshots, two in quick secession followed moments later by a third. Kyle hustled down the metal steps imploring Ayumi to move faster. When he'd reached the bottom of the stairs on the main deck, Kyle turned to reach up and help her down the last few steps. Without warning, a thick braided line wrapped around his neck and pulled him away from the stairs.

Ayumi saw the crewman attack Kyle from behind. A second seaman appeared and approached Kyle from his front with a fire ax. Without hesitating, she leapt over the rail and onto the sailor with the ax, knocking him down and separating him from his weapon.

Kyle twisted his waist and then hammered home two fist shots to the sailor's ribs. The seaman loosened his grip on the line around Kyle's neck and doubled over in pain. Kyle spun another quarter turn and then brought his knee up quickly, driving it into the crewman's face.

The sailor that Ayumi had tangled with was back on his feet with the ax in his hand. She stood in a defensive posture waiting for him to make a move. The sailor raised the ax above his head and charged at her. When he was in striking distance, he brought the head of the ax down hard.

Ayumi moved, but only slightly. Keeping her balance and composure, she shifted her weight to her left leg while using her right arm to deflect the ax at its handle on its descent. She then spun to her right and brought her left arm up and placed her elbow into the face of her attacker. The ax continued its downward momentum at a new angle that ended in the sailor's leg, just above his left foot. The follow through with her left arm put him flat on his back.

With both crewmen incapacitated, Kyle led Ayumi toward the stern of the boat. Strapped to a cradle just over the port railing were two, white, three-foot-long, fiberglass containers. The containers were split into two halves, held together and secured to the cradle by a nylon lashing. A length of line poked out of the seam in each half and was anchored to a bolt on the cradle. An identical pair had been spotted on the stern's starboard side. Kyle had seen them when he first boarded the ship and recognized them as the ship's inflatable life rafts.

Printed in blue paint on the outside of the containers was the number 10. Kyle read a label affixed to the container and discovered that the fiberglass container weighed 87 kilograms. He did a quick mental conversion and figured the ten-person raft's weight to be just less than 200 pounds.

Kyle called to Ayumi. "Give me a hand." He undid the lashing that secured the container to its cradle.

Ayumi positioned herself across from Kyle on the other end of the container. He doubted whether she could lift the container up in her weakened condition so he convinced her not to try.

"All we have to do is roll it off its cradle over the railing. Don't lift, just push," he said.

Ayumi nodded her head, placed her hands on the back of the container and then waited for Kyle to give a signal.

"On the count of three. One...two...three." With that, they pushed the fiberglass container over the railing.

The container had tumbled a quarter of the way to the sea below when the painter line that was attached to both the cradle and the raft became taut. The sweet sound of compressed air being released was unmistakable as the painter line pulled the plunger out of the gas cylinder and began inflating the life raft.

Fifteen seconds later, the raft was fully inflated and bobbing on the waves below them. Kyle turned to help Ayumi up over the railing, but he was too slow. She had already wriggled through the rungs of the railing and had jumped into the dark waters below. He looked down and saw her swimming with conviction toward the raft. He threw his legs over the railing, steadied himself and then joined her in the choppy sea.

Niko emerged on the observation deck, having come up from the starboard side. Winded and stained purple from the borscht soup, he scanned the fore deck frantically for any signs of the American and the woman. They were nowhere to be seen. He searched aft. Nothing. He scanned the port side and that's when he saw them, out in the water, climbing into an inflatable life raft and drifting quickly away from the *Revolyutsiya*.

He had no choice. Starting from the starboard end of the observation deck, Niko took off running as fast as he could. He made a strong jump when he neared the end of the deck and pushed off of the railing with his right foot. He needed to clear a span of less than six feet from the edge of the observation deck above to the railing on the main deck below. Having jumped from a height of over four stories above the main deck, he let out a primal scream as he lunged for the cold waters of the Atlantic below.

44

K yle put his right hand on Ayumi's backside and pushed. Weak from the events of the last twenty-four hours and exhausted from battling the choppy waves of the Atlantic, she tumbled face first and rolled to a stop in the middle of the raft. Kyle followed, pulling himself up the flimsy nylon ladder and crawling through the entrance flap into the large life saving device.

Ayumi was lying still on her back, her eyes were closed and her hair matted across her face. Her stomach strained to rise as she inhaled against the heavy, wet sweatshirt that pinned her down to the raft.

Kyle knelt over her and brushed her hair aside. "Are you okay?"

She nodded and lifted a cold, delicate hand to touch his face. "Thank you."

Ames voice crackled in Kyle's earpiece. "Talk to me son."

"Give me a couple minutes, captain," Kyle replied.

He took Ayumi's hand in his and gave it a gentle squeeze. "I'm going to get you home," he said. "I promise you."

Next to the entrance flap and fitted to the raft where the

canopy met the floor, an emergency survival and repair kit was situated. The pack contained signaling torches, food, drinking water and a first-aid kit, a fishing kit, seasickness bags, a whistle, a floating knife and tools and material to repair the life raft. On the other side of the entrance flap were a pair of oars and rescue line with a rubber ring attached to the end. This last item is what Kyle was looking for.

He went about letting out thirty meters of stiff nylon rope. Ayumi got to her knees and helped keep the half inch thick line from tangling. Kyle used his knife and cut off the rubber life-saving ring on the end. He would save that for later. In the meantime, using a pair a scissors from the first-aid kit, he proceeded to cut small holes in the thick canopy every ten inches, careful to make the openings as circular as possible.

Kyle stood in the opening of the enclosed raft and Ayumi fed him safety line from within as he fished it through the holes he had just cut from the outside. When they had threaded all of the holes, Kyle cut two more in the top of the canopy and fed more line through and fashioned it into a strangle-knot with two-foot diameter loop. Inside the raft he reattached the rubber safety ring to the end of the rope to be used as a pull.

Outside, hidden by the waves, a dangerous predator inched closer to the raft.

"What is that going to do?" Ayumi asked.

Kyle adjusted one of the lines. "Hopefully, get us out of here."

Ames' deep voice boomed through Kyle's earpiece, "Time's up, soldier."

"Got it, Captain," Kyle said. "Now, how good is that pilot of yours?"

"Sidwell?" Ames did not hesitate. "He's the best."

"I hope so."

"What have you got in mind?"

Kyle explained, "I need him to thread the needle."

"Keep talking." Ames was patient.

Kyle went on, "I've fastened a snare with a two-foot opening. It's attached to the raft six feet above sea level. I need you to let out enough line from the windlass through the cargo hatch, and then I need Sidwell to thread the hook through the loop."

Silence.

Up in the Coast Guard's jet, Ames buried the flexible mouthpiece in his fist. He turned to Dunn. "He's joking right."

Dunn shook his head and covered his mic, "I don't think so."

"Sidwell," Ames called.

"I hear you captain," the pilot answered.

"Is it possible to-"

"Thread the needle. Yes, sir. Been there, done that."

"What about retrieving cargo?" Ames asked.

"Did it in a seaplane once," the pilot answered.

"What are the odds?"

"It's bad luck to announce the odds before you roll the dice Sir."

"Shit," Ames said. For the first time in a long time, Ames looked to another man for confirmation. "Richard?"

"We should probably make sure our life vests are secure." Dunn offered.

Ames positioned the microphone just below his bottom lip, "Sidwell, you know how I feel about gambling."

"Yes, sir," the pilot answered. "You hate to lose, sir."

"That's right," Ames replied. "Kyle, I hope you know what you're doing."

Kyle's voice scratched over the crew's headsets, competing with the stiffening North Atlantic breeze. "We'll find out soon enough."

The Ocean Sentry roared loudly overhead, banked hard to the north, and set about coming around for a run at the raft.

Everything must be timed correctly. Kyle would stay where he was, standing in the opening of the raft with the entrance flap licking the back of his legs. From here, he could make certain that the hook on the end of the cargo cable found its way into the loop of the snare.

Kyle ducked his head into the darkened confines of the raft. Ayumi was kneeling in the center and had threaded her slender left arm through the center of the rubber rescue doughnut. Nylon rope snaked around her torso and under her arms. If the raft's canvass did not hold, at least Ayumi would still be rescued.

Kyle could see her shivering hard against her wet clothes as she gripped herself tightly in a bear hug. Her bottom jaw twitched uncontrollably. Her eyes found Kyle's and locked in, pools of obsidian hidden behind scattered strands of black hair. She nodded her head to indicate that she was ready to go.

He straightened up outside the shelter of the raft and held the precious loop with both hands. Mother Nature was not playing nice. Kyle squinted against the spray of saltwater that pricked at his face. He leaned heavily against the polypropylene wall of the life raft trying to absorb the impact of the waves as they lifted and then dropped the raft. Keeping the rope erect and maintaining its shape was proving to be a challenge. He hoped that Sidwell would get there soon.

Niko kept going. Although he could no longer feel his extremities, he forced them into motion, refusing to be denied his ultimate goal. He would rather die, consumed by the Atlantic, than not reach it. He was only five meters away now. The American was standing with his back to the water, the raft's entrance flap draped down in front of his legs concealing the inside.

He swam harder performing a crude, but effective, variation of the breaststroke. He was careful not to have his entire head exposed for any length of time. The American still had his back turned, oblivious to his presence. He filled his lungs with chilly Atlantic air and then ducked beneath the waves. He swam the last two meters underwater until the blurred outline of the life raft's red nylon ladder came into view.

Niko hung onto the ladder, a flimsy rung tucked under his left arm. He breached the surface silently. The crown of his head surfaced first, dark wet hair camouflaged against the blackened sea. Slowly, he raised himself. When his nose finally cleared the waterline, he resisted the urge to hastily empty and then refill lungs. No need to announce his arrival. The floor of the raft was raised a foot and a half above sea level. From his vantage point, he could not see inside the raft. He did not need to. He knew she was in there.

Niko was ready. He was ready to lunge up, grab the American, and pull him into the dark water. He would hold him under like he would a stray cat, until there was no more movement, no more bubbles, and no more frantic clawing. He would enjoy it.

His pleasant thoughts were interrupted by the sound of a low flying aircraft. The plane approached from the north and seemed to be making a course right toward the raft. A cable dangled and trailed behind the jet. Niko kept low in the water. He did not want to be spotted. As the plane came near, he took a chest full of air and submerged himself under the raft.

"Get ready!" Kyle shouted above the lapping waves and the approaching din of the Ocean Sentry.

"Ready," Ayumi answered from inside the raft. She braced herself.

Sidwell was bringing the aircraft in as low and as slow as was possible. From his vantage point, it looked to Kyle that the end of the cable was on a direct course with his snare. Ames had been right about his pilot.

In a matter of seconds, the jet was on top of them. The cable trailing out of the plane's cargo hatch was speeding toward the raft.

Kyle kept his nerve. He had to be sure that the huge hook at the end of the cable was going to hit its imaginary target in the center of the snare.

It did.

In the cockpit, Sidwell's fingers danced on the throttle. His senses were on alert, prepared to counter the resistance of the raft the instant he felt the plane struggle. "Hold on," he said. It was more suggestion than command.

Ames and Dunn each took hold of a pair of overhead handles. Ames forced a nervous smile.

"Now!" Kyle dove into the raft and held on to Ayumi.

The snare caught and the raft lifted out of the sea with a loud "pop". A half second later she and Kyle were thrust into the bulkhead of the raft. G forces kept them there. The polypropylene roof creaked in protest, pinched savagely by the nylon rope, but ultimately held strong.

Ayumi lay pressed against Kyle as the raft gained altitude. He had one arm around her waist and his other arm and one leg tangled in the braided nylon handholds that lined the inside perimeter of the raft. Ayumi kept her head buried in his chest as the raft spun like a wind sock on a breezy autumn day. She kept her eyes closed to avoid its dizzying spell.

"How are you doing son?" Kyle's earpiece suddenly came to life at the sound of Ames' voice.

"Pinned down at the moment, but otherwise in good shape," Kyle answered.

Ames said, "As soon as Sidwell levels off the aircraft the G forces will subside and you won't be so restricted. You might be able to move around a little bit."

Kyle tucked his chin in and caught a glimpse of Ayumi. Her eyes were shut. She was not squinting as if forcing her eyes closed. She looked relaxed. Her lips were parted and puckered slightly from having her cheek pressed against his chest. "We're in no hurry captain," he answered.

"How is the woman," Dunn asked.

"She's-." Kyle started to speak and then stopped. Ayumi had opened her eyes and gave him a smile. "The woman is fine," he said.

Ames cut in, "Alright. In just a few minutes we'll start reeling you in," he said. "In the meantime, enjoy the ride."

45

VanRoy got in the back of the taxi and slammed the door. "Twenty third and first, please." As the cabbie pulled away from the curb, he cursed under his breath, "Bitch."

The driver made eye contact via the rear-view mirror and VanRoy stared back at him until the driver looked away.

It was one thing when Ingrid rebuffed his invitation to dinner, even if her excuse was a lie. It was quite another to ignore him altogether. It was time to find her and speak with her in person, make sure that everything was "okay." Of course, he knew that wasn't true.

In truth, he cared little about her well-being. Ingrid didn't make for much of a girlfriend. In the several months that they'd known each other he hadn't received so much as a peck on the cheek. Not that it mattered, as he preferred his "girlfriends" a bit younger.

The problem with Ingrid was that she was an extremely dedicated family member as well as a highly trained member of the Colombian Special Forces. He'd heard that she helped rescue Señora Béntancourt from the FARC and protected U.S.

Presidents George Bush and Barack Obama when the two men had visited her country.

VanRoy had bombarded her with nonsense magazine cover modeling offers and parties with the city's elite to distract her and prevent her from investigating her niece's disappearance. Meeting her on the flight from Medellín to New York and bumping her up to first class was a stroke of hubris and genius. He'd done his best to keep her close in order to prevent her from discovering any of the extracurricular business that he was involved with. As well as to find out how much, if anything, she knew.

Now, the events of the weekend were causing him concern. He had been scheduled to meet with a business associate, Mr. Welke, to discuss the particulars of his upcoming trip to Chacachacare, Trinidad and Tobago. Unfortunately, Mr. Welke was killed in an accident outside the UN Millennium Hotel late yesterday afternoon. Right around the time that Ingrid began making excuses not to see him.

It might be his paranoia, but he couldn't take the chance that she had managed to somehow uncover his dirty laundry. His phone calls to her were going unanswered and the sudden lack of communication made him more than a little anxious.

He took solace in having stolen Welke's briefcase. The dirty bastard liked to brag that he'd never get caught via the internet because he didn't do any business or correspondence online. All of his business was done old school, in person and all his contacts were in hardcopy form in his briefcase. The one that was now on the floor of a cab in New York city between Edward VanRoy's legs.

VanRoy stuck his hand in his pocket and felt the flat, rigid outline of the key to Ingrid's apartment. It would be easiest to wait for her there. Maybe she'd actually been looking after a friend like she mentioned when they last spoke. Or maybe she had spoken to the police. He kept an eye on the driver through the rear-view mirror while he pulled on a pair of tight-fitting leather gloves and clenched his fist. Either way, it was always better being safe as opposed to being sorry.

Ingrid was just outside of Queens when she realized that it had been quite some time since she'd last heard from Edward. The man was nothing, if not annoyingly persistent. Reaching into her back pocket, she pulled out her cell phone to check for any missed calls. With one hand on the steering wheel, she punched in her security code to unlock the phone. Nothing. She tried again. Nothing. She had three more tries to get the code right. Holding the phone close, she got a better look. The phone wasn't hers. She had taken Kyle's by accident. "Dammit." She pounded the steering wheel.

She hadn't spoken to VanRoy since last night back at her apartment. Given his personality, it was likely that her recent disappearing act would be perceived as suspicious. He would probably have a lot of questions for her as soon as he had the chance so, she decided to continue to play it cool. She didn't want to tip him off. Not yet.

After getting him to take the bait on the flight from Medellín to New York and keeping him on the hook for months, Ingrid didn't want him to swim free, now. If he got spooked by her sudden lack of communication, it might mean that he had come to the realization that she had discovered who he really was.

She'd pretended to be friends with this monster for nearly four months in order to discover the whereabouts of her niece. Now that the *Chilean* also known as, Tobias Welke, was dead, Edward VanRoy might be the only one left who could tell her where Marlena was. She ran her fingers over the handle of

Kyle's gun on the seat next to her. So, she had a lot of questions for him too.

D mitri stood outside the garage and drew in a heavy lungful of cigarette smoke. Ilya had done a masterful job ensuring that it would be impossible to identify the remains of the garage's previous owner, Andrily Vasilyev. He'd cut off every fingertip with a pair of tin snips and knocked out every tooth with the air chisel. Using an acetylene torch, he burned off all of Andrily's tattoos. Lastly and most brazenly, he used a hacksaw to remove Andrily's head. Ilya casually mentioned dissolving the head, fingers and teeth in a bath of lye and disposing the rest of body in the East River. "Without its essentials," Ilya had said. "A body could not be identified. No need to waste time fucking with it." The young man was psychotic. Dmitri was very impressed.

Ilya opened the side door to garage and stuck his head out. "All is completed," he said matter-of-factly, before closing the door.

Dmitri took another draw on his smoke. He liked Ilya. The young man was efficient and pragmatic. Unlike the former Alex, who was wild and unpredictable, Ilya seemed to Dmitri to understand self-control and discretion and he was impressed at how quickly and dutifully he'd taken care of Andrily with only the slightest of suggestion. He'd make a good soldier, for sure.

He hadn't yet been able to get in touch with Niko and was becoming personally concerned about his inability to provide proof that the Japanese woman was alive and unharmed. He'd sent an urgent email to the *Revolyutsiya's* captain with instructions to have Niko contact him immediately. In the meantime, he was desperate to receive payment from Koba for the hit on Mr. Sakai.

As if on cue, his cell phone rang.

"How are you my friend?" Koba asked.

Dmitri didn't let the conversation get too far before cutting him off. "Enough with the bullshit," he said. "I want the money, now."

"My, how quickly you've lost your dignity," Koba said. "I'll need proof that you've held up your end of the contract."

"Turn on your television set," Dmitri said.

"I've seen the news reports, you fucking *Khokhol*." Koba said. "I'm happy to hear the woman has gone *missing*. However, dead is a much more permanent state of being."

"Give me the rest of the money and you will also hear reports that she has died," Dmitri answered.

The phone went silent for several moments. Long enough for Dmitri to question if the call had been disconnected.

"Very well. I can deliver the money to you today, in person," Koba offered.

He must be in New York City, Dmitri thought. "That's more like it. Have my money ready and meet me at the apartment building at twenty third and first avenue. Apartment two, zero, zero, four."

Koba paused before answering. "As you like. I look forward to finally meeting you."

With the call ended, Dmitri dropped his cigarette to the pavement and extinguished it with the heel of his shoe. To hell with the window washer. If he happened to be at Ms. Garcia's apartment, so be it. If not, Dmitri did not care. He would deal with Koba for the last time.

"This is Cavasano." The detective pressed his cell phone to his ear. He was in the waiting room with a cluster of weary faces that sat slumped in chairs all around him. He had refused to sit down, choosing instead to pace back and forth amongst the somnolent masses like a polar bear cast adrift on an ice flow. Only a few dared to make eye contact with him.

It was not like Cavasano to strut around like this, his body language bordering on aggressive. Today was the first time he had ever shot somebody. And in the course of doing so, he killed a man, two of them, to be exact. The adrenaline still rushed through his body and there was a feeling within him that if someone in the waiting room looked at him the wrong way, he might not respond in the most appropriate way.

"Alright, thanks again, Moses." Cavasano hung up and strode through a set of doors into a tiled hallway. A train of gurneys lined one side of the hall, most of them empty, a few were occupied. Frank Merylo occupied one of them, two places from the head of the train. Cavasano sidled up next to him.

"Jesus Frank, they still got you out here," Cavasano said.

"There talkin' to my insurance, something about bullet wounds and preexisting conditions or some shit," Merylo said.

"What?"

"I'm just kidding. A little health insurance humor."

"Jesus, Frank."

"So, what's the story?" Merylo asked. "I heard your damn phone ring all the way in here."

"That was Moses. He's still trackin' Murdoch's cell phone. According to Moses, the guy's on his way into Queens at this very moment. I'm gonna take the unmarked, Moses said he'll be able to give me a turn by turn."

"That sounds like a plan," Merylo said.

"Yeah. I also got a surveillance photo from the hospital of the woman that we saw at the Armsport Apartments last night."

"Excellent work, detective."

"Uh, huh. And now I'm gonna make a scene to get you out of this hallway and into a room," he said. "Is there a doctor in here?" Cavasano yelled. "This officer's got a fucking bullet in him."

The ruckus got everyone's attention. Startling the patients in the hall and turning the heads of a number of nurses and clinical staff.

Merylo grabbed his partner's arm. "It's all right, Joe. I'm okay out here." He lowered his voice, "They got me on Demerol."

"What's Demerol?"

"It's amazing stuff," Merylo said. "Just wait 'til the first time you get shot."

46

The Ocean Sentry leveled off at an altitude of just under 1,000 feet. The raft's maniacal spinning had slowed to a calming rocking motion and the G-forces that had held Kyle and Ayumi tight, finally loosened their grip. Kyle took advantage of the reprieve and maneuvered away from the canvas bulkhead, giving himself a little more room. Ayumi stayed on top of him, clinging to his chest and in no hurry to move.

The entrance flap whipped against the side of the raft allowing for brief glimpses of the gray sky outside. The roar of the Ocean Sentry overhead was constant and smooth. Even with all the external stimuli bombarding him, Kyle could feel Ayumi's heart beating against his chest.

The entrance flap caught a side breeze and flapped loudly against the side of the raft startling Ayumi. She slid up his chest a little until the two were face to face and then she propped herself up on her elbows. The line was still secured under her arms. A strand of wet black hair fell off of her shoulder and touched his neck.

"Thank you," she said.

"You're welcome." He didn't know what else to say.

They laid in calm silence studying each other. She traced the outline of his face with her hand and tried to smooth the crow's feet from the edge of his eye. She caught a glimpse of the man as a young boy in the process. Her fingers ran slowly over a day's worth of stubble on his shaved head. Her brow furrowed when she came his injury and she was careful to stay away.

"It's ok," he said. "It doesn't hurt."

Kyle took her face in his free hand, tucked her hair behind her ear and gently inspected the cut on her chin. He moved his hand down, felt the soft curve of her neck. She leaned into his touch. A droplet of seawater ran from her hairline down to the tip of her nose where it balanced delicately before it fell off and landed on the corner of his mouth.

Before Kyle could do anything about it Ayumi pressed her lips to his. Her lips were soft and full and salty. Her black hair tumbled from behind her ears and brushed the side of his face. He closed his eyes and pushed his lips into hers.

Dunn's voice suddenly pumping through his earpiece killed the mood. "I got some info on Tora," Dunn said. "It's not the woman's name."

Kyle pulled his lips away from Ayumi. "No?"

"No. It's a logistics company." Dunn was on to something and the enthusiasm in his voice was noticeable, even over the earpiece. "And apparently, they've been sanctioned in the past for violating U.S. Iranian policy," he said. "They shipped some Iranian oil to Japan a few years ago and pissed off the White House."

"No kidding?"

"No, sir," Dunn replied. "Haven't figured out how it relates to your friend down there though. Maybe she could shed some light."

"Maybe," Kyle answered. "I'm sure we'll find out."

"Roger, that," Dunn said. "See you when you get topside."

Kyle turned his attention back to Ayumi. "Sorry about that," he said. "What were we talking about?"

"We weren't talking," Ayumi said. She pressed her lips back against his.

N iko had managed to stay attached to the raft by entwining himself into the raft's nylon ladder. The idea had worked, but the circulation in his left arm was starting to get cut off. As the jet leveled off and the G-forces relaxed he repositioned himself and allowed his arm to regain its sense of feeling. There would be nowhere for the American to run from him now.

Once he'd managed to catch the bottom rung of the flimsy ladder with his boot it, he pushed himself up and held on with wobbly arms. He could now see into the raft. The Japanese woman was lying on top of him. Kissing him.

He lunged forward and grabbed her ankle pulling her as hard as he could, yanking her out of the life raft and sending her over the edge. He nearly went with her were it not for the hand-holds sewed around the perimeter of the raft. He caught his balance and lurched himself through the opening in the raft.

I n an instant she was gone. Pulled out of the raft. The nylon rope trailed behind. Kyle shot up to follow the rope. The entrance of the raft was blocked by the shivering mass of the big Russian from the *Revolyutsiya*.

"Not you again."

Kyle wasn't going to wait for him to get comfortable. He gripped the handholds on the inside roof of the raft with both hands and swung his right leg catching Niko in the face with his boot.

Deja`vu.

Niko was undaunted and made a frenzied rush into the life raft, crashing into Kyle's midsection and bringing him down. He landed a hard blow to the side of Kyle's head.

Kyle's earpiece crackled with the sound of Ames' voice, "Is everything alright down there?"

Niko had Kyle by the ears and was raking his wounded head against the thick seam of the life raft's bulkhead. He absorbed two more blows to the head before a well-placed knee temporarily halted the Russian's assault.

Ames continued, "It looks like something is tailing from the life raft. Repeat. Is everything okay?"

Kyle threw Niko off of him and into the crease of the raft where the floor met the sidewalls. The Russian's weight threw the raft off balance and into an uneasy rocking motion.

Kyle held onto the overhead grips. When Niko staggered to his knees, Kyle was able to deliver another kick that sent his assailant tumbling onto his back. Again, Niko got up, and again Kyle met the Russian's face with the heel of his shoe.

A quick look out of the entrance flap and Kyle saw Ayumi spinning ferociously at the end of the dangling line.

Inside, Niko lie dazed with his head in the crease of the raft. The survival knife that had come with the life raft was just inches from his face. He saw it, pulled the knife from its sheath and stood up in the shallow confines of the raft.

Kyle turned in time to see Niko coming toward him, knife in hand. Ames' voice again came through his earpiece, "We're going to begin pulling you in with the winch, hang tight."

"Make it quick," Kyle barked.

Niko swung the knife at him and missed. The big man's left eye was beginning to swell. A trickle of blood ran from his nose. He lunged across the raft and narrowly missed as Kyle dodged out of the way.

Kyle braced himself against the swaying raft. Niko slashed at him with a backhand slashing motion, grazing his abdomen and thigh. He looked down to confirm that his dry suit was compromised and felt the telling, belated sting that accompanied such a cut.

The raft was unstable and both men had trouble keeping their balance. Niko swung again wildly and missed, this time, falling to the floor. Kyle dove and landed in front of the entrance trying to get out of the way. Niko spun around and brought the knife down hard toward Kyle's shoulder. Kyle guided Niko's hand and knife away from his body and into the body of the raft. The raft's tubular frame popped and hissed, blowing compressed air into Niko's face. Kyle placed both feet into his attacker's midsection and launched him through the opening of the raft.

A scream.

Now, it wasn't just Ayumi dangling from the end of the line. Niko was holding on to one of her legs. She held on to the safety doughnut with all her strength, but she was beginning to slip through the harness that Kyle had tied around her. The G-forces and the weight of Niko clamped to her leg pulled at her in one direction, the windlass bringing the raft up seemed to pull at her the other. Her arms burned and it felt as though the line would cut right through her.

She raised her free leg and kicked down hard on Niko's head. He didn't respond. She grunted as she kicked again and again and again to no effect. The gray sweatpants that she was given to wear aboard the cargo ship were beginning to slip down. She finally reached down and pulled the tie that gathered the sweatpants. She gave her captured leg a violent shake and, in an instant, the sweatpants came off and Niko was left flailing his arms in vain as he fell into the cold, hard water below.

It took a few minutes, but Kyle managed to pull Ayumi up

and into the raft. She collapsed, shivering on top of him. He held her as Ames and Dunn brought the deflated raft up through the cargo hatch and into the hold of the Ocean Sentry. Once everyone was safely inside, Ames raised the aircraft's cargo ramp sealing off the back of the plane.

She clung to Kyle. He wrapped both arms around her and pulled her close to maximize their body heat. Dunn covered them with a thick blanket while Lawrence Ames finished locking the cargo hatch. Kyle held her tight. For a moment, he felt as though he might have been placed on this earth for a reason.

47

VanRoy threw a five-dollar bill at the driver and then stepped out of the cab. The cabbie swore at him in a foreign tongue as he pushed the door closed, cutting the driver off mid insult. Standing on the corner of 23rd and 1st, he considered the consequences should Ingrid go missing. Surely, he would be the main focus of any investigation. He imagined the firestorm that would follow if he, as a hot shot New York magazine publisher were questioned as the main suspect in the disappearance of his girlfriend. Stepping inside the apartment building's modest lobby, VanRoy smiled as it occurred to him that such a story would sell a ton of magazines.

He boarded the elevator and punched the button that would take him to Ingrid's floor. In his hand was the key that he'd stolen from her during one of their first "dates." After an afternoon of helping her deliver some of her mother's unwanted belongings to a local donation center, he'd helped her comb through an assortment of keys left by her late father. After trying all of the keys in the apartment door, VanRoy found that four of them were to the apartment. He surreptitiously kept one for himself and gave Ingrid three.

He stepped out of the elevator the 20th floor. Ingrid's apartment on the top floor was down the hall to the right. He was still smiling at the thought of his own magazine running a story about his missing girlfriend as he stuck the key to her apartment in the lock and opened the door. He called for her as he entered the apartment.

He stood motionless in the doorway waiting for a reply and listening for any sound of movement from within, but there was only silence. Silence and a faint, almost imperceptible odor. He inhaled trying to place it. The scent didn't seem organic, but he thought that there might be some garbage that had begun to ripen in her absence.

He set Welke's briefcase down and located the trash can under the kitchen sink. The bin was only half full and from what he could tell, lacked any decaying food. He changed the bag anyway and tossed the old bag out into the hall. Any decent apartment complex would have a service that would come by and dispose of it.

He peeled his gloves off his gloves as he made his way into the living room area. Nothing in her apartment seemed out of the ordinary. Then again, her apartment never appeared lived in to begin with. He checked his phone once more for any messages from her. There were none. The faint odor lingered. The apartment could use some fresh air.

VanRoy walked over to the sliding glass door that accessed the tiny balcony. He parted the curtains a little and cracked open the door to let in the cool damp breeze. If one knew where to look, the view from Ingrid's cramped balcony was actually quite good. To the northwest, the iconic Empire State Building rose against the clouded gray backdrop. To the north, its art deco rival, The Chrysler Building shone like the sun on an old black and white TV.

VanRoy closed the door and put the curtain back in place.

He flared his nostrils a little and inhaled deeply. The nagging odor that greeted him when he entered the apartment ebbed and flowed, carried on the draft that he'd just let in the house.

T he suit was new, but it was already wrinkled. He kept the jacket on much too late in the day he had been told more than once. He walked with a slight, but noticeable limp and supported himself with a curved handle cherry wood cane. The dying embers of a cigarette were wedged between the first two fingers of his free hand. On the corner of 23rd, a gust of wind finished off what was left of his cigarette and thrashed his unruly hair. He threw the empty butt to the pavement and clawed at his hair in an attempt to keep it straight. He gave up when he realized he'd reached his destination.

In the lobby of the apartment complex, he was met by an older concierge who nodded politely in his direction. He responded by smiling back, exposing rows of little teeth. Leaning on his cane, he raked at his hair some more before locating the elevators at the back of the foyer that would take him where he needed to go.

Room 2004 was on the top floor and as the elevator took its time, he pondered what it was that drove people to live at these heights. Tokyo, his current home, was remarkable in its vertical dependency. He wasn't a fan of heights. Luckily for him, his apartment in the Japanese capital was on the first floor.

The elevator door opened and he stepped out into the hall-way. To his left, a solitary maintenance worker was setting up a step ladder in the threshold of an open doorway. A burned-out exit light that led to the rooftop patio had required his attention. Room 2004 was to his right.

. . .

VanRoy lifted the toilet seat and unzipped his pants. It was too bad about his business associate, Tobias Welke. The little prick didn't deserve to die. He was scheduled to meet with him this weekend to discuss the details of his trip to Chacachacare Island. VanRoy had an interest in acquiring a Brazilian glossy and was traveling to Rio De Janeiro next week and had arranged to stop by the private island off the coast of Trinidad on his way to mix in a little pleasure with his business. It would be his first chance to meet little Marlena in person since he bought her from Welke four months ago.

Chacachacare Island was purchased from the government of Trinidad and Tobago by a private investor for 25 million U.S. dollars a few years back. The little island off the north west corner of the country was once a cotton plantation and more recently, a leper colony that was finally abandoned in 1984.

Welke's passing posed little problem as VanRoy had already verified the contact information for his arrival on Chacachacare. He'd no longer have to pay Welke to act as a liaison and considered the timing of his associate's death as nothing more than a price break. VanRoy and the island's owner knew each other, even before Tobias Welke introduced them. Shared tastes, he supposed.

He was eager to indulge in the islands rumored amenities. All of the cigars, alcohol, and drugs that one could want were allegedly included in the purchase price along with the guaranteed, exclusive access to "dates" of one's choosing. The whole trip promised to be a carnival of taboo activities. It had been eight months since his surgery and all was looking good and feeling good. He zipped up and flushed the toilet. He couldn't wait to try it out.

As he washed his hands he enjoyed the fresh aroma of toasted vanilla and sugar. He cupped a handful of water and splashed some on his face. While he dabbed at his with the hand towel that hung next to the sink, the persistent, nagging odor returned. But this time it was much stronger than before. So much so, that he was no longer at a loss about what the odor was.

It was paint.

He set the towel down and stood up straight. In the mirror's reflection, he noticed a man standing behind him. The man was a few inches shorter and was wearing a gray long-sleeved shirt. His hands were placed behind VanRoy's neck. The man's face was expressionless. Puzzled, VanRoy thought about turning around and asking the man what he was doing in Ingrid's apartment. Then he noticed the wire and knew what was going to happen next.

A lone white kitchen garbage bag sat outside apartment 2004. He poked at it with his cane. Dmitri, the criminal that he'd hired, demanded to meet him here. He'd received word from Captain Drogzvic of the *Revolyutsiya* the night before that Dmitri had brought the Japanese woman aboard the cargo ship and that she wasn't dead.

It didn't matter in the short term as he had no intention of paying anyone anyway, least of all, Dmitri. When the *Revolyutsiya* reached Kaliningrad, that giant bastard Niko would find this out as well in a most unpleasant way.

Turning his cane over, he removed the rubber end from the bottom and placed it in his suit pocket. He took the pocket square from his jacket and placed it over the handle of the door. It was unlocked. He took that as a sign that Dmitri was indeed already inside. He smiled. He had a plan in mind for Dmitri and wished to deliver it in person.

48

Kyle still had one arm around Ayumi, but she was sitting up straight now and had stopped shivering. Her hair was still wet and splayed out over the blanket that draped over her shoulders. The blood from the cut on her chin had dried and a yellowing bruise had formed under her left eye. Ames had provided her with a headset so that they could communicate when she was ready.

Ames was the first to speak. "Can you tell us your name Ms.?" He had a clipboard and was filling out paperwork. His position required it.

"Ayumi Kagawa," she answered.

"Thank you, Ms. Kagawa." Ames was aware that his tone of voice was naturally intimidating. Mindful of this, he toned it down as he spoke to Ayumi. "Are you a United States citizen?" Ames continued.

"No." Trust did not come easy for Ayumi. So, even though the men had helped rescue her, she tread cautiously with their questions. "I'm from Japan," she said.

"You're a Japanese national?"

"Yes."

"Thank you." Ames noted the information. "Ms. Kagawa, do you know who the men are or were that abducted you?"

"Bratva," she said.

Kyle and Captain Ames shared raised eyebrows before turning to Dunn.

"Russian mafia," Dunn clarified. He turned to Ayumi. "How are you certain they were Bratva?"

"By their tattoos."

"Any idea where they might be from?" Dunn asked. The collapse of The Soviet Union gave rise to hundreds of criminal enterprises. It could be nearly impossible know which one, if any, was responsible.

"No." She answered quickly, then thought about the question a little more. "Maybe Vladivostok."

"Kostenaya?" Dunn asked.

"Possibly."

Dunn was intrigued. "You're familiar with Russian organized crime?" He looked closely at her. The sweatshirt she was wearing was heavy with sea water and sagged around her neck exposing a small portion of skin on her left shoulder. A collage of colorful ink mingled with strands of hair.

Ayumi tugged at the sweatshirt, pulling it up toward her neck. She held it in place with her arm. "Yes."

"Any idea what they may have wanted?" Kyle asked.

Ayumi didn't answer.

"Ms. Kagawa, what was your reason for coming to the United States, to New York?" Ames asked.

"I came at the request of a family friend."

"Did-does this family friend work at the UN for the International Atomic Energy Agency?" Dunn asked.

"Yes."

Kyle slid his arm out from behind her so that he could look at her straight on. "Ms. Kagawa, I'm afraid that Mr. Sakai-"

"I know," Ayumi said. "They killed him."

Kyle placed his hand on top of hers. "I know this is difficult, but can you think of any reason why they would want to kill Mr. Sakai?"

"He knew about the *Orso*," she said.

"What is the *Orso*?" Ames asked.

"It's a ship," she answered.

"What kind of ship?" Dunn asked. "Is it a cargo ship, passenger ship?"

Ayumi recalled her conversation with Mr. Sakai. She repeated what he'd told her. "It's an I-N-F-class three vessel," she said.

The detailed description caught the men off guard. Kyle looked at the Coast Guard Captain for an answer. "What is that?"

"It's an Irradiated Nuclear Fuel ship," Ames said. "One that's certified to carry high level radioactive waste." He softened the tone of his voice and then asked, "Mr. Sakai briefed you on that?"

Ayumi nodded.

"Mr. Sakai was worried about Nuclear waste?" Kyle asked.

Ames jumped in. "The classification of the vessel is important," he said. "The ship is certified to carry an unrestricted amount of aggregate plutonium waste or spent fuel." Ames eyed Ayumi to gauge her reaction, then continued. "Japan has a surplus of spent nuclear fuel on hand. A lot of which is plutonium from their breeder reactors."

Dunn adjusted the mouthpiece on his headset. "What else did Mr. Sakai tell you?"

"He said he found a discrepancy in the shipping logs of a company called Tora that commissioned the *Orso*," she said.

Dunn eyed Kyle. Ayumi just validated his earlier discovery that Tora was a logistics company.

Ayumi continued, "The *Orso* is set to be loaded with one hundred and fifty thousand pounds, or ten casks, of nuclear fuel waste. It's going to be shipped from the port in Aomori Prefecture to Vladivostok. From there it will be transported by rail for reprocessing at the Mayak facility in Ozyorsk, Russia."

"Is that normal?" Kyle asked.

"Yes, sort of" Ames said. "Japan has *a lot* of spent fuel nuclear waste and so ships it to a number of countries such as England, France and Russia, where it goes through a vitrification process. They basically turn the waste into glass, before it's shipped back to Japan for storage or disposal."

"Sounds legit, so far," Dunn said. "Mayak is a large reprocessing plant capable of handling large amounts of spent nuclear fuel. It also happens to be the birthplace of the Soviet Union's atomic bomb project. So, lots of equipment and nuclear technology there."

Ayumi continued. "Mr. Sakai's concern was that, after Mayak reprocesses the nuclear waste, only eight of the ten original casks are set to be shipped back to Japan for disposal."

"They're keeping the other two?" Kyle asked.

"No. Mr. Sakai didn't think so."

Ames looked concerned. "That could be problematic. Powdered plutonium is a by-product of reprocessing. It's relatively safe to handle, but is a huge proliferation concern."

"How much plutonium are we talking?" Kyle asked.

"About one percent of the total waste load, probably" Dunn said. "But a little plutonium goes a long way."

Kyle turned to Ayumi. "The Russian mafia is trying to make nuclear weapons?"

"No. The Bratva were only hired to kill Mr. Sakai because of what he knew."

"And then they found out that he'd spoken to you," Kyle said.

"Yes."

Dunn asked, "Ms. Kagawa, did Mr. Sakai mention anything about Tora having been sanctioned for importing Iranian oil in violation of U.S. policy?"

She shook her head. "No. But he did say that he spoke to the Chairman of Tora and that they had decided to stop the shipping of nuclear waste for the foreseeable future. They were instead concentrating on their recent acquisition of a section of the Azadegan oil field in Iran."

Dunn mulled these new facts over in his mind. "That's interesting."

Turbulence caused the Ocean Sentry to drop suddenly and lurch to the side. Ames and Dunn braced themselves against the bulkhead. Kyle held Ayumi tight.

"Sorry about that," Sidwell's voice crackled over their headsets. "Hope you're all wearing your seatbelts."

When the Ocean Sentry stabilized, Kyle said, "Okay. So, doing some quick math, we're missing two casks of approximately thirty thousand pounds of reprocessed nuclear waste."

Dunn and Ames agreed.

"Of that, roughly one percent, or three hundred pounds, is powdered plutonium which can be used to make a nuclear warhead. Is that right?"

"That's correct," Ames said.

Kyle looked at Dunn. "How much plutonium did you say it took to make a nuclear weapon?"

Dunn hadn't said, but he did know the answer. "About five kilograms or just over ten pounds."

Ames let out a deep breath. "Jesus."

Kyle turned to Ayumi. "Did Mr. Sakai have any thoughts on where the plutonium might be going?"

"Yes."

"Where?"

"He said, he suspected Tora was shipping it to the Iranians."

"That might explain the acquisition of the oil field," Ames said.

Dunn sat up straight and stroked his jaw. "Shit. No wonder the Iranians are meeting all their obligations under the Joint Comprehensive Plan of Action."

"While everyone was hand-wringing over their nuclear facilities, they were developing a ballistic missile delivery system. Hell, they've already launched a military satellite into space," Ames said.

"And the IAEA officials walking around haven't found any indication that they're burning fuel for plutonium production," Dunn said. "Their heavy water limits are low and their uranium stockpiles are within compliance. They're getting their material in through the backdoor." He looked at Ames. "All the while, like you said, they've been developing their missile delivery systems."

"So, they must've completed their nuclear weapons program and are just waiting for the plutonium to arrive," Kyle said.

"I'll be damned," Ames muttered.

"Is there anything else?" Kyle asked. "Anything at all that you can think of that might help us."

Ayumi thought for a moment, then remembered what Niko had said while they were looking over the railing on board the *Revolyutsiya.* "The Bratva, they think we are working together," she said.

"Who's *we*?"

"You and me," she said. "And a Ms. Garcia? He said they were going to kill you two."

"Who is going to kill us?" Kyle asked.

"The third Bratva," she said. "He was not on board the ship. He stayed back in the city."

Kyle braced himself as turbulence again buffeted the plane.

As far as he knew, Ms. Garcia was back at his family home in Montauk where she should be safe until he and Dunn got back. He doubted the authorities had found her, let alone a Russian mobster.

Still, he felt responsible, knowing that she was in unfamiliar surroundings, mainly his home, and thought it best to check up on her now that they had rescued Ms. Kagawa.

He pulled out her phone from the pocket on his dry suit. "I'll try to give her a call on my phone." he said.

Dunn leaned forward toward Ayumi as the plane danced through more turbulence. "You said that Mr. Sakai spoke to the Chairman of Tora?"

"That's right."

"Did Mr. Sakai happen to tell you the Chairman's name?"

"Yes," she answered. "He's a former U.S. Ambassador to Japan."

"Really?" Dunn's interest was piqued. "And who might that be?" He asked.

"Everyone calls him Koba," Ayumi said. "But his real name is James Brewer."

49

The door to apartment 2004 pushed open without any resistance. He tucked his handkerchief back into his suit coat. His initial impression was that the apartment was small, not unlike a lot of the ones in Tokyo. Moving through the kitchen, he gave it a quick once over. Standard fare, he mused. The place wasn't going to win any interior design awards.

Stepping into the living space, he was struck by what he encountered. Two men, neither of whom, was Dmitri. The Russian bastard had insisted on meeting him here, but it now seemed that he sent someone else sent in his place.

One of the men, wearing a gray, long-sleeved shirt under black denim overalls had a garrote around the throat of a taller, much nicer dressed man. Given his unfortunate situation, the taller man's face was twisted grotesquely and tinted an unflattering purple. It looked as though an eye might come loose. By the looks of it, the shorter man had managed to drag his victim backward down the hall and out into the living area where unbeknownst to him, James Brewer sat, relaxing on the arm of the couch.

Brewer was transfixed by the man's clawing and thrashing about, trying to free himself from the wire around his neck. He cocked his head to the side, watching intensely. He never failed to be captivated by the way in which men responded to the realization that they were about to die. Some thrashed about wildly like the man at the end of the garrote. Others let go with a bit more resignation, were more dignified. He supposed religious belief played a part in it. As the tall man quit his thrashing about and finally expired, Brewer couldn't help but wonder how his tormentor would handle the same situation.

"And what is your name?" Brewer asked.

Startled by the voice behind him, the man in the gray shirt turned around. He was surprised to find someone else in the apartment with him, but did his best not to seem alarmed. "Ilya," he answered.

Edward VanRoy had died lying on his stomach, his face buried in the shag carpet. Ilya casually slid the wire out from under his neck.

Ilya. A Russian name? Ukrainian at the very least. Clearly this is who Dmitri sent in his place. "Tell me, Ilya," Brewer said. "How did it feel?"

"How did what, feel?"

"Killing this man. How did it make you feel?"

"I feel nothing," Ilya said.

"No?" Brewer smiled. He was intrigued by Ilya's casual demeanor.

"No." Ilya wiped the wire off on the back of Edward's pant leg before coiling it up and stuffing it in his coat pocket.

"Not even the slightest tingle of satisfaction?" Brewer asked.

"No."

Brewer pushed himself off the arm of the couch, careful not to step on the dead man that lay on the floor in front of him. He ran a cool hand down the length of his cherry wood cane. "Well, that does seem to be the problem these days, doesn't it?" He said. "Nobody's passionate about their work. Everyone's just a bunch of mindless zombies."

Ilya stood up straight. The delicate looking man with the cane was inching toward him, like a starving rat that was happy to bite off more than it could chew. He brushed his arm up against the gun hidden in the pocket of his overalls.

"Everyone's so sloppy," Brewer said. He poked the dead man with his cane. "So... messy." He looked at Ilya. "That's how mistakes happen, you know."

The thought began to occur to Ilya that he may have killed the wrong man. That maybe the little man in front of him was the one Dmitri had sent him to kill.

"I was once asked to kill a man," Brewer said. "But I couldn't do it without first learning all that I could about him beforehand." He smiled. "What was his name? His hair color? Was he a big man?" Brewer paused for effect. "Or a *short* man?" With his smile gone, Brewer continued. "I wanted to make sure that the man I killed deserved it."

Brewer took a step closer to Ilya. "I suppose you could argue if one ever truly *deserves* it. After all, some of the worst men among us get to live out the remainder of their lives once they've been apprehended, even if it is from the inside of a prison cell." Brewer continued. "Still, when it was all said and done, at least I was confident that I hadn't made a mistake. That I had in fact, killed the *right* man."

Brewer raised his cane, examined it. The finish was perfect. He tilted his head to the dead man lying on the floor. "You do know that that was supposed to be me."

Ilya stood slack jawed.

Brewer looked up from his cane. "I really do hope Dmitri paid you up front."

I ngrid was in the city. The cell phone on the seat next to her rang. Instead of the electronic version of "Despacito" to which she was accustomed, it was the dowdy ring of a bygone era.

She answered, "Hello, Kyle? Where are you?"

"We're on our way back." Kyle shouted over the din of the aircraft. "We rescued the woman. Are you still at the house?"

The connection was poor. Kyle's voice came across the air waves in short choppy bites. Unintelligible chatter that Ingrid could not piece together.

"Can you repeat that?" Ingrid said. "I can't understand you."

"Listen to me," Kyle said. "Stay where you are. Do not go back to your apartment."

In addition to the intermittent audio, the static and noise from the aircraft were too much to compete with. "You're breaking up," she said. "I'm going to go back to my apartment. I'll call you back in a few minutes."

"No. Ingrid, don't do that," Kyle shouted. "Do not go back to your apartment."

It was too late. She didn't hear him.

"Ingrid?" Kyle turned to Dunn. "She hung up."

Dunn turned to Ames. Before he could say a word, Ames cut him off.

"No," Ames said. "Don't even ask, Richard."

"Come on Lawrence," Dunn begged.

"We're even, Richard. And lucky too."

"Captain Ames, please," Kyle said.

"I would be indebted," Dunn added.

Ames looked around the aircraft. No one said a word, but all eyes were on him. "Oh hell, Rick. You're gonna owe me big time," Ames said.

"Thanks, Lawrence."

"Sidwell. Request permission to land at JFK," Ames bellowed over the headset.

"Yes sir," the pilot answered.

Kyle squeezed Ayumi tight. She rested her head on his shoulder.

Ames glared at Dunn. "Big. Time."

I lya hadn't realized it, but he had unconsciously been backed up against the wall by the small, unkempt man in the wrinkled suit.

"Have you ever wondered what it must feel like to die?" Brewer asked. "To have the rest of your life reduced to mere minutes?" He nodded to the dead man on the carpet. "Or seconds. Whatever the case may be."

Ilya did not respond. He understood that the question had no correct answer and that continuing the conversation was pointless. He had learned to recognize when words were used merely as a mechanism for buying time. He reached into his jacket pocket to draw his gun.

The young man that Dmitri had sent was quick, there was no doubt about that. But Brewer was already in position with his cane at shoulder height. Before Ilya could raise the gun, Brewer had pushed the end of his cane into the young man's neck. A trigger was located on the underside of the cane's handle. He pulled it. With the pop of a small pistol, a small white pellet was expelled and delivered neatly into Ilya's neck.

Brewer stepped back as Ilya dropped his gun and clawed at his neck trying in vain to work the pellet out from under his skin. He slid down the wall until he was sitting on the floor, clawing, scratching. His eyes were wide and darted wildly.

Brewer knelt down and picked up the loose gun. While he

was kneeling, he looked deep into Ilya's eyes. The ricin pellet that he had just injected into Ilya's neck wouldn't kill him right away, but it would kill him. Just as it had the others, beginning with an American spy in Romania in 1989. And although Ilya maintained that killing another human being personally did nothing for him, the same could not be said for James Brewer. He absolutely loved it.

I ngrid made a left on 23rd Street and then a left again into the parking garage. Valerie, the attendant on duty, got out of her booth with a clipboard and pen and met Ingrid as she pulled up to the booth.

"New ride, Miss Garcia?" Valerie asked.

"Oh, hi Valerie. No. I just borrowed it from a friend. It'll only be here for a day."

"Okay, but you still have to fill out a form for it." Valerie gave the vehicle a good look over. "Wish I had a friend like that," she smiled.

Ingrid took the clipboard and pen and filled out enough information about the Mustang to satisfy the attendant, thanked her and then found the nearest parking spot closest to the elevator.

Riding the elevator up to her apartment, Ingrid fidgeted nervously with her keys, uncertain if she had reached the end of the line in the search for her missing niece or if the journey had only just begun. Welke's death could prove to be a blessing or a curse.

The elevator arrived unabated at the twentieth floor. Ingrid got out and strode down the hall to her unit. To her left, a main-tenance man stood on a folding ladder working on the exit sign that led to the rooftop patio. In front of her, a half full, white kitchen garbage bag rested against the wall outside of her apartment door gave her pause. She hadn't put any trash out. She put the key in the lock and the catch felt slack. Her apartment door had already been opened.

50

C avasano pulled the unmarked over to the left-hand curb on First Avenue and jumped out of the car. He'd blocked the bicycle lane completely and partially obstructed the left turning lane, quickly drawing the ire of a passing motorist who honked and flipped him the middle finger.

Luckily for that prick, he had more important priorities. After the day he'd had, he wasn't going to put up with any more bullshit. He used his gun for the first time in his career today. He wouldn't hesitate to use it again.

The tracking that Moses had done on Kyle Murdoch's cell phone had led him to this apartment complex on the corner of 23rd and First. He craned his neck to get a look up to the top. He guessed the building to be about 20 floors. The property next door was being renovated and a tower crane stood idle between the two structures.

Cavasano stepped into the lobby and inspected the rows of mail boxes that decorated one wall. Unfortunately, no names were listed. Opposite the mailboxes, an old, serious looking concierge was perched behind a circular station eyeing him with suspicion. Cavasano stood up straight and strode over to the apartment gatekeeper without ever taking his eyes off of him. By the time he'd made it to the concierge station, the older man had started to shrink.

"Excuse me," Cavasano said. "I need to know if a Kyle Murdoch is a tenant of this apartment building?"

"I'm afraid I can't-," the man said.

Cavasano didn't give him any points for his politeness. Instead, he pushed his badge within a centimeter of the man's face, cutting him off. "Yes, you can," he said. "On second thought, I'd like a list of all the tenants who reside in this building."

That was all that was needed to inspire the concierge to quickly produce a printout of all the apartment's tenants. After scanning the list and finding no one with the last name Murdoch, Cavasano called Moses back at the station.

"Yeah, Moses this is Cavasano. Hey, you're sure about the location of Murdoch's cell phone?"

"Yeah," Moses said. "I don't know if he's there, but his cell phone sure the hell is."

Just then, a loudmouth in a pair of khakis waltzed into the lobby. "Who's the dipshit that parked their car ass sideways in the street out front?" He said.

"Thanks, Moses. I gotta go." Cavasano hung up.

He walked over to the man. "I did," he said. "And I'm gonna give you to the count of three to get your ass out of here."

"Hey, who the-"

"Three." Cavasano pulled out his gun and fired three quick shots into the floor next to the man's feet. Tile shattered and bullets ricocheted out into the street.

The concierge ducked behind the counter. The man danced frantically out of the lobby to avoid the bullets, swearing to call the police as he did so.

"Call 'em," Cavasano shouted. He walked calmly back to the concierge station. The old man took his time standing upright. He had a phone receiver in one hand.

"How many floors?" Cavasano asked.

"Twenty," the trembling doorman answered.

"And you don't know any Kyle Murdoch that lives here?"

The old man shook his head.

There was no way Cavasano could check every floor by himself. Moses was positive that Murdoch was here, or as he had made a point of stating, Murdoch's phone was here. He was almost resigned to going floor to floor when he remembered the surveillance photo of the woman that had visited Murdoch in the hospital. He pulled it out of his pocket.

"How about her?" He asked the doorman. "You know this woman?"

"Yes," the doorman said. "That's Ms. Garcia."

"Really? Which apartment does she live in?"

"She's on the Twentieth floor. Room two, zero, zero, four."

"Thank you," Cavasano said. Then, "You calling the cops?"

The old man nodded that he was.

"When they get here, just send them up to her apartment." He pushed the list of tenants at the concierge. "While you're at it, tell them they're probably going to need an ambulance."

Ingrid crept into her apartment. She left the door open behind her on purpose, in case she had to exit in a hurry. A titanium briefcase sat up against the wall opposite the kitchen. From this vantage point she could see into part of the living room and saw a body lying face down on the floor.

She moved closer quietly, not wanting to give away her presence in the apartment. There was a gasping sound coming from around the corner and out of her immediate view. It sounded as if someone was in distress and struggling to breath. As she approached the man lying on the floor, she could see that it was Edward VanRoy. His eyes were open and seemed to be staring deep into the carpet, unblinking, bulging. His face was red. She covered her mouth to prevent any noise from escaping.

She crept out into the living room and was able to see down the hallway toward her bedroom. On the floor in the hall, a second man was struggling for air as if being choked by an invisible hand. The man clawed at his neck furiously while a smaller man in a rumpled suit and propped up by a cane, stood by, watching the horrific scene.

Ingrid paused to process what was transpiring in her apartment. VanRoy was dead on her living room floor and she had no idea who the two men in the hall were. She reached in the back of her waistband and felt the cool textured handle of Kyle's gun. One shot would be all that she'd get.

Suddenly, a hideous noise erupted at her feet. She looked down to see Edward VanRoy appearing to rise up off of the floor. A yawning, guttural moan escaped from his mouth. He flattened out and then was still again. Ingrid looked down the hallway. The short man in the suit was looking her way.

"Fascinating, isn't it?" he said. "You don't get to see that every time, the death throes." He turned so his whole body faced her. "Don't worry. Our friend there is still dead. That was just air escaping his lungs." Taking a step in her direction, he leaned on his cane for support with his left hand. He held a gun in his right. "He'll probably shit himself for an encore."

"Who are you?" Ingrid asked.

"Me?" He inched closer. "You can call me Koba." The man smiled and flashed tiny, pointed teeth. "I was just here to meet Dmitri." He stopped and opened both arms for effect. He turned to look at both men sprawled out in the little apartment. "Seems I've met everyone but."

Ingrid noticed that the man struggling to breath on the floor in the hallway had crawled incrementally closer toward the man who identified himself as Koba. He reached out and grabbed his pant leg. Without looking down, Koba kicked his hand away. "I'll assume this is your apartment?" He stepped closer to Ingrid.

"Yes," Ingrid replied.

"Finally." The man feigned relief. "Now, we're getting somewhere." He took another step toward her. "It was starting to get crowded in here." He flashed a disingenuous smile and nodded over his shoulder. "I really hope you can help me with my next question." Koba dipped his head, rolled the gun over in his hand to make sure the safety was off. Keeping his head down, he rolled his eyes in Ingrid's direction. "You wouldn't happen to know where Dmitri is, would you?"

She didn't. She also knew that she wasn't going to become the third dead body at the hands of this little man. Her apartment door was open and available for her escape. She took a step backward toward the door. Her muscles tightened, ready to react to anything. She answered, "I do not."

Koba followed her. He lifted his head and pursed his lips in disappointment. "That's too bad," he said.

Ingrid's mind raced. She had been caught off guard by the whole scene. Edward VanRoy was dead on her living room floor. Another man was moments away from death, grasping his neck and crawling on the floor in front of her. She didn't know *who* Dmitri was, let alone *where* he was. She reached down and picked up the briefcase and held it in front of her chest. If he was to shoot at her, the titanium case might slow a bullet enough to avoid being killed by it.

The little man chuckled and to Ingrid's surprise, he put the gun in his coat pocket. Instead, he raised his walking cane and ran his hand down the length of smooth, cherry wood. He opened his mouth as if he were going to speak and then his brows furrowed and a gasp of pain escaped him instead.

Ilya was still alive and able to manage one last act of violence. He had crawled close enough to grab James Brewer by the ankle and had sunk his teeth into the man's Achilles tendon. It was all the distraction that Ingrid would need as she turned and ran out the door.

Out in the hallway, her options were limited. The elevators were simply too slow and couldn't be counted on as a means of escape. The stairs were too far down at the end of the hall and would only offer a slightly better option *if* she could get to them in time. A gunshot echoed out from her apartment.

The maintenance man working on the exit sign that led to the rooftop patio had been startled by the blast and scrambled to come down off his ladder. Ingrid decided that this was her best option and ran for the door.

51

The elevator couldn't go any slower. Cavasano tapped his ring finger anxiously against his leg. Both he and Merylo believed that Murdoch was the key to solving this case, but for some reason, the man hadn't shown an interest in talking to them. Considering the body count and chaos that's surrounded him in the last 24 hours, one could be excused for thinking that Murdoch might be happy to park his ass inside the safety of police headquarters for a while.

When the elevator finally stopped at the 20th floor, he held the door open with his foot and scanned the hallway in both directions. The hallway was empty, but for a lone stepladder in the middle of the hall to his left. Room 2004 was ahead to his right and from here, Cavasano could see that the door was open.

He moved cautiously. From the hallway, there wasn't any discernible noise coming from inside the apartment, but he kept his entrance discreet and stepped in with his gun leading the way. He'd only managed a few steps into the kitchen area when he saw a man lying face first in the shag carpet. Dead.

Farther in, another man. This one was on his back in a puddle of blood with both hands around his neck. He was still alive, but seemed to be just barely so. Cavasano stepped over him and checked the single bedroom and bathroom to make sure the rest of the apartment was empty.

Out in the living room, Cavasano stopped in front of the dying man. "How many?" He asked.

The man could hardly breathe, let alone talk. He held up one finger and then pointed toward the door and scratched weakly at Cavasano's pant leg as if silently begging for help. The detective moved his leg out of reach. The man didn't have long.

Cavasano called dispatch and ordered a meat wagon for two. Then he called Moses. "I'm in the apartment and I've got one, possibly two dead guys. But no Kyle Murdoch," he said.

"Murdoch's phone is about fifty feet away," Moses answered. "You sure you're in the right apartment?"

"Shit." Cavasano stayed on the phone with Moses and stepped out into the hall. He considered knocking on doors, but decided it was a waste of time. The beat cops could handle that. He ran a big hand through his thick hair. The stepladder caught his attention. It stood in front of a door that was advertised as an exit to the rooftop patio. The door was held open by a pair of boots. There, he found another man lying face down on the concrete floor, partially encircled by a fresh pool of his own blood. With all these dead bodies it seemed a good bet to Cavasano that Murdoch was not far away. "I've got to let you go." He hung up with Moses and called dispatch for a second time.

The rooftop patio was two tiered and included a number of all-weather type bistro furniture that looked straight off a Parisian sidewalk café. A stone outdoor fireplace occupied the southwest corner and was accompanied by a wrought iron bench and concrete coffee table. A dozen or more arborvitae bushes gave the area a park-like atmosphere.

The recent weather had covered all with a thin layer of snow and rendered the patio vacant. All was quiet, but for a helicopter chopping air in the distance. Ingrid hid, crouching behind an eight-foot-tall arborvitae planted firmly in a terra cotta colored cement pot. A three-foot-high brick wall kept her safely on the rooftop. For a moment, and without reason, she wondered why she had never taken the time to come up here.

Being on the second tier, Ingrid had a view of the man from her apartment searching the patio below. He walked with a limp and was making his way toward the steps that would lead him to the second level and after that, right to her. She shifted her weight to make sure she could square up on her target, should he come within range. There was nowhere else to run and nowhere else to hide. She had Kyle's gun in hand and knew it contained only one cartridge so, she'd better make it count.

The heavy, rhythmic smacking of helicopter blades pushing air was suddenly closer and was starting to become almost deafening. Rising up behind her, a red and white Coast Guard helicopter hung in the air as if dangling from an invisible string. The turbulence whipped her hair across her face and thrashed the arborvitae back and forth. Snow blew off the patio ledge.

Kyle Murdoch was hanging out of the open cabin on the starboard side, holding on with one hand to a length of cable from the rescue hoist mounted overhead. His other hand reached out for Ingrid as the helicopter floated slowly toward her.

She stood up and was about to make a move for the concrete railing when a succession of shots rang out from the lower level patio. She ducked and saw Kyle fall from his perch. She turned away, thinking that he had been shot. When she turned back to look, she saw that he had jumped and landed safely on the idle tower crane that was erected between the two apartment buildings. She watched as he shimmy through the steel lattices of the jib toward the safety of the operator's cab.

J ames Brewer missed. The man had jumped onto the crane and was now hidden, darting among the steel lattice. He fired two more shots at the helicopter and it immediately dipped and presented its underside, angling away from his gunfire. He was about to shoot some more, when a voice echoed from behind, instructing him not to move. He ignored the order, turned in the direction of the patio entrance and fired three more shots.

Cavasano ducked into the doorway. "Mother-," he started. He got on his belly in an attempt to change the sight level of his assailant. Sticking only his arm out, he popped off two rounds, aiming in the vicinity of the man's legs.

Kyle had the crane running and began to swing the jib in Ingrid's direction near the top of the terrace patio wall. He stuck his head out of the side window of the operator's cabin and shouted to her, "Come on."

"I can't reach," she yelled over her shoulder while keeping an eye on the man with the gun.

The jib was too high. Kyle engaged the trolley that was attached to a large hook, used to carry the crane's load. He was sending it out to the end of the arm of the crane in hope that Ingrid would be able to grab hold of it.

With the briefcase in hand as a shield, Ingrid stepped out from behind the arborvitae. The man with the gun was facing away from her toward the patio entrance. She set her feet and took a shot, placing the one bullet through the top of the man's left shoulder causing him to spin 180 degrees in her direction.

She ditched the empty gun and made a run toward the crane

while still clutching the briefcase. The crane arm was still a few feet from the ledge as the trolley eased out to the end of the jib.

Ingrid didn't wait. She leapt from the ledge and landed with two feet on the massive hook and grabbed hold of the braided steel cable with her free hand. The assembly swung under the transfer of her weight.

"Hold on," Kyle shouted. He began to draw the trolley in toward the center of the crane as the jib arm rotated counter-clockwise, away from the terrace patio.

Brewer fired two more shots at the woman as he climbed up the stairs to the second level of the patio. The shots were wild and off the mark.

The helicopter had drifted away and gave a wide berth as it circled back around the top of the apartment building.

Richard Dunn was growing anxious as Lawrence Ames steered the aircraft back into position. He raised a pair of binoculars and aimed them at the man on the second level terrace. When the lens focused in, he was surprised at what he saw. "I'll be damned," he said.

"What's that, Rick?" Ames asked.

"I know that piece of shit." Dunn kept the binoculars to his eyes, watching the man in the wrinkled suit move toward the tower crane. "Romania. Nineteen eighty nine," he said. "The Athénéé Palace Hotel." As Kyle was rotating the jib arm away from the terrace patio, the little rat climbed up onto the terrace wall and jumped for the crane. "You still got that gun on you? I left mine back at the station."

"You know I do," Ames said. "Why do you ask?"

Dunn put the binoculars down. "I've got a promise to keep that's been a long time coming."

.   .   .

he trolley wouldn't move any faster. Ingrid held tight to the braided cable. Her hand was black with soot and her clothes soiled with grease. The man in the suit had jumped onto the crane. He was on his stomach, hugging the crane and trying not to fall off. He pointed the gun in her direction and fired. Metal pinged and sparks flew off a crossbeam just over her head.

"Hang on, tight." Kyle shouted. He reversed the direction of the jib arm suddenly, causing the crane to jerk back in the other direction.

Ingrid coiled her legs around the cable for extra insurance. The hook and cable swung wildly from Kyle's maneuver. The action loosened Brewer's grip and his legs fell off the side of the jib arm. He struggled to reestablish his hold.

Kyle steadied the crane to give Ingrid a chance to get off. The trolley had brought the hook and cable in toward the operator cabin. Kyle opened the front window to let Ingrid climb in.

Desperate to get off of the trolley, she nearly lost her footing, slipping as she reached for the window. She threw the briefcase through the open window first and then jumped in herself.

Kyle caught her and fell backwards with her in his arms. "Are you okay?"

"I'm fine." She brushed a lock of hair from her face. "But you really need to get some more ammunition."

Cavasano was on the second terrace with his gun drawn. He had his sights on the man in the suit who had gotten back to his feet and was now walking toward the center of the tower crane. The Coast Guard helicopter had come back around and from Cavasano's perspective was positioned right behind his target. He tried to wave the chopper off. "Get out of the way. Police!" He shouted. He didn't want to endanger any innocent lives, but the helicopter wouldn't move.

Dunn's sights were set. The crane had stopped moving and

James Brewer was limping his way toward Kyle and Ingrid in the cabin of the tower crane. "Hold still."

Brewer continued to move toward the cab. The dirty air from the helicopter whipped his hair around. He remained fixed on his target. He could see the woman on top of the crane operator. He was holding her in his arms. He lifted the gun and pointed it to the open window. He had a clear shot.

Dunn steadied his hand and exhaled slowly. "This one's for you, Thomas."

The bullet hit James Brewer on the right side of his head, just above the ear. He didn't even feel it. The gun fell from his hand and clanged through the crossbeams of the crane. His left knee went weak first causing him to list to that side. He fell off the tower crane head first and cart wheeled a full one rotation before hitting the back end of a concrete mixer on his way to the ground.

52

I ngrid rented a room on Lexington Avenue at one of the international chains around the corner from the 17th precinct until authorities could advise her that her parent's apartment was cleared to occupy again. The titanium briefcase sat opened on the hotel room bed. Ingrid sat in front of it and stared. The faint scent of a cigar lingered and tickled her nostrils.

So far, she'd been unable to bring herself to go through its contents. She had immersed herself in the effort to find her niece so thoroughly and without hesitation, that now, she wasn't sure if she was ready to learn the truth. Her instinct and training drove her to search for the answer, but she hadn't given herself time to grieve. Speculation had seemed much easier to deal with than the truth.

A pile of manila folders sat at the bottom of the briefcase, fastened in place with a buckle style adjustable strap. Ingrid fought back the urge to sneeze, resorting to only a quick sniffle as she undid the straps and lifted the folders out of the briefcase.

In total, there were more than ten folders. Each folder contained photos of stolen children paper clipped to pictures of the pedophiles that paid to steal their innocence. Deviant animals in suits and ties, turbans and toupees.

Welke had kept records of his client's likes and dislikes. He recorded their preference for boys or girls or both, and what age. Did they like dark ones, light ones, skinny ones or fat ones? He made notes about their professions, occupations or royal status. A perverted biographer, Welke's notes were disturbingly detailed.

Ingrid took her time looking through each of the folders one after another. Each the same book with a different cover. Sick men with sick smiles. The poor children. There was an Arab prince, smiling grotesquely, a dark Brazilian girl from Sao Paulo, no more than ten years old, paper clipped to his photo. A banker from Luxembourg with a pre-teen Peruvian girl clipped to his picture and bio. Fat, disgusting men with young boys. Short, bald men with older girls. Monsters, all of them. And then she stopped. And for a moment, her heart stopped with her.

In the fourth folder, a beautiful twelve-year-old girl with black hair and brown eyes set upon a soft, round face. The little girl was from Medellín and was holding the hands of her mother and her aunt.

Marlena.

Tears rolled down Ingrid's cheeks. She knew what to expect next, but it didn't make the viewing an easier. Attached to the photo, in suit and tie, lips twisted in a sick, arrogant smile was an American magazine publisher named Edward VanRoy. Ingrid clutched the picture of her niece to her chest and began to weep uncontrollably.

At the Consulate General's office on the 18th floor, Ayumi sat with her head in her hands, looking out the window onto Park Avenue. Arrangements had been made by the Consulate and she was waiting for her ticket back home.

She had been interviewed more than once for a total of some 20 hours by detectives regarding her ordeal and was assured that she would be able to go home soon. She only answered the questions as they were asked and resisted the invitation to speculate where facts proved inadequate. She agreed to make herself available should any other questions arise, but for now, the authorities in New York were satisfied with her answers.

By way of the tattoo on his neck, she was able to positively identify the body of Alex as the man who first attacked her in her hotel room and one of the three men responsible for her abduction and the murder of Mr. Sakai.

A Coast Guard search and seizure of the *Revolyutsiya* in the Atlantic, south of Long Island resulted in the discovery of a cache of stolen American vehicles, as well as a dead captain and several injured crew members. The vessel was brought back to New York and the Russian crew was jailed on transporting stolen goods charges.

The body of the large Russian, Niko, was not found on board the *Revolyutsiya,* nor was he found during a brief search of the surrounding waters and is presumed dead. The third Russian mafia member that Ayumi had described remained at large.

In the course of her questioning by the American detectives, Ayumi had been able to avoid any discussion pertaining to her family's relationship and membership in the Yamaguchi-gumi. It wasn't relevant, she reasoned, because in the case of the vessel the *Orso,* even though her family controlled the docks, the stevedores were hired by the shipping company.

She was happy to bump into Kyle Murdoch on one occasion

while both were at the 17th precinct assisting with the investigation. He bought her a cup of coffee and they reminisced about their incredible experience. She enjoyed his company for one last time and couldn't help stare at his dimples every time he smiled.

Richard Dunn's credentials and contacts within the agency helped shed some light on the details of James Brewer's less than patriotic existence. From what Dunn could tell, the man had made a living working against American interests.

An opportunist in the extreme, he most recently sought to take advantage of the American sanctions policy against Iran as well as Japan's dependence on Middle Eastern petroleum, exacerbated by the Fukushima nuclear disaster of 2011. Brewer's position on the board of logistics company, Tora, saw him intending to do an end run around United States sanctions by smuggling inexpensive petroleum from Iran in exchange for spent fuel nuclear waste. Specifically, weapons grade plutonium waste from Japan's breeder reactors.

Thankfully, the *Orso* never made it to Vladivostok. The tropical storm that battered Japan stalled between Honshu and Hokkaido, dumping record amounts of rain and keeping all ships moored for three days. By the time the weather broke, the *Orso* had been surrounded by Japan Maritime Self Defense Forces at the dock.

Digging deeper into Brewer's past, Dunn traced his beginnings back to his employment as a Foreign Service Officer stationed in Bucharest during the Cold War. While he was there, Brewer came under suspicion of selling information about United States intelligence personnel to the Nicolae Ceausescu regime. The preliminary inquest was dropped once

Romania fell and the Iron Curtain collapsed onto the dust heap of history.

Dunn remembered his brief encounter with Brewer well. He had been directed to his best friend, who was found dead in a hotel room, by the little man. The autopsy results on Thomas Murdoch revealed that he had died as a result of liver and kidney failure as well as pulmonary edema. Symptomatic of having been poisoned.

At the moment, Ilya Golubev was lying in a hospital bed suffering the same fate and fighting for a life that he was ultimately going to lose. He was able to lead the investigators to a cane recovered from the crime scene in apartment 2004, that he said he was assaulted with by James Brewer. The cane was outfitted to perform like a gun, utilizing a trigger under the handle and the long shaft as the barrel. At its tip, a single ricin pellet was chambered like a bullet, ready to be fired into the next victim. And although the gunshot wound he received from Brewer hadn't killed Ilya, the ricin poisoning most certainly would.

James Brewer was a murderous and deceitful human being. A man that Richard Dunn unknowingly spent decades of his life hunting down. A man that he always knew he'd eventually find.

Parked off the side of the road in a little cemetery in eastern Brooklyn, Dunn waited for Kyle as he paid his respects at the gravesite of his former coworker. He wasn't sure if he should tell Kyle that it was James Brewer that killed his father. He wasn't sure it would even matter now. But he did feel that the longer he waited, the less trusting of him, Kyle would become. Against his better judgement and for reasons he couldn't fully understand, he decided to wait.

Kyle's buried his chin deep into the collar of his pea coat. It was still early morning and the cold front that had gripped the eastern seaboard had yet to fully subside. He dug his hand into his coat pocket and pulled out a series of pictures that he'd printed off his cell phone. In one of them, the subject looked unaware and unprepared, as if he had accidentally taken a picture of himself while trying to operate the camera. The next one was deliberate. The man was smiling as wide as he could. He had a huge smile. In both photos the man was cast in front of a spectacular view of the New York City skyline. The third one was an ominous shot of a well-defined line of gray clouds.

The inscription on the small granite stone laid in the grass and covered with snow said that he was loved by all. Kneeling down and to tuck the second picture in next to the stone, Kyle smiled. He had only known Carl McCree for a few days, but suspected that the statement engraved on the stone was true.

Not wanting to linger, he brushed off his pants and started to walk up the slight incline back to his car. Another car had pulled up behind the Mustang and a woman dressed in a warm, knee length jacket stood outside its driver's door. There were more than 200 plots in the tree lined memorial park, but it seemed as though she was waiting her turn to visit this one.

She didn't move as Kyle approached her. Instinctually, she knew who he was and he in turn, knew her.

"He would be happy to know that you stopped by," the woman said. "He told me that he thought he had finally found a friend in you." She spoke tentatively, as if she were giving away a secret.

Kyle smiled. He would have never guessed that Carl thought of him that way.

She went on, "Carl said you seemed like the kind of man that could use a good friend too."

Kyle smiled, surprised at Carl's level of insight having only known each other for a few days. He nodded his head in agreement. "He was right."

He said his goodbyes to Kim, Carl's girlfriend, and got into the car with Uncle Rick. He started up the Mustang and took a long last look out the window toward Carl's burial plot. Kim had walked down to Carl's gravesite and was now kneeling in the snow in front of his headstone. He turned to Dunn. "Do you ever wonder about the meaning of life?"

Dunn paused before speaking. "I used to," he said. "But I think that over the years I've learned to accept what it means to me."

"What would that be?" Kyle asked.

"For me, it means to live life with purpose," Dunn said. "And embrace all the people, challenges and craziness that comes into your life. Learn to enjoy the experience. Don't run away from any of it."

Kyle thought about it. "That's not a bad philosophy," he said. 'I think I might adopt that as my own."

"I think you might already have," Dunn said.

The car started off down the little hill and around the corner of the winding, tree lined path.

"There is one more very important thing," Dunn said.

"What's that?"

"You don't want to always obey all the rules." He shot Kyle a wry smile. "The great Katharine Hepburn once said, if you obey all the rules, you'll miss all the fun."

53

F rank Merylo had already been in the hospital for a
month and was told he would need to stay a few days
longer. He had been shot twice during the incident at
Josef's grocery store and one of the bullets had broken his pelvis
and was the main reason for the extended hospital stay. The
second bullet had gone in and out of his body cleanly, only
cracking a rib along the way and was a minor irritation by
comparison.

Cavasano had come to see him almost every day and had
kept him informed of the investigation in all of its detail. He
appreciated his partner's commitment and wasn't sure he'd be
able to show the same devotion if the roles were reversed.

At night, when he was alone in his room, he often wondered
how it was that someone as miserable as himself, was blessed to
have a partner like Joe Cavasano. But at the moment, he was just
happy to have a partner with whom to antagonize the lead nurse
stationed on his floor.

"Please slow down." The request echoed down the hall,

emanating from a nurse in powder blue scrubs who chased fruitlessly after her patient.

"Aw, quit your moanin'," Merylo called over his shoulder. He looked up at Cavasano. "That's all she does is complain."

"You're going to run into someone," the nurse protested.

"I think we got it," Merylo replied. "Don't listen to her, Joe. You're doing fine. Take a right turn, right here."

Cavasano had agreed to be the getaway driver with his partner's wheelchair en route to the cafeteria on this day. He slid a little on the tile floor as he rounded the corner at maximum speed. "I see it, Frank."

"Gentleman, please." The nurse gave up. "Ugh."

Merylo craned his neck, checking the rear view. "You out ran her. It's all that NYPD offensive driving skills paying off."

"You know it, partner," Cavasano said.

The elevators were on the left-hand side of the hall. Cavasano rolled Merylo's chair forward and let his partner push the call button for service. The doors opened immediately and Cavasano pulled Merylo's wheelchair backward into the elevator. The old detective selected the first floor and the doors began to close.

"You're never gonna believe who sent me flowers," Merylo said.

"Somebody actually sent *you* flowers?"

"Yes, sir."

"Who was that?" Cavasano asked.

"Shirley."

"Shirley, the one with the big-?" Cavasano held his hands out in front of his chest.

Merylo smiled. "That's the one."

Ingrid stood in front of the window at terminal #4 tapping the boarding pass against the palm of her hand. A light snow was falling and the little flakes that melted on the window pane and trickled down looked like tears against her reflection in the glass. There was nothing left here for her. Weeks had passed and the detectives were satisfied with the information she'd given them. There was no reason for her to have to stay, they'd told her.

She'd made copies of everything she'd wanted from Welke's briefcase before turning it over to the police. Detective Cavasano promised to keep her informed. If anything came up that would help her find her niece, he assured her that he'd contact her. Her sister needed her now and if she were honest, she'd admit that she needed her sister too.

Edward VanRoy was gone, but that didn't mean all was lost. A monster like that must have left a trail of evidence in his wake, wrongly believing that he could get away with whatever he wanted while in a foreign country, without repercussion. Ingrid doubted he practiced the same sort of discretion abroad that he did while at home. Men like VanRoy rarely did. Whatever evidence he had left behind, Ingrid was determined to find.

She managed to pack all of her belongings into one carryon, opting to travel light. A laptop bag was slung over her shoulder. With the exception of what she was currently wearing, she dropped off the remainder of her clothes with the local Salvation Army. The rest of her possessions were given to the newlywed couple that lived down the hall or thrown out. She sold the car for cheap. She saved the family photo that Edward VanRoy had inserted himself into for herself, hoping it might be useful in helping her track down her niece once she got back to Medellín.

When the red and white Avianca Airbus A330 finally rolled

up to gate B35 an hour behind schedule, Ingrid's heart sank for a moment. In a little over five hours, she would be back home with her family, and leaving the United States behind. She had exchanged email with Kyle during the course of their interview sessions with detective Cavasano, but she hadn't told him when she was leaving. As the passengers waiting to board began to queue up, Ingrid started to feel as though she might regret that decision. It would have been nice to have seen him one more time.

She was both anxious to get home, yet reluctant to leave as she shuffled with the group toward the ticket agent. Checking her watch, she was suddenly, uncomfortably, reminded of one more thing that she needed to do. She noticed a waste receptacle at the end of the ticket counter. After presenting her boarding pass to the gate agent, Ingrid smiled politely, removed the expensive, gaudy watch and tossed it into the bin.

Snow fell gently outside on K Street as John Coltrane and Duke Ellington's "In a Sentimental Mood" whispered longingly in the background. Dunn sat alone at the end of a thick mahogany bar, admiring its deep, mirror-like finish. This was possibly his favorite place in the whole world. It was also a favorite of the Embassy crowd and as a consequence, a place where intelligence seekers came to ply their trade.

He swirled a few ice cubes around the bottom of the rocks glass before taking one last sip and pushing the glass forward across the bar. A raised finger and a nod of the head was all it took to let the bartender know that he'd like one more. He ran a hand over the smooth bar rail.

Lately, he'd found himself indulging in this practice on a more regular basis. One more bourbon on the rocks turning into two or three. It felt good having reconnected with Kyle, regardless of how fleeting and chaotic the circumstances might have been. The son was a lot like his old man and he was reminded of the good days gone by. Even so, he felt more alone now than he had in a long while. Thankfully, there was still bourbon.

His drink arrived and he thanked the bartender with a tip of his head. Both of them seemed to prefer nonverbal means of communication. He took a sip of bourbon and then checked his phone for any messages he might have missed. Nothing. He set the phone face down next to his drink in an attempt to keep himself from looking at it.

Staring straight ahead, he noticed a woman in the reflection of the mirror behind the bar. She was standing just off to the side, behind him, and rested a hand on the back of the seat next to his. Dark curls flowing over the top of a soft winter coat.

"Is this seat taken?" Her accent sounded Jamaican.

Dunn wasn't sure he'd ever met a Jamaican spy before and so concluded that she must be a diplomat. He decided not to turn around in his seat. "That depends on who's asking?" he answered her via the mirror.

"Victoria."

It was a Nigerian accent, not Jamaican. And it was pleasantly familiar. He spun around on his bar stool and his heart raced as he stood up to greet her. Droplets of water from melted snowflakes clung to her shiny black curls. Her red lips curled into a smile.

"Victoria." Dunn desperately tried to conceal his emotions. "How long has it been?"

"Too long, Richard."

He pulled out a seat and helped her out of her coat. The night was still young and had just gotten better. He ordered two more drinks and smiled, enlivened by the arrival of an old flame and inspired by the intimate melody of John Coltrane playing on in the background.

The fire crackled and popped and Kyle sat on the couch in his stocking feet enjoying the warm, shimmering orange glow. Snow fell more heavily today and had covered everything in a soft blanket of white. Both hands kept warm wrapped around a cup of hot coffee as he stared deeply into the picture above the fireplace. Chopin played in the background while the shadows cast from the fire danced and flickered, seeming to animate the faces of his parents in the photo. For a second, it looked as though his father had looked down and winked at him.

Unexpectedly, the doorbell rang and broke the tranquility of the moment. Before getting up, he checked the grandfather clock and wondered who would be stopping by at this late hour unannounced. Maybe someone accidentally put their car into the ditch across the street or it might be a couple of neighborhood kids hustling to make a buck shoveling driveways.

Whatever the case, he put his coffee down and shuffled to the foyer. He opened the door with low expectations and so, his heart was moved when he saw her standing there. It had been weeks since they'd last seen each other. Last he knew, she was flying back home and didn't have any intention of ever coming back. Her black hair flowed out from underneath a gray knit hat and rested on top of her thick winter coat. She was prettier than he remembered.

He took her hand and led her out of the cold and into his home. Instinctively, he put his arms around her and pulled her close. She put her hands on the back of his neck and brought his lips down to hers. They kissed for a moment before stopping and staring into each other's eyes. He touched her cheek and ran a finger down the contour of her face.

"It's good to see you again." She smiled. Her bruises had disappeared and the nick on her chin had healed, leaving only a tiny scar.

"It's good to see you, too."

THE END

EPILOGUE

Vladivostok, Russia

It was a two-hour flight from Incheon International Airport in Seoul to Vladivostok International in the Russian far east. The flight was smooth and the meal was welcomed, but neither could fill the void inside him. He trudged in silence with his fellow travelers in a single file line up the jetway with only a small leather bag slung over his right shoulder. Spilling out into international Terminal A, they were greeted by an audience of empty seats. The airport was practically abandoned at this hour and the lack of human activity only served to add to his feelings of emptiness and isolation.

He hadn't made the money the money he'd expected to, save for the minimal down payment he received before the ordeal began. He'd barely enough money left to make it back to his home country and even at that, he was still thousands of miles away from where he had started in Moscow.

There was no reason to go home, now. There was nothing left for him there. He thumbed his phone and pulled up a picture of his daughter. He was always surprised at how much she looked like him. It seemed as if she looked more like him with every year that passed. He was equally surprised at how much he missed her. How was it possible to have loved another human being so much? He wondered if this was normal, and if other people had these feelings as well.

He continued on through the airport, clearing customs without hassle, keeping eye contact to a minimum. He exchanged the remainder of his American dollars for rubles and then bought a copy of Sport Express for when he might need to keep his mind distracted.

He was right to have killed Alex and should have known better than to trust him in the first place. The wiry drug addict was loyal to no one and had sold him out to the only organized criminal enterprise in the world that did not have a mutual respect for and understanding of the Russian Mafiya, the Yakuza.

Alex had reached out to the Yakuza and negotiated a 2.5-million-ruble deal in exchange for details of their operation. He sold personal information about the parties involved. Including the names and locations of loved ones and friends.

He had never heard his daughter's mother scream like that before. She had been angry at him plenty of times and he was often reminded that she despised him. But never had he heard the primal scream of a mother whose child had been ripped from her arms. For the first time, he felt sympathy for the woman. For the first time, he knew what it meant to hurt.

He exited the airport and stood outside where a line of cabs idled patiently, plumes of condensing exhaust rising into the frigid air. The wind was coming down from the north and brought with it all the pleasantries of the Siberian winter. He zipped his coat up to his neck and pulled a wool beanie over his ears.

He had a choice to make. Moscow was 6 days and 6,000

miles away by train via the Trans-Siberian Railway. It would be a slow, painful reminder of what he had lost, but he could get lucky and Tomo, the man who killed his daughter, might still be in the city.

He cupped his hands around the end of a cigarette, lit it, and drew in a heavy lungful of smoke. Conversely, the Japanese mainland was only 500 miles to the East. The Yakuza woman and her family lived on the island. He exhaled, letting the smoke trickle out of his nose and the corner of his slightly parted lips.

He always considered himself to be a pragmatic man. Not given to bouts of impulsiveness. He knew when the odds were insurmountable and when to cut his losses. And so, he was surprised that he felt compelled to go against his better judgment, to ignore logic and reason and dive headlong into imminent self-destruction.

He now knew what drove some men to unimaginable consequence. The total lack of regard for one's own self in the single-minded pursuit of retribution. He put the cigarette to his lips and inhaled some more. His purpose in life had been defined for him. His goal had never been more clear. Dmitri Korychnevy felt reckless. And that made him a very dangerous man.

ACKNOWLEDGMENTS

I would like to thank the following individuals for their assistance, inspiration and encouragement with writing this book: My sons, Kyle and Ryan and my parents, Terrence and Beverly. Karen Casper, Christina Rooy, TKO, Cate Grimm and Tom Murdoch. Any errors are solely of my own making.

ABOUT THE AUTHOR

Christopher Anthony was born in Cleveland, Ohio. Please visit his website: thechristopheranthony.com or follow him on Parler @CAnthonyBooks

instagram.com/c_anthony71

twitter.com/CAnthonybooks